Tread Softly

Melanie Loveridge had been a looker too. Shenfield could still remember, as if it were yesterday, the shock of seeing the vandalised beauty of that first young body, the obscenity of her long auburn hair fanned out around her on the grass, reflecting the twinkling fairy lights, as if one part of her, at least, were still alive.

And now O'Driscoll was back. Seven murders in the past twelve months. The similarities in the injuries, the choice of one attractive redhead after another; it had to be O'Driscoll.

All Shenfield was lacking was a single shred of proof.

About the author

Tread Softly is Georgie Hale's first novel. She has spent most of her life in Coventry, although many of her family live on the Isles of Scilly. She studied at Liverpool University before working first as a social worker, then at the University of Warwick. She has a strong interest in the criminal justice system. She is married, with two grown-up daughters.

Tread Softly

Georgie Hale

To Nancy,
with best wishes,

Georgie Hale

NEW ENGLISH LIBRARY
Hodder & Stoughton

Copyright 2000 by Georgie Hale

The right of Georgie Hale to be identified as the Author of the
Work has been asserted by her in accordance with the
Copyright, Designs and Patents Act 1988.

First published in Great Britain in 2000 by
Hodder and Stoughton
First published in paperback in 2000 by Hodder and Stoughton
A division of Hodder Headline

A New English Library Paperback

10 9 8 7 6 5 4 3 2 1

British Library Cataloguing in Publication Data.
A CIP catalogue record of this book is available from the British
Library.

ISBN 0 340 76852 5

Typeset by Phoenix Typesetting, Ilkley, West Yorkshire.

Printed and bound in Great Britain by Mackays of Chatham, plc

Hodder and Stoughton
A division of Hodder Headline
338 Euston Road
London NW1 3BH

To Clive, without whom nothing.

Acknowledgements

The author is grateful to A. P. Watt Ltd for
permission to quote from two poems by
W. B. Yeats: 'Her Praise. Wild Swans at Coole'
in Chapter Four and 'He Wishes for the Cloths
of Heaven' in Chapter Fourteen.

Sunday 4 October

The voices came again last night. Like a tiny scratching, no louder than the rustling of a mouse behind the skirting. But soon they filled the room, seeping through the cracks like poisoned gas, stopping my ears with poison, like Claudius, until I slept. And dreamt of blood. Always so much blood.

Aye, there's the rub.

Now I must wait until tomorrow. Tomorrow, I shall buy the papers and read what I have done.

Chapter One

Eight-thirty a.m.

Falkner Square, a terrace of once-gracious town houses now sub-divided and well past their prime, was starting to come round. Rather later than most, but that was the kind of area Falkner Square was.

The street-girls who graced its corners by night and slept in its underheated bedsits by day wouldn't be seen again until dusk. The newly-returned students whose rusty Minis and battered VWs cluttered its kerbs wouldn't be up and about for hours; the term's lectures hadn't started yet. And anyway, it was Sunday.

A dog trotted jauntily along the pavement. An elderly woman, a reminder of the area in better days with her felt hat and Sunday best coat, shuffled her way stiffly to morning prayer. A boy delivering papers pierced the stillness with his loud, tuneless whistle.

Suddenly, the door of number twenty-five Falkner Square crashed open. A man hurled himself out into the street, his hair awry, his eyes wild.

The dog stiffened, its hackles rising. The elderly woman glanced around nervously, then put her head down and quickened her pace. The paperboy stopped whistling and stared, open-mouthed.

The man's dressing gown, his hands, his slippered feet, were soaked in blood.

'Help me!' he shouted into the silent street. 'For God's sake, somebody help me!'

A mile away, in the canteen of Blackport Central police station, Detective Chief Inspector Dave Shenfield was having his breakfast. He was a big man, his powerful build belying his fifty-five years despite the beginnings of a paunch. His bullet head above the thick, muscular neck was so closely cropped it was almost shaved. His face had the flattened, coarse features of a boxer gone slightly to seed.

As he ate, he looked through the sheaf of photographs that had just arrived from the pathologist. The first showed the swollen, distorted face of a young girl. Auburn curls formed an incongruous frame to her marble, bloodied features. Dave Shenfield took a swig of tea and turned to the next, a close-up of the butchered remains of her torso. He glanced at it dispassionately, then bit into his bacon sandwich.

'Sorry about your holiday, Guv.'

Shenfield looked up at the man who was taking the seat opposite and shrugged. 'Never did like gardening.' He lit a cigarette and blew out a long plume of smoke. 'So, tell me all about it.'

Ray Whitelaw was flicking through the photographs, pausing to look closely at the injuries to the girl's torso. He was shorter than Shenfield, rounder-edged, with grey moustache, a worn grey suit and shoes so highly polished he would have stood out anywhere in the world as a policeman. 'Helena Goscott. Found just after midnight, down by the docks. She'd been at some start-of-term disco, had a row with her boyfriend and stormed off alone.'

Shenfield shook his head. 'Nice-looking kid. Or was. Beats me how they can still be stupid enough to be about on their own.' His mouth twitched as he added, 'By the way, I met our new recruit on the way in. How's he shaping up?'

'Medlock?' Whitelaw grunted. 'How do you think? Knows it all. Flash clothes, flash car. Into computers.' He made it sound as if it were an indictable offence.

'Lambert's happy then. Still,' Shenfield stubbed out his cigarette, 'give him time. We'll soon knock him into—' He broke off as a loud, breathless voice in the corridor outside called, 'Sir! Sir!'

Whitelaw closed his eyes and muttered. 'Talk of the devil . . .'

Tall and sharp-suited, his yellow hair flopping from its fashionable centre parting as he ran, Detective Constable Neville Medlock was sprinting across the canteen towards them.

'They've found another girl, Sir,' he panted, managing, despite his urgency, to smooth back his hair as he came to a halt in front of them. 'Flat near the university campus.'

'Jesus Christ! Two in one night! What's this bloke on, piecework?' Shenfield jumped to his feet. 'Another redhead?'

'I don't know, Sir. Forensic are on the scene now.'

'Address?'

'Falkner Square.'

Shenfield stopped, one arm into his jacket.

'Number twenty-five. She was found by one of the other occupants. A Dr . . .' Medlock consulted his notebook, '. . . Christopher Heatherington.'

Shenfield and Whitelaw exchanged glances, then Whitelaw said quickly, 'Guv, if you want me to go—'

'Right,' Shenfield cut across him. 'Tell them I'm on my way.'

The basement flat was a scene of utter carnage. Blood splattered the walls from floor to ceiling. Hardly a piece of the cheap, meagre furniture in the living room had not been overturned. This one must have put up one hell of a fight before she died, Shenfield thought.

He pushed his way through the mêlée of police and forensic officers, removed his jacket and threw it over the back of a chair, then squatted down beside Tanya Stewart's lifeless body.

'Time of death?' he queried.

'Doctor reckons between one and three a.m., Guv,' a uniformed officer responded. 'She was found just after eight. Man from the flat upstairs came down to fetch the papers and noticed her door ajar. He wasn't expecting anyone back till today, so he went in to investigate. Harding's taking his statement now.'

'Tell him I'll be up in five minutes.' He waved Medlock across, noticing the faint sheen of perspiration on the man's upper lip. 'Anything strike you?'

Medlock turned a greenish-white. He glanced hastily at the body and looked away.

'Similar mutilations,' he mumbled.

'True. Spot anything different? Apart from the hair. Take a closer look.' Shenfield pulled the younger man down beside him, and murmured. 'This is what CID's about, lad.'

The stench of death was overpowering. Shenfield had learned long ago to take shallow breaths, to avoid it feeding too deeply into his lungs. Medlock might be a graduate fast-tracker, he might have come with glowing references from the Met, but there were some things he'd only find out the hard way. With a gabbled, 'Excuse me,' he barged his way from the room. The uniformed officer let out an ill-concealed snigger.

'That'll do.' Shenfield watched as Medlock disappeared, then turning back to the mangled body, said, 'What do you reckon, Ray?'

Whitelaw sucked pensively at his moustache for a few moments, then answered slowly, 'Extensive injuries. Battered about the head, which isn't his usual style.' He paused. 'And the cuts to the torso look different.'

'Precisely. They're shallower. Almost half-hearted. Look,' Shenfield pointed to the blood-soaked shirt. 'He's moved that aside before he's cut her. It wasn't part of the main attack. An afterthought, almost.'

'Copycat?'

'It crossed my mind.'

She certainly wasn't his usual type. Whatever else you could say about the bastard, he had good taste in women; all the others had been lookers, not that that counted for much when they were laid out on a mortuary slab; they were all sisters under the skin. This one was plump, heavy-featured. More to the point, her hair was dark, and short.

Turning his attention back to Whitelaw, he said, 'But what are the chances of two killers striking on the same night, within a mile of each other? No, it's got to be the same bloke.'

'O'Driscoll?'

Shenfield gazed slowly around the room. No sign of forced entry, and yet she'd hardly have let him in willingly; she'd died within an hour or so of Helena Goscott, and the killer, whoever he was, would most probably still have been stained with her blood. Could she have been near the scene of Helena's death? Followed home and murdered because of what she'd witnessed?

As though echoing his thoughts, Whitelaw asked, 'But why indoors this time? All the others he's taken out at random. Sees them on the streets, creeps up behind them . . .' He made a lunge forward, his hands encircling an imaginary neck, '. . . and does the business. He ran a hell of a risk of being seen. Recognised, even . . .'

Which only added weight to the O'Driscoll

theory, Shenfield thought. Even after all his years in the force, he still felt the knot of excitement in the pit of his stomach that told him they could be on to something. It was over six years since Gavin O'Driscoll had rocked the genteel foundations of Blackport University by stabbing his girlfriend to death after the May Ball. Melanie Loveridge had been a looker too. Shenfield could still remember, as if it were yesterday, the shock of seeing the vandalised beauty of that first young body, the obscenity of her long auburn hair fanned out around her on the grass, reflecting the twinkling fairy lights, as if one part of her, at least, were still alive.

And now O'Driscoll was back. Seven murders in the past twelve months. The similarities in the injuries, the choice of one attractive redhead after another; it had to be O'Driscoll.

All Shenfield was lacking was a single shred of proof. On bad days, he could almost make himself believe that all the murders had in common was his own sense of outrage at the waste of it all.

He looked back down at the body. Could O'Driscoll have taken Tanya Stewart out deliberately, because she'd somehow recognised him? Then given the body his sickening trademarks to cover his tracks? Speculation, he told himself firmly. And for the moment he had enough on his hands dealing with the facts. He pulled himself to his feet and squared his shoulders.

'Right. Flat upstairs, you say?'

*

Medlock was waiting in the communal hallway, wiping his mouth with a handkerchief. Shenfield noted the dark patches on his smart new trousers, where he had knelt in Tanya Stewart's blood, and murmured as he passed him, 'We've all been there, lad. It does get easier, I promise you.'

They made their way up the curved, crumbling staircase to the first floor, where a PC opened the door and stood aside to let them into a large, high-ceilinged room. It smelled damp and unlived-in. Shenfield glánced around, taking in the untidy, book-filled shelves, the table cluttered with the half-eaten remains of a meal, the chipped sink with its haphazard jumble of unwashed plates and mugs. In one corner of the room, an open suitcase spewed books, papers, crumpled clothing.

'Christ,' he muttered under his breath. 'What a pigsty.'

'In the bedroom, Guv.' The PC gestured to a door leading from the main room. 'He's pretty shaken up.'

On the edge of the unmade bed, hunched over a mug of tea, sat a thin youngish man, his face, as he looked up, surprisingly boyish beneath his receding hairline.

Shenfield stood motionless in the doorway, trying not to remember the last time they'd seen each other.

'Hello Christopher,' he said at last.

It was not until they got back to the waiting car, and Shenfield had gone on ahead to the mortuary, that Medlock had the chance to ask the question Whitelaw could see he'd been busting a gut to ask for the last hour.

'What the hell was all that about?' he wanted to know, jerking his head back towards the house. 'There was definitely some sort of sub-text there.'

Whitelaw wondered briefly whether to blank him out, but decided against it; Medlock didn't strike him as the type to be easily snubbed. Instead, he asked in an excessively neutral tone, 'Sub-what?'

Medlock raised an eyebrow. 'Let me rephrase the question. There wasn't exactly any love lost between Shenfield and that lecturer. I might have guessed he'd have it in for anyone with an education, but—'

'And why's that then?' Whitelaw could feel his hackles rising.

Away from the scene of the crime, Medlock had regained his cockiness along with his colour. He gave a dismissive laugh. 'We were warned about traditionalists like Shenfield back at Police College.'

'Chief Inspector Shenfield to you.' Whitelaw looked at Medlock's soft pink face. He stank of after-shave, although he probably didn't have to take a razor to those pudgy cheeks more than once a week. 'Good at summing people up, are you?' His tone might have dented a more fragile ego.

'I reckon so. A degree in psychology helps.'

'Right,' Whitelaw nodded. 'Nothing surprises you too much, then?'

'Not often.'

'Well, try this for size, sunshine. Christopher Heatherington is Dave Shenfield's son.' Whitelaw watched with satisfaction as the younger man's jaw dropped. He had the feeling it wasn't often that Neville Medlock was lost for words. 'How does that fit your . . . what was it? Your sub-text?'

Chapter Two

The blood was sticky, already congealed, pools and pools of it, impeding his progress, his shoes making an obscene, squelching noise as he moved forward. From under the sheet protruded a small hand, hardly bigger than a child's. The blue-white fingers were curled, like the petals of a flower. He knew he had to face what was under that sheet. Slowly, reluctantly, he lifted one corner.

A high, insistent scream split the silence. The petal-hands reached up to him, the nails stretching into talons as they clawed at his flesh, dragging him down, down, down . . .

Christopher Heatherington shot up in bed, drenched in sweat, and stared wildly around him as the screaming gradually translated itself into the shrilling of a kettle in the flat above. He sank back against the pillow, his heartbeat subsiding as the familiar bedroom took shape in the dull light filtering through his curtains, a half-unpacked rucksack lurking like a sleeping animal in the corner. He closed his eyes, opening them abruptly as the vividness of the nightmare swept over him again.

Any hope of further sleep banished, he got up, pulling on a jersey and going through to the living room, averting his eyes from the black plastic sack that held his bloodstained clothing. He busied himself with making tea and toast, then, his back to the bin-liner, he sat down at the table and turned on Radio Three. The measured strains of a Schubert string quartet filled the room. Humming softly, he crossed to the window and looked down on the shabby street below.

Apart from the striped tape that still cordoned off the front of the house, it all looked terrifyingly normal, like a placid sea the morning after a storm. The feeble rays of sun slanted through the trees and freckled the dusty glass. A fly buzzed languidly in the corner of the sash. From the flat above came the faint clatter of pans as cupboard doors opened and closed. A distant babble of breakfast television competed insistently with the Schubert. An answering glimpse of monochrome flickered in the window opposite. The unevenly-drawn curtains jarred against the symmetry of the once-gracious Georgian façade; the wood around the sash windows was beginning to rot.

Christopher closed his eyes, then glanced back into his shabby room.

'The whole place is beginning to rot,' he murmured to himself. Going back to the table, he cleared a space amongst the toast crumbs and butter smears, and took out the CV he had been working on the previous evening.

Name: Christopher David Heatherington.
Age: Thirty-five.
Qualifications: St John's, Cambridge: BA
(1985); MA (1987); PhD (1989)
Current Employment: Lecturer in English
Literature, Blackport University.
Publications Include: 'The Wild Old Wicked
Man; Self Portraiture in the Poetry of W. B. Yeats'
in S. Castledine (ed.) Contemporary Irish Litera-
ture, *Cambridge University Press (1991)*; 'A
Divinity that Shapes Our Ends; Shakespeare's
Heroes' in C. Muldoon (ed.) Elizabethan and
Jacobean Literary Theory and Criticism,
Blackport University Publications (1992) . . .

The list of dry-as-dust articles and papers that
represented more than a decade of academic
endeavour ran to another two sides of A4. He hesitated for a long moment, pen poised, then turned
instead to the last section on the form.

Other Achievements: . . . Christopher looked
around the untidy living room again, and began to
write, 'I work in a second-rate department at a
northern red-brick university, where the majority of
students would rather drink in the Union bar than
study Shakespeare. I have a book of published
poetry to my name that few will read and fewer
understand, a flat that needs redecorating, and a
father with whom I have nothing in common other
than the deepest mutual contempt. That is the sum
of my other achievements.'

He screwed the paper into a ball and hurled it across the room. Then he lifted his face to the weak autumn sun and began to weep.

'Thought the education budget had been cut.'

Later that afternoon, Dave Shenfield was standing with Medlock in the wood-panelled anteroom of the Vice Chancellor of Blackport University's office, waiting for an audience. He glanced at the ornately-framed paintings of previous Vice Chancellors and shook his head. 'Different world.'

'So, counting last night's victims,' Medlock said, producing a file from his immaculate leather briefcase, 'four have been students, and three prostitutes.'

Shenfield nodded. 'Mind you, these days it's not always easy to spot the difference. From the description of what Helena Goscott was wearing at that nightclub, anyone could've mistaken her for a tom. Black Lycra skirt half way up her backside. Some of these girls are asking for it.' He watched Medlock bite back a number of possible responses, and waited. Political correctness was one failing he would not tolerate in his officers.

The younger man coloured slightly, but said merely, 'Precisely my point, Sir. The students could just as easily have been taken for prostitutes as vice versa, bearing in mind the university's proximity to the red light district. In which case, the O'Driscoll theory becomes rather more tenuous, doesn't it?'

Shenfield suppressed a twinge of irritation. Nothing wrong with Medlock having a point of view of his own, he told himself. Even if he had only been on the case for a couple of days, when the rest of the team had spent the last twelve months slogging their guts out on it. 'The university authorities would like to think so,' he said. A far more worthy cause for his ill-humour. 'The last thing they want is a psychopathic ex-student on the loose. After all, he might damage their application rates. Christ, what a bunch of tossers.'

'Isn't that a slight generalisation?' Medlock replied stiffly, the 'Sir' that he added delayed just long enough to suggest a touch of insolence.

Shenfield looked at him hard. Intellectual snobbery; so that was going to be young Medlock's blind spot. He was robbed of an adequate chance to respond by the arrival of the Vice Chancellor's secretary.

'It's Guv, not Sir,' he threw over his shoulder, as they followed her through to the adjoining office. 'You're not at school now.'

It was a large room, expensively furnished and dominated by a huge walnut desk, behind which sat the Vice Chancellor, a small, pink man with half-moon spectacles, translucent ears, and a mouth already puckered in distaste. Shenfield looked at him with instant dislike. Since yesterday morning he'd been doing his best to pull strings with the top brass by all accounts, but if he thought Shenfield was going to dance to his tune by playing down the university angle to the press, he could think again.

Christopher was perched uncomfortably on the edge of one of the armchairs arranged in a semi-circle in front of the desk. Shenfield tried and failed to catch his eye.

'Dreadful business, dreadful,' the Vice Chancellor said, when he had seated them and ordered coffee. 'The Senior Tutor's been run off his feet, and the SU president has already given a most ill-advised interview to Radio North West, complaining about security. And that this . . . incident took place on the doorstep of a member of staff . . .' He took out a silk handkerchief and dabbed his nose fastidiously as he glanced at Christopher, as if fearing that the other man's proximity to violent death had made him contagious. 'You've already met Dr Heatherington, I believe.'

Christopher nodded curtly. Shenfield lit a cigarette and regarded him through a curtain of smoke almost as thick as the atmosphere of antagonism between them.

'I do trust I can rely on your discretion in this investigation Chief Inspector?' the Vice Chancellor addressed Shenfield. 'As I have already discussed with your Chief Constable, the fact that our new students are just arriving . . .'

'. . . Means you don't want them turning up to find the place crawling with police. I can see what an inconvenience that would be, Sir,' Shenfield said blandly.

Medlock glanced across with a slight frown. 'As a graduate myself, I quite understand your concern. The prospect of a clearly deranged killer . . .'

18

'DC Medlock did "deranged" at college,' Shenfield said dryly. The comment would have raised a chuckle of amused contempt at Blackport Central.

'Really?' Christopher's voice was icy.

'Psychology. Warwick, as a matter of fact, Vice Chancellor.' Medlock smiled engagingly. 'My professor spoke of your time there with enormous respect. You're something of a legend.'

The Vice Chancellor, mollified, offered him a biscuit.

'At this stage, there's no conclusive evidence of a connection between either Helena Goscott or Tanya Stewart and their killer.' Shenfield struggled to control his rising anger. Two of their own girls – four, if you counted Jennifer Moore last February, and Nicola Collett in June – snuffed out within a mile of this room, and they were carrying on as if they were at a bloody garden party. 'Not that that'll stop the press trying to find one. They've been having a field day. "Beast of Blackport Strikes Again" and all that crap. And speculating on the link with the May Ball murder, of course.'

Christopher breathed in sharply.

'Nothing like a serial killer to boost circulation,' Shenfield went on, goaded by his son's undisguised disapproval. 'Especially if he turns out to be middle-class and well educated. Still, as young Medlock here was saying before we came in, we could just as easily be looking at a disgruntled punter knocking off what he imagines is a few toms. Tarts, in case you don't watch *The Bill*,' he added, helping himself to the only chocolate digestive. Biting into it thoughtfully and scattering crumbs over the shining surface of the desk, he asked, 'Don't suppose you'd happen to know if young Helena was supplementing her grant with a bit of street work, by any chance? Quite a sideline with students these days, according to the *Echo*.'

'And you'd be the expert on tarts,' Christopher muttered quite audibly. The Vice Chancellor stared at him nonplussed as he went on, 'Murder may be a laughing matter to you, but for the rest of us . . .'

Ignoring the ashtray the Vice Chancellor had manoeuvred towards him, Shenfield stubbed his cigarette into his saucer and leaned forward. 'If you had to face what I do, day after day, you might find you needed a sense of humour to stay sane. I have to live in the real world, *Dr* Heatherington.' He made the title sound like an insult. 'I do a hard job. Maybe that makes me hard.' He glanced at the heavy brocade curtains and plush carpets. 'Sorry if my attitude doesn't fit in with the decor. Now, shall we get down to business?'

Shenfield knew he was handling the meeting badly. He had the distinct feeling that he was in a minority of one, that the others were all members of a private club that he was unqualified to join, bandying jargon and acronyms that he was buggered if he was going to ask them to explain. Medlock, a model of diplomacy, made all the right noises, while Shenfield, in his discomfort, found himself using every available opportunity to put him down. Then, angered by his own unprofessionalism, he began to bluster and bully. He could hear himself doing it, describing the girls' injuries in ever more graphic detail, seeing the disgust in his son's expression but unable to stop himself. It was unnerving, observing Christopher on his own territory. In a position of authority. Somehow, in his mind's eye, he still saw him as a kid, inept and helpless.

By the end of the meeting, Christopher had lapsed into stony silence. The Vice Chancellor barely managed to maintain a façade of civility as he saw them off the premises, promising tight-lipped to take up the discussion with their Chief Constable.

Shenfield stumped ahead, elbowing his way through the drifting crowds of students. He reached the car first, turning the radio up, as Medlock climbed in next to him, to a volume that precluded conversation.

Medlock stretched out his long legs, folded his arms, and said nothing.

By the time they got back to Blackport Central, Shenfield had begun to calm down. So he'd been made to feel like a pork pie at a bar mitzvah, and had ended up making a prat of himself. But even so . . . He glanced across at Medlock, trying to gauge whether his continued silence meant he was nervous, embarrassed, or simply pissed off. Whatever, they'd hardly got off to a good start.

'Listen,' he said, as they parked the car and made their way back through the ranks of panda cars. 'I'm sorry about all that back there.'

'All what?'

'I don't make a habit of slagging off fellow officers. Not in public, at any rate.'

'I'll survive. Like you say, I'm not at school now, Sir.' Shenfield could detect no sarcasm in Medlock's sudden grin as he added, 'I mean Guv.'

Thank Christ at least he was going to be thick-skinned enough to take a few knocks. Shenfield respected that.

'Right,' he said briskly, relieved to have got the apology out of the way. 'I want you to get to work on finding everything you can about Tanya Stewart. Trace her movements since she arrived back here yesterday morning, then look into her background. Back to infant school if necessary. See if there's any way we can link her to O'Driscoll.' Shenfield took the front steps two at a time, then paused as he reached the door. 'You mark my words, if we can track that little bastard down, we'll have our Beast of Blackport.'

Monday 5 October

I keep her memory in a box inside my head. Safe, where I can spread it like a fine, precious cloth and examine its minutest stitch. My Melanie. Her bloodless, oval face turned up to me. The waxy purity of the roses against the whiteness of her shoulder. The tiny hairs dusting her slim arms like pollen. Her long, red hair. So beautiful.

But beauty is not truth, it is corruption. Writhing limbs and open, greedy mouths and slippery darkness.

And so it started.

Two this time. Omniscient now; redeemed, they stare out from this morning's papers.

The first deserved to die. Bold-eyed and predatory, with her short skirt and tight, revealing blouse. Just looking at her picture, I can taste the hot, musky smell of her, like a bitch on heat.

But not the second. Poor girl, you had no beauty. I would not have hurt you for the world, but how can you forgive me? I cannot blame the voices for your death, and now I am beyond redemption.

Chapter Three

Flora Castledine, caught in the swell of bodies, allowed herself to be swept forward across the road, not caring whether she should be turning off to right or left.

Blackport afternoon rush hour was unlike anything she had ever experienced. The main street in St Mary's boasted perhaps a dozen shops, three pubs and a post office. The nearest equivalent to a rush hour was the holiday-makers' ten o'clock saunter to the quay each day in summer to pick up tripper boats to the off-islands. The only crowds were the squabbling gulls on Penninnis Head. Nothing she had seen or read about Blackport had prepared Flora for this clamorous assault on her ears and eyes.

On the far pavement, the crowd split in all directions, leaving her in a shop doorway like a piece of driftwood washed up on the shore. She dropped her ton-weight suitcase, a present from Simon. He had always been Simon. Never Father. And certainly never Dad. She visualised his frail, hunched figure, still waving as the plane took her up and away from the Scillies, standing alone, getting smaller and smaller, and was filled with a wave of love mixed with compassion, and, she allowed herself the luxury of admitting, resentment.

A taxi hooted, its window down as the driver called out, 'Want a lift, duck?'

She picked up the case, unable to suppress the grin of sheer excitement she could feel spreading across her features.

'I'm here,' she mouthed at her reflection in the taxi window. 'I've done it!'

She felt in her pocket for the letter from the Accommodation Officer. In the same envelope, she had pushed a scrap of paper bearing the name: 'Dr Christopher Heatherington, department of English', and a phone number. Simon had made her swear she would contact this old friend of his as soon as she arrived. She hesitated, then screwed the paper up and dropped it onto the floor, with a mental apology to her father.

'Thirty-one Aigburth Street, please.'

The driver nodded. Expertly manoeuvring a series of turns, he nosed into the traffic and away from the station, following signs to the university. As they turned into a broad square on the edge of the campus, the taxi slowed down. It was just the sort of place that she had envisaged, each house sub-let, she could tell from the ranks of doorbells, into several apartments. She tried to imagine the exotic mix of occupants, craning to see which was number thirty-one. She was disappointed when they did not stop, but drove on through a maze of narrowing streets, passing row upon row of identical, increasingly grimy terraces, punctuated by derelict, boarded-up factories and stretches of scrubby wasteland. Finally, they came to a halt outside an Indian take-away. Its flickering neon sign, The Royal Bombay Palace, enlivened the corner of a row of dingy shops. One of its windows was boarded up and covered in graffiti.

'But . . .' Flora stammered, checking the address.

'Flat above the shop,' the driver grinned, pointing to an upper window draped with sagging net curtains. ''Spect you get in round the side. Look on the bright side, duck. At least you'll be all right for your tea.'

As Flora hauled her case out, she became aware of another girl standing on the pavement, a rucksack and several carrier bags balanced against her sturdy legs. Her shock of red hair, jacket of vivid Aztec patchwork, and trailing scarlet scarf lent her the appearance of a plump, exotic bird against the drab shopfront.

'God, what a dump, eh?' The girl nodded at the window. 'The woman in the curry shop's rung the agent and he'll be along in two minutes. Or at least that's what she said quarter of an hour ago. I'm Meg, in case you hadn't worked it out,' she beamed from behind round wire spectacles. 'You must be Flora.'

Flora nodded, too confused to ask questions, feeling as if she had landed an unwitting part in *Alice in Wonderland*.

'They did tell you we'd be sharing? God, they

didn't, I can see by your face. The bastards. I tell you, that bunch in Accommodation need putting up against a wall. Still, there you go. Let me give you a quick CV. I'm Meg Evans. Welsh, see,' she added unnecessarily. 'Fourth year medic. I've no nasty habits, or none you need worry about. I don't smoke, I'm not a vegan, I don't suffer from PMT and I'm not in the habit of setting fire to holiday-makers' cottages, despite the accent. In fact, I'm just about your ideal flatmate, and anyway, you'll never find a place on your own now term's started.' She stopped to draw breath and grinned. 'My only vice is the size of my gob. You come from a family as big as mine, once you manage to get a word in you don't stop till someone shouts louder than you can. But I don't get offended if you tell me to shut up. Everyone else does.'

'So where did you live last year?' Flora asked cautiously. 'I mean, why are you . . . ?'

Several minutes later and Flora had received the life-history of Meg's last flatmate Bernadette, together with a detailed report of Bernadette's violent and, in Meg's opinion, ill-advised passion for Jamie, a fourth-year vet, whom she had now invited to share her bed on a more permanent basis.

'And her a good Catholic!' Meg shook her head and continued without a trace of irony. 'Anyhow, to cut a long story short, I told Bernadette I didn't fancy having some great oaf leaving his toenail clippings in the soap and his socks in the breadbin. Get quite enough of that sort of thing at home, see. "It's him or me, Bernie", I told her. Reasonable enough, that seemed to me. So now I'm homeless. So much for friends!' she finished cheerfully. 'Shall we give it a go here, then?'

Flora looked at Meg's round, friendly face and felt secretly relieved that Bernadette had chosen the vet. Thirty-one Aigburth Street had already begun to seem a less romantic prospect than when viewed from the safety of St Mary's.

Before she could answer, a voice behind her asked uncertainly, 'Are you the s . . . students?'

She turned, and was startled by the contrast between the timid voice and its owner, a bulky man of about forty, with a solid, fleshy face overlaid by a patina of blackheads and the battle scars of teenage acne. He exuded a faint aura of curry.

'N . . . N . . . Norman,' he stammered, by way of introduction. 'I'm the c . . . c . . .'

'Curry shop owner?' Flora hazarded. She could feel the corners of her mouth begin to twitch, and stared studiously at him, avoiding Meg's eye. He appeared to be moulded into his blue suit, the straining fabric settling into the greasy folds and shining hillocks of his large body. His huge hands protruded from his fraying cuffs as though grateful for escape. He stared back at Flora for a long moment, before offering her a hand by way of greeting. It felt like a fish, clammy and boneless to the touch.

'Caretaker.' He bent and picked up her case as if it were a feather. 'I l . . . look after Mr Singh's p . . . properties. He owns m . . . m . . . most of the houses round here.'

He led the way down the entry at the side of the shop and fiddled interminably with a bunch of keys, before finally throwing himself against the door, which gave way abruptly, catapulting him inside. Meg crossed her eyes at Flora as, trying to suppress their giggles, they followed him up the stairs. At the top, he squeezed himself against the wall to let them through.

'The k . . . k . . .'

'Kitchen,' Flora finished desperately, ignoring Meg's stifled guffaw as best she could.

The cheap sink and grease-encrusted cooker stood incongruously against garish nursery paper; spaceships and men in spacesuits floated at regular intervals across the wall, sharing the gaps between the flimsy kitchen cupboards with the figure of a small beaming chinaman.

'One moment, please. My friend and I need a word.' Meg shut the door in his face, and they exploded into helpless laughter. Finally regaining some self-control, she whispered, 'Leave this to me.' Arranging her features into an expression of righteous indignation, she threw open the door and said sternly, 'This is appalling. The Accommodation Office said "newly-fitted kitchen".' She stuck her head into one of the bedrooms. 'There's damp on that wall.'

The caretaker looked crestfallen. 'I could d . . . d . . . decorate it for you. I'm only just across the road.'

'And we were told there was central heating,' she said, pointing to a grimy gas fire.

His dark, button eyes darted away from her, as though his big frame were inhabited by some small creature looking for a way out.

'It'll be fine.' Flora could bear his discomfort no longer. She turned to Meg and muttered, 'Come on, it's not too bad. And you did say we'd never find anything else now term's started.'

Meg gazed around, then shrugged elaborately. 'It'll do, I suppose.' She gave the caretaker a shrewd look. 'Provided you have a word with your Mr Singh about the rent.'

He insisted on bringing up the rest of their luggage, and, despite Meg's increasingly unsubtle hints, hung around while they unpacked, checking the locks and rearranging the sparse furniture, then disappearing briefly, to their relief, only to return with a rickety bookcase from the house next door.

'Are you d . . . doing English?' he asked, picking up a stack of Flora's books.

'No.' Unable to maintain Meg's level of abruptness, she added reluctantly, 'I just like reading.'

'The M . . . M . . . M . . .'

Flora took the book he handed her and placed it on a shelf, wishing he'd selected something a little easier to pronounce than the Metaphysical Poets.

'*Love, all alike, no season knows, nor clime, Nor hours, days, months, which are the rags of time.*'

The words came out entirely without impediment. Flora glanced up at him in amazement, which turned instantly to embarrassed remorse as she realised how patronising she must appear. Why should she imagine she had the monopoly on poetry?

As if sensing her thoughts, he said, 'I l . . . like reading too.' A dark flush suffused his features as his eyes flicked away from her and fixed on a hole in the threadbare carpet. 'I'll t . . . try to find you a rug.'

At last he went, promising to come back the following day with some tins of paint.

Meg watched him lumber down the narrow stairs and shook her head. 'Strange man. Anyway, never mind him, I'm starving.'

Half an hour later, they settled down to celebrate their first evening in the flat with a take-away and a bottle of tepid white wine. Meg plugged in the ancient television, while Flora spooned out soggy rice and poked around in a foil container of pungent, violently orange sauce in a futile search for some trace of anything remotely identifiable. She checked the scrawl on the lid of the container and shook her head as she peered dubiously at the already-congealing mixture; Balti it could be, for all she knew, never having eaten curry before. Chicken it most certainly was not.

The six o'clock news had just started. A burly middle-aged man in a well-pressed shirt with a collar that looked too small for his beefy neck sat at a table, in front of which was ranged a barrage of reporters and photographers.

'Do you think the killer could be from the university, as some of the tabloids have suggested, Chief
Inspector?' a voice called.

'I am unable to comment at this stage.' The man
leaned forward self-consciously to speak into the
microphone. 'But I would advise all students,
especially female students, as they return from their
summer holidays, to be extremely vigilant . . .'

'You don't want to watch that stuff, do you?' Meg
flicked to another channel.

'Doesn't it bother you, knowing there's a killer on
the loose?' Flora shivered.

'Not if I don't think about it,' Meg grinned. 'No
point in worrying, is there? A quarter of a million
people live in this town, see. The way I look at it,
you're more likely to get run over by a bus. Or get
salmonella from this muck.' She pushed away the
remains of her meal and poured them both more
wine, which, in the absence of any glasses, they
were drinking from chipped enamel mugs. 'Anyway, this is supposed to be our house-warming
party, girl! So here's to us, and sod the Beast of
Blackport!'

Flora thought of the polished crystal and
freshly-starched linen that Mrs Menheniott, the
housekeeper, would be laying out at that moment
in the big, silent dining room overlooking the sea.
Simon's usual half-bottle of Sancerre would be
chilling in the ice bucket.

'To Blackport.' She raised her mug. 'And to
freedom!'

33

Chapter Four

'Do you reckon Shenfield gets a kick out of going into the gynaecological details?' Medlock asked.

'You what?' Ray Whitelaw looked up from his copy of the *Blackport Echo*.

'Or did he put on that exhibition yesterday for the benefit of his son?' He sauntered over to Shenfield's desk and picked up the photograph which stood beside the orderly bundles of files. 'The Shenfields *en famille*, one supposes.' A much younger, leaner Shenfield, complete with knitted tie and flared trousers, stared back at him. His arm was clamped possessively around the shoulders of a slight, pretty girl, with bare feet and a dress of flowing Indian cotton. She'd even got a flower in her long hair. They made an incongruous couple. He looked at the solemn toddler slung across her hip and said, 'Christopher Heatherington, presumably. So why the different surnames? Mrs Shenfield been playing away from home, had she?'

'Watch it, you,' Whitelaw snapped.

Medlock let the photograph fall from his fingers.

'Christ, what an appalling thought. Shenfield in the Swinging Sixties!'

Whitelaw snatched the photograph up and re-positioned it beside the files with a carefulness bordering on reverence. 'Dave Shenfield's a first-class policeman. One of the best. And don't you forget it. You might think you can come up here from London and blind us all with science, but let me give you a word of advice. You'll get nowhere in this force unless you learn to show some loyalty. And some respect. Now why don't you do something useful, like put the kettle on? Or haven't you got an A level in making tea?'

'OK, OK. Keep your shirt on.'

'You've got a big mouth, Medlock. If you spent a bit more time with it shut, and your ears open, you might just learn something.'

'And if you lot took advantage of my expertise, instead of taking the piss all the time, you might learn something.'

Leaning back in his chair, Whitelaw folded his arms and asked, with a sarcasm lost on his younger colleague, 'And what expertise would that be, then?'

'Psychological profiling.' Medlock perched himself on the edge of Shenfield's desk. 'Assuming Shenfield's on the right track with his murder investigation, we should be trying to understand Gavin O'Driscoll's mental state.'

'His mental state?' Whitelaw laughed bitterly. 'We heard enough about that last time round. Bloody barristers. Even if we do nail him, some do-gooder judge'll probably find diminished responsibility and send him off for therapy sessions in the south of France.'

He glanced up. Shenfield was standing in the doorway.

'Nothing.' He slammed the pathologist's report on Tanya Stewart down in front of Whitelaw, while Medlock slid hastily off the desk. 'If I had my way, I'd put the bastard down, same as I'd put down a mad dog.' He jabbed a finger at Whitelaw. 'It's *when* we nail him, not if. And this time we'll make bloody sure we hang on to him.'

Even after all these years, he still couldn't quite believe the stupidity of the court that had released O'Driscoll from custody while he awaited trial, on no more than his lawyer's trumped-up plea of psychological hardship.

As if reading his thoughts, Whitelaw said, 'If he'd had a crew-cut and an earring, they wouldn't have given a toss. They just couldn't hack the idea of a nice, clean-cut, middle-class boy like any of their own sons in a remand centre.'

'So why come back to Blackport, where he's known, when there's a warrant out for him?' Medlock reached for the file. 'Would anyone of O'Driscoll's intelligence seriously be prepared to take the risk?'

'You're the trick cyclist, sunshine,' Whitelaw snorted. 'You tell us.'

'OK, OK, break it up.' Shenfield turned to Medlock. 'It's not difficult to buy yourself a new identity. He could have changed beyond recognition in six years, if he'd put his mind to it.'

They'd always assumed O'Driscoll had headed back to Belfast when he skipped bail. All the usual enquiries had been made at the time, but Belfast was an easy place to disappear in, and the RUC, whilst co-operative, had had more pressing matters on their hands. Six years on, the trail was stone cold. O'Driscoll would have had no problem reinventing himself, especially as he had no family left over there. His father, a local GP, had died of a heart attack a few months after the murder; his mother had committed suicide last year, which, Shenfield suspected, was what had set him off again.

'As to motive, who knows? Grudge against the university is a possibility,' he continued. 'They threw O'Driscoll to the wolves. No backing, no character reference, nothing. Damage limitation was the name of the game . . . then as now. He could be trying to get his own back.'

And succeeding, if the headlines in today's *Echo* were anything to go by, he thought. 'A Campus that Lives in Fear.' The university authorities must be wetting themselves.

'Or a grudge against you, of course.' Medlock looked him in the eye. 'Forced confession, police brutality . . .'

Shenfield met his gaze for a long moment. Fair enough, he thought. He'd tried to get Medlock to rise to the political correctness bait yesterday. He quite admired the lad for playing him at his own game with the police brutality routine. He'd never been one to bow and scrape to more senior ranks himself. And in the O'Driscoll case . . .

'Instead of speculating ourselves up our own backsides, let's get down to the facts, shall we?' he said, mildly enough. 'Tanya Stewart's movements last Saturday, for instance.'

Medlock evidently wasn't going to push it. Reaching for his pocket book, he said, 'Not exactly a party animal. Spent the day in the library. Ate in the Students' Union. Called in at the disco, but left before ten-thirty, which blows a hole in her having witnessed the Goscott murder. A neighbour saw her returning home around eleven.'

Shenfield grabbed the pocket book. 'You mean we can place her in the same initial location as Helena Goscott? Why didn't you say so?'

'Half the university was there.'

'Including, most probably, her killer.' He crossed to the board on which photographs of the two dead girls were pinned, and drew a line joining them to the third likeness above. He paused to examine the unsmiling, slightly gormless face staring back at him, and wondered why identification photographs, like passports, seldom did their subjects justice. Gavin O'Driscoll's evil nature certainly hadn't shown in his face; even Shenfield had to admit he'd been a good-looking lad.

'All three of them were at the disco.' He nodded slowly, the excitement beginning to bubble up again. 'I'll stake my reputation on it. And, as we already know, Student Union cards had to be shown on the door. They were adamant about that. You realise what this means?' He turned to Whitelaw and Medlock. 'We're not just talking about Gavin O'Driscoll back in Blackport. We're talking about him back in the bloody university.'

The Senior Common Room was empty, apart from Professor Sommerville from Classics, who was dozing over *The Times* crossword, and Professor Muldoon, Dean of the English department. Clarence Muldoon was an expert on Jacobean tragedy and the internal politics of the university in just about equal measure. He held a burning ambition for public life, and an entrenched dislike of undergraduate students, surpassed only by his own unpopularity amongst his colleagues.

On entering the Common Room, Christopher nodded briefly in his direction, poured himself a coffee and selected a seat as far away as possible, then pulled out the letter that had arrived that morning and began to reread it.

'One wonders if the poor old chap has been here since last term.' Clarence glanced across at Professor Sommerville, then sat down, uninvited, beside Christopher. He lowered his voice, 'Between you and me, the Vice Chancellor is looking into the whole area of Classics. The Funding Council was none too happy about their performance, frankly.' He bent to put his coffee cup down on the table in front of them, taking the opportunity, as he did so, to glance inquisitively at Christopher's letter. 'Anything interesting?'

'An old acquaintance.' Christopher folded the

letter and put it back in his pocket. 'A personal matter.'

'Really?' Clarence, never noted for his thin skin, looked at him expectantly.

Christopher sighed. 'His daughter is coming up this term. He wants me to keep an eye on her.'

Clarence pursed his lips. 'Need to be careful about that sort of thing, in my opinion. Always a mistake to get involved with the undergraduates. Remember Alford?' He shook his head. 'Blighted what could have been quite a promising career.'

Dr Alford had been a rival candidate for the Deanship. The rumours concerning his relationship with one of his female students had been widely ascribed in the Senior Common Room to Clarence Muldoon himself.

'The last time I set eyes on her, she was a grizzly, ginger-haired toddler,' Christopher said stiffly. 'If it were not for the fact that her father will hound me with phone calls, faxes and God alone knows what else until I reassure him of her safety, I would have no hesitation in ignoring his letter entirely. This term has started unpleasantly enough for me, without having to pander to the whims of over-anxious parents.'

'Of course!' Clarence leaned forward, his eyes gleaming with renewed interest. 'Appalling experience for you, old chap. Now tell me, is it true that—'

'Will you excuse me please?' His coffee unfinished, Christopher got up and left the Common Room.

'Extraordinary fellow.' Clarence shook his head. 'One would have thought a sympathetic ear was exactly what he needed at a time like this.'

Across the room, Professor Sommerville slumbered on, undisturbed.

Flora was feeling dazed as, marshalled by an officious third year, she and her fellow freshers piled into the corridor outside the History secretary's office and over to the pigeon holes, already crammed to overflowing with registration documents and letters of welcome. They had followed obediently all morning and she was getting bored.

'Your timetables will be over there,' their leader was explaining.

As the rest of the group surged forward and fanned around the noticeboard he was indicating, Flora edged away and gazed out of the window onto the square below, orange and yellow with a bright patchwork of fallen leaves. Knots of denim-clad figures sat in the October sun; the atmosphere was full of anticipation at the start of a new term. Timetables could wait, Flora decided. She had had enough of being inside.

'Miss Castledine? Flora Castledine?'

The voice made her jump and she turned around guiltily, as though her thoughts had been read. Its owner was standing in front of the main group, who had all turned towards him expectantly, like fledglings awaiting the next worm.

'That's me.' She moved hastily back towards the

noticeboard. The man's cords, crumpled shirt and ancient sandals marked him as an academic, and Flora had no desire to get on the wrong side of one of her lecturers before she had even started.

'I wonder if I might have a word?' The group parted to let them through and looked on with curiosity as he drew her towards the door and introduced himself as Dr Heatherington.

'I was meant to ring you, wasn't I?' She tried to suppress the irritation in her voice. 'I only got here last night.'

'I . . . I just wanted to say hello . . .' His voice faltered. He looked so uncomfortable that she couldn't help smiling.

'Hello.'

'I . . .' He sighed. 'Listen, Miss Castledine. Whatever your father may have told you, I have no intention of playing chaperone. Now, I mustn't keep you . . .'

'Poor Simon!' She caught the answering glint of humour in his eye, then they both laughed. Glancing back towards the group, she whispered, 'I think I've reached saturation point actually. We're supposed to be on a tour of the library next, but what I really need to find is the nearest bank. There's a stack of things I need to buy already.'

As they walked, Flora described the flat above the take-away, making him laugh again with her thumbnail sketch of Norman-the-caretaker.

They passed the bookshop. Flora glanced at the window then stopped dead. 'That's you!' She squinted through the glass at the stacked volumes, topped by a large, grainy photograph of her companion, looking mildly embarrassed. 'Poetry! That's brilliant! Have you had a lot published?'

'Not much,' he blushed. 'It's more of a hobby, really. I haven't achieved anything like your father's output. But I do enjoy writing.'

'He doesn't.'

They walked on for a few moments in silence.

'What *I'd* really like to try is acting.' Flora said suddenly. 'I wanted to apply to drama school, but the headmistress threw a fit, and Simon was dead against it. You know how he can be.'

'There's a very good drama society here. Why don't you audition? I could find out the details, if you like. Kieran Willerton, one of my second years, is a leading light. I could ask him . . .'

'Would you? Thanks, Dr Heatherington. That would be great.'

'Oh, please, call me Christopher,' he smiled awkwardly. 'Everyone else does.'

'You know, you're not a bit what I expected.' She looked up at him, her head on one side. When she had been given the phone number, she had imagined some desiccated, fussy intellectual; a carbon copy of her father, in fact. Christopher Heatherington was sweet, she decided. 'When Simon said you'd been at Cambridge together, I thought you'd be old.'

Christopher waited until she had disappeared into the bank, then turned towards the student coffee bar. He scanned the crowded, fuggy room, then fought his way to a bench by a low table, already awash with cigarette ends and empty wrappers. Some wit had written, 'Is Muffin the Mule a sexual offence?' in red felt-tip across the Formica top. Student humour was one of the few statics in a fast-changing world; Christopher had read the same line in a Cambridge rag mag.

He reached into his briefcase for a copy of the book that had been awaiting him on his return from holiday. *'C.D. Heatherington: Collected Poems 1992–99.'* He turned to the flyleaf. *'To Susannah'*, the dedication read. He ran his hand gently over the pristine page, his lips moving silently as he stared into the distance.

'They say it's the first sign, talking to yourself. How're you doing, Christopher?'

'Kieran!' Christopher looked up at the sound of the familiar Manchester accent and put the book down on the table with an embarrassed laugh. 'Sorry. I was just running through some Yeats for a lecture this afternoon.' He repeated the lines aloud. *'Like a man who has published a new book. Or a young girl . . .'*

'. . . *dressed out in a new gown.* "Her Praise. Wild Swans at Coole". Ask me another.' Kieran Willerton swept the rubbish from the table and sat down, careless of the cigarette ash and spilt coffee. 'It's good,' he nodded towards the book. 'You must be dead proud.'

'You've read it then?' Christopher looked pleased.

Kieran said with a grin, 'Read it? First thing I bought out of my student loan. Can't say fairer than that, can I?'

He looked around the coffee bar, raising his hand in greeting to several groups at other tables, then turned his attention back to Christopher, the grin vanishing as he said soberly, 'I heard about what happened. Have the police any idea who—'

'Do you mind if we don't talk about it?' Christopher cut in. 'Everyone seems to want the grisly details, and I . . .' He looked up apologetically. 'I know you weren't trying to . . . It's just that I . . . I'd rather try to put it out of my head, at least while I'm here. When I'm back at the flat, of course . . .' He shuddered.

'Sure.' A small silence. 'So, what've you been up to all summer then? Apart from getting yourself published.'

'I spent a couple of months in Florence.' Christopher smiled, with effort. 'The Uffizi is absolutely breathtaking, although parts of it are still closed, unfortunately. It's a marvellous city. Visually stunning, of course, but it's the sounds around those impossibly narrow streets.' He closed his eyes. 'And the smells . . . garlic, fresh-baked bread . . . All darkened by the sour breath of the River Arno. Ordinary, everyday life underpinned by the sluggish dankness of who knows how many past centuries. The whole city an amazing juxtaposition of the then and the now.' He opened his eyes abruptly and gave an embarrassed laugh. 'That was all very poetic, wasn't it? Sorry!'

Kieran tapped the book. 'You're allowed to be poetic. You're a poet.'

'Yes.' Christopher smiled. 'Yes, I am, aren't I?' He picked it up, measuring its satisfying weight. 'It's an incredible feeling, you know, actually holding it, here in print. I've had stuff published before, of course. Chapters in literary criticisms . . . well, you know that, you've read some of them. But this . . .' His expression suddenly became anxious. 'Oh God. Does that sound terribly conceited?'

''Course not. It must be brilliant. I'm really chuffed for you.'

'Thanks I . . . I value your opinion.' Christopher cleared his throat. 'So . . . how about your summer. Did you manage to get any travelling in?'

'Some day.' Kieran glanced down at his shabby jacket and cheap, scuffed trainers with a wry smile. 'I think I might have to make do with reading about the Uffizi, for the time being.'

'No, of course not. The state of student funding these days . . .' Another embarrassed laugh. 'What were you doing then?'

'This and that. Got a job in a bar for a bit . . .' Kieran glanced at the clock. 'Anyway, time I wasn't here. I've got a ten o'clock with Prof Muldoon, if he can spare us the time. He hardly turned up for a lecture last year. "Lunch at the Arts Council, frightful bore." ' Kieran mimicked the nasal minor-public-school twang and fingered an imaginary bow tie; the most talented actor the university had seen in years, he collected mannerisms the way others might collect stamps.

'I was wondering if you could do me a favour, actually,' Christopher asked, as Kieran stood up to go. 'A first year, who wants to audition for *Romeo and Juliet*. Her father's a friend, of sorts. Would you keep an eye on her for me?'

'Why? Is she dangerous? Sounds promising!'

'I was thinking of Myles Delahunt. She's had a very . . . sheltered upbringing. Her father's a writer – one of my lecturers from Cambridge, actually. Her mother left them when Flora was hardly more than a baby, and he absolutely fell apart. Took himself off to deepest Cornwall. He writes novels, now. Quite popular, I believe. I tried one once but I couldn't get on with it. To be honest, I came to the conclusion the isolation must have blunted his intellect, and from what Flora's intimated, her father seems to be as unimpressed as I was by what he does. He always was prone to bouts of the most appalling depression. It must have been a very strange household for a little girl to be brought up in.' He shook his head. 'I doubt that she's very worldly-wise. I wouldn't want Myles . . .'

'. . . homing in on her like a heat-seeking missile. *"Why sweetie,"* ' Kieran leered, ' *"has anyone ever told you you'd make a devastating Juliet? "* '

'Something like that.' Christopher grinned, despite himself. 'Tell me, Kieran, don't you ever get confused with all those rapid shifts of character? It's quite amazing. You even looked like Myles for a moment.'

'Bloody hell, I hope not!' He got to his feet.

'I was wondering if you needed any advice about

the text, as a matter of fact,' Christopher went on. 'I'd be happy to drop in on a few of the rehearsals.'

'Sure. All contributions gratefully received.' Kieran gathered his books and looked down at Christopher with a quizzical smile. 'Flora, eh? And you're asking me to take on the role of Nurse? Shame that. I'd quite fancied myself as Romeo.'

Chapter Five

It was dark and pouring with rain as Flora stepped off the bus and into a puddle, cursing as she checked the damage to her new shoes. She had bought some trendy clothes, a bright red lipstick, and a packet of Benson and Hedges. After a couple of hours practising in front of the bathroom mirror, she had just about perfected the art of talking with a cigarette smouldering suggestively between scarlet lips. Tonight, she had decided, she was going to take the drama society by storm.

She shook the droplets of water from the map of the campus that seemed to have been hardly out of her hand in the week she'd been at Blackport. Her brain felt as sodden as the tattered sheet of paper, with all the information that had been rained down on them. She still couldn't visualise where the drama studio was. 'Turn left at Senate House, past the Health Centre, right at the Students' Union', she read from the note Christopher Heatherington had posted in her pigeon hole.

Finally, half an hour later, wet through and wondering if she wouldn't have been wiser to stay in for a take-away with Meg and her bunch of medic friends, she located the studio. Christopher Heatherington obviously had trouble with his rights and lefts.

She stepped inside, blinking as her eyes adjusted to the blazing lights. In one corner of the barn-like room, a couple were practising stage-hits. A thin boy in denim dungarees and an embroidered skullcap was sitting on a table, a copy of the play balanced on his knee as he shovelled the contents of a poly-styrene container into his mouth at ravenous speed. On the stage at the far end of the room, a tall figure with curling dark hair stood on a chair, his back to her, surrounded by a small knot of people who were watching him intently. As she watched, they erupted into a sudden burst of laughter.

'Hello! I don't believe we've met.'

Flora turned, to be met by a pair of dazzlingly blue eyes. Their owner was dressed in immaculate denims and a fashionably distressed leather flying jacket. Offering a well-manicured hand and a con-fident smile, he tossed back his mane of wavy blond hair and added, 'Myles Delahunt. Second year Law.'

He squeezed Flora's hand warmly as she intro-duced herself.

'Flora! What a lovely name! And what kind of flower *are* you, I wonder? A snowdrop, maybe? No, something more exotic, I think. A tiger lily?' He gave a roguish wink. 'Or are you a Venus flytrap?'

Unable to think of a suitable response, Flora smiled.

'But you're wet through, sweetie. Allow me to get you a coffee, and then you can tell me all about yourself.'

She had to start somewhere, Flora told herself, as he reappeared with two plastic cups. And he was undeniably handsome. Meg had observed that the only men she'd met from the drama society were either gay, or so irredeemably odd that they could only communicate from behind the safety of a set of footlights. At least Myles did not appear to fit into either of those categories.

'I'm the director, for my sins,' he beamed modestly, pulling up a couple of chairs. 'I have to say, Flora, that you have exactly the look I have in mind for Juliet. Now what I suggest, sweetie, is that you—'

'So are we finished for tonight then, or what?' a voice floated over from the stage.

With an elaborate sigh, Myles stood up and shouted back, 'I'll be with you in one minute. This *is* supposed to be a social function too, you know. You're not at the National yet.' Sitting back down, he whispered to Flora, 'Kieran Willerton. Absolute pain in the proverbial. Takes these wretched auditions desperately seriously. Now, just you sit and watch for a while and then we'll see what we can do for you. Here's a copy of the text. Why don't you read through a few of Juliet's lines while you're waiting? Act three, scene three,' he called out to the assembled company. 'Damien, do you think you could possibly tear yourself away from whatever is in that disgusting carton and work the lights?

Thank you so much.' Turning back to Flora, he explained, 'All you need to know for now is that Romeo's about to find out he's been banished. Don't worry yourself about why. I'll explain the plot later.'

Flora resisted the temptation to reply. Myles might be insufferably patronising, but he was also, as he had pointed out, the director. And Flora had already decided that the drama society had potential.

Up on the stage, the shadowy figure flicked through his copy of the play then, stepping into the glare of the lights, he dropped to his knees. Flora stopped reading, transfixed, as he poured out his anguish at his banishment, his face white, his voice choked with emotion. The studio was quite silent as he reached the end of the speech. Then he pulled himself to his feet, rubbing the dust from the knees of his jeans, and squinted across the footlights. A hum of conversation started; a couple of people applauded.

'He'll get the part, won't he? He's brilliant,' Flora whispered.

Myles raised an eyebrow and called up to the stage, 'You'll have to do something about that accent. It's still coming through. Don't want the punters thinking they've walked in on *Coronation Street* by mistake, do we?'

Kieran jumped from the stage and strode towards them. Myles, looking slightly alarmed, clapped his hands in an officious manner and announced the audition over and that a cast list would be on the board the following week.

'And I won't stand the bickering we had last time. You'll all take the parts you're allocated.'

'Oh Myles, I just love it when you're masterful,' Kieran breathed, tossing his head in flawless imiation, to the obvious delight of the couple of dozen people scattered around the studio.

Ignoring him, Myles put a hand under Flora's elbow and steered her towards the door, murmuring, 'Now what do you say to a drink back at my place? You can read through a few lines for me . . .'

'I need a word about the text.' Kieran caught his arm.

'Not now, chum. Can't you see I'm busy?'

'Now. I promised Christopher Heatherington we'd decide what cuts we want, so he can work on it over the weekend. Sorry love,' he added to Flora, who had turned to take a better look at him. He was gorgeous, she decided.

'I was going anyway,' she said, shrugging Myles off, stung to think that anyone could imagine she had been taken in by him.

'I'm not completely naive,' she muttered crossly to herself as she headed out into the rain.

It was not until the bus ploughed splashing up the hill to where she waited that she realised she did not have her bag. The studio was in pitch darkness by the time she'd squelched back. Unable to find the light switches, she fumbled around, bumping into tables, feeling amongst the detritus on the floor, crumpled tissues, cigarette butts, sweet papers, before withdrawing her hand from something damp and sticky. By the time she gave up the search, she was feeling thoroughly unnerved.

She headed for the brightly-lit Students' Union. Maybe there would be someone there she recognised from whom she could borrow the fare. Feeling the first twinge of homesickness since she'd arrived in Blackport, she scanned the crowded bar for a familiar face. No use; she'd just have to hope for a sympathetic bus driver.

As she reached the stop, a bus sailed off up the hill in a wave of spray. She hung around for a few minutes, stamping her feet against the cold as her fingers went numb and the rain poured down her face in rivulets.

'To hell with this,' she muttered at last, and set off on the mile-long walk home.

The high tenements on either side of the broad road looked even grimmer than in daylight. Litter on the pavements bunched in soggy heaps at the feet of the lampposts. A mangy Alsatian paused briefly in its foraging to sniff at her and raise a half-hearted growl. She side-stepped it and ran into a group of youths who, careless of the rain, were lounging against the wall outside a pub. They whispered obscenities as she backed away, laughing and catcalling after her as she quickened her pace.

The street ahead of her was deserted, the lights around the campus well behind her now. Her back straight, she tried not to think of the warning Norman had given them about walking alone at night. Gruesome snippets from the newspaper reports flashed through her head as she hurried along the dark pavement, eyes down, not looking to right or left.

At first, she told herself that the footsteps were in her imagination. She walked a little faster. The footsteps speeded up. The skin on the back of her neck prickled. She did not dare turn around. By now she was walking so quickly that she could hardly hear the steps for the sound of her own ragged breathing, but she knew they were gaining on her. A voice shouted from behind her. It sounded harsh and urgent, and it was getting closer.

She glanced in desperation at the blank, curtained windows on either side of the road, trying to reckon whether she should risk stopping to bang on one of them to attract attention. But what if no one came? She hesitated for a second and the voice shouted again. Giving up all pretence of controlling her panic, she broke into a frantic, lurching run, sobbing for breath as the steps behind thudded through the puddles towards her. Tripping over an uneven slab, she stumbled, almost falling. A hand grabbed her arm. With a desperate cry for help, she turned and lashed out with all her strength, bringing her knee up sharply.

The figure collapsed to its knees and doubled up, groaning. Across the street, a face appeared briefly at a window then vanished, the curtain twitching a thin shard of light along the pavement as Flora regained her balance and started to run, straining for the sound of the footsteps. Not slackening her pace, she forced herself to glance back over her shoulder. The figure was still on the floor. Picked out in the light from the window, there was something familiar about the dark, bent head. To her horror, she saw that he was holding up, as if in self-defence, her handbag.

She stopped dead, the full realisation of what she'd just done flooding over her.

'Oh my God!' She ran back and dragged him to his feet. 'Are you all right? I thought you were following me. I mean . . .'

He leant against the wall, coughing. 'I'd not realised you'd taken up kickboxing as well as acting,' he wheezed, when a little of the colour had returned to his face. 'And there was me worrying you weren't safe out here on your own.'

'I thought you were . . .' She stopped, feeling increasingly foolish. Tears of relief welled in her eyes. Her teeth were still chattering. 'Are you OK?'

He nodded, grimacing as he finally straightened himself. 'Sorry if I frightened you. Did you not hear me call?'

'I . . . I . . .' She could hardly admit that she'd thought he was the Beast of Blackport. She'd made enough of an idiot of herself as it was. Glancing back, she said, 'There were some yobs. Back there by the pub. I thought . . .'

'I'll try to remember me Oxford accent next time.'

'I didn't mean . . .' she flushed, wishing the earth would swallow her up. 'It's . . . it's Kieran isn't it?' she floundered.

'Kieran Willerton.' He grinned and held out his hand, her bag still looped over his wrist. 'Here, I think this'd suit you better than me. D'you fancy a pint? I promise I don't bite. Well, not unless I'm provoked.'

He wove his way back through the crowded bar of the City Arms and plonked a glass in front of her, as she tried surreptitiously to rub the streaked mascara from her cheeks.

'I thought you were terrific at the auditions,' she stammered. 'Really, I'm not just saying that to . . .'

'Thanks . . . sorry, I didn't catch your name while you were trying to castrate me,' he said, easing himself gingerly onto a stool.

The elderly men at the next table looked up from their game of dominoes with interest.

Kieran was a good listener, voracious for every small detail of the life that struck her as so dull, as she described the Scillies, and the bleak, Devon convent school which had been as far as she'd made it from the islands until now. Finally, to her own surprise, she started to tell him about Simon.

'*The* Simon Castledine? You're kidding! Bloody hell, Christopher said he was a writer, but . . .'

'You don't want to hear about me. It's boring,' she said, embarrassed to realise that she had been doing all the talking. 'What about you? You're a bit older than the rest of us, aren't you?'

'Yeah. Twenty-four.'

'How come?'

'I'm not sure. It just sort of happened after I'd been twenty-three. So tell me about the rest of your family. You've only mentioned your father. Is ziss of significance, I vonder?' He crouched up over her on his stool, pen poised, peering over imaginary spectacles. 'Plees lie down on ziss couch, Miss Castledine, unt tell me all about your past.'

One of the old men stopped, his glass to his lips, and stared.

Gradually, with prompting from Kieran, Flora recreated the anxious little girl always trying to live up to Simon's overwhelming love and dependence; the uncertain teenager behind the confident exterior, never quite fitting in, with her expensive clothes and famous father as old as the other girls' grandfathers. All the time haunted by the shadowy mother whose name she was never allowed to mention.

At last, the barman bawled time, breaking the spell. Flora glanced at her watch and shivered; Kieran had almost had her believing this psychiatrist thing.

'Come on,' he said, helping her into her coat. 'I'll walk you back.'

As they neared the flat, Flora wondered whether she should invite him in for a coffee. The trouble was, with Meg's noisy friends monopolising the lounge, she'd have to take him into her bedroom. Would that look a bit presumptuous, she wondered? She wouldn't want him thinking she was trying to chat him up.

Damn it all, she told herself at last, it's only a coffee I'm offering him. Anyway, the whole idea of being here is to start having a bit of fun.

She glanced up at him, the straight features, high

cheekbones and strange grey-green eyes fringed by long black lashes that she would have killed for. She'd invite him in, she decided, as they stopped outside the curry shop.

'This is it,' she said, gesturing to the upstairs window.

'Cheers then. Keep hold of that handbag next time.'

She watched him amble off down the street, not even turning back to wave.

'So much for the seduction routine,' she muttered ruefully.

At the corner, he turned and flung himself down on one knee on the wet pavement.

'*Sleep dwell upon thine eyes, peace in thy breast,*' his voice rang back through the quiet night air.

'*Romeo and J . . . J . . . Juliet.*' Norman appeared from the side entry, carrying a toolbox.

Flora spun around. 'God, Norman! Don't do things like that. I've had enough shocks for one evening.'

'I've been f . . . fixing a new . . .' He looked at her in agitation. 'W . . . what shocks? Are you all right?'

'*Would I were sleep and peace, so sweet to rest.*' Kieran blew her an extravagant kiss. 'Ta-ra then, Juliet. See you at the next rehearsal.'

'I'm fine.' Flora began to laugh. 'Just fine, thank you Norman.'

Chapter Six

'Where's Shenfield?' Superintendent George Lambert roared as he slammed into the incident room.

It took one look at the memo he was carrying for Whitelaw to know what was coming next.

'Out of the office, Sir. Can I help?'

'A request for DNA testing on every male student at Blackport University? For God's sake, what's Shenfield trying to do? First we have the Vice Chancellor complaining to the Chief Constable about the, and I quote, "unpleasantly confrontational" manner of his senior officers, then there was that outrageous press conference . . .'

'With respect, Sir, all DCI Shenfield said—'

'I heard what he said. The entire bloody nation heard what he said. The Chief Constable made it perfectly clear at the time that until there was evidence, *concrete* evidence,' he repeated, overriding Whitelaw as he opened his mouth in protest, 'the *possible* link with the Loveridge case was to be played down. So what does Shenfield do? Working on what appears to be nothing more than one of his so-called hunches, he takes it upon himself to issue a statement to the effect that a serial killer is rampaging around the campus masquerading as a student. And now this.'

Whitelaw stifled a yawn. The last time he'd actually put on his pyjamas and slept in a bed, as opposed to snatching an hour here and there with his head on his desk, was four weeks ago. Once Shenfield got the bit between his teeth, minor matters such as eating and sleeping didn't seem to occur to him.

'Am I boring you, Detective Sergeant?' Lambert glared at him. He slapped Shenfield's memo down on the desk. 'I assume I don't need to spell out my decision?'

'No, Sir.'

'Where is he, anyway?'

'I'm not quite sure, Sir.'

It didn't seem the appropriate moment to tell him that, as they spoke, Shenfield was with the Vice Chancellor, demanding to check the admission lists.

'Well tell him I want him in my office,' he snapped. 'The minute he gets back. Is that clear?'

'Might I have a word, Sir?' Medlock, who had been following the conversation from the safety of his desk, leapt to his feet as Lambert turned to leave. 'I've been doing some research of my own into the Loveridge case, and while I tend to agree with Chief Inspector Shenfield that we're probably looking at a single killer, I think we may have overlooked something.'

'Always good to have a fresh viewpoint,

Constable,' Lambert nodded his encouragement. 'Let's hear it then.'

Funny how he found time to listen every time Medlock stuck his oar in, Whitelaw thought sourly. But then some whiz kid from the Met was always going to have Lambert's ear.

'As you know, Sir, Gavin O'Driscoll always maintained his innocence. And it would seem—'

'He confessed the same night,' Whitelaw interrupted. 'I should know. Dave Shenfield and I interviewed him.'

'But then withdrew the confession the next day. Didn't he claim he'd been under duress? I think I'm right in saying he sustained a broken nose.'

Whitelaw stared at him with unconcealed contempt. 'Shouldn't have resisted arrest, should he?'

In fact, the ferocity of Shenfield's rage that night had shaken him. He'd never seen him lay a finger on a suspect, before or since.

'Gavin O'Driscoll confessed because there was no point in doing anything else. He was seen with Melanie Loveridge less than an hour before her body was discovered. His fountain pen was found at the scene, and traces of his semen were found on her. There was so much bloody evidence, we didn't need a confession.'

If the powers that be put half the resources into active policing that they did into 'image improvement', as Lambert was fond of calling his various PR initiatives, the case could have been solved months ago, Whitelaw thought; Medlock was barking up entirely the wrong tree with six-year-old allegations of police brutality. Suggestions that an investigating officer had beaten the tripes out of a suspect had no place in 'image improvement', even if they were correct. Whitelaw was gratified to see Lambert glance at his watch.

'I've been checking on the security guard.' If Medlock had noticed the impatience of the gesture, he chose to ignore it. He flicked through a file until he found his place. 'Norman Ackroyd, the man who found Melanie Loveridge's body. Was it known at the time that he has a number of convictions for sexual offences?'

'Yes. Surprisingly enough, it did dawn on us to check him out,' Whitelaw said dryly. 'But then if we ran in every sad bastard who'd been caught flashing in the park when he was a teenager, we'd probably have half of CID behind bars.'

He was the only one who laughed.

Medlock continued as if he had not spoken. 'The problem is, Sir, that O'Driscoll simply doesn't have the right psychological profile. All the statements taken from his friends at the time paint the picture of a sociable, well-adjusted young man, who had had any number of girlfriends, none of them serious . . .'

'Sociable and well adjusted? That little shit claimed they went down to the boating lake for a quickie and that he then buggered off back to the beer tent to find his mates, leaving Melanie to find her own way back. If that's the definition of sociable and well adjusted these days, I'm bloody glad I haven't got daughters.'

'A lack of old-world charm doesn't necessarily make him a murderer. If one looks at the latest studies coming out of the States on sexually motivated murders, a common feature is the protagonist's polarised concept of womanhood. Whores or Madonnas. Mothers or lovers. Very many men carry the view, in a less extreme way, of course. Most settle for a respectable wife and a bit on the side.' The smile he gave Lambert reminded Whitelaw of the crocodile in Peter Pan, as he went on, 'He could be homosexual, either latently or actively, but it's equally possible he maintains an ostensibly normal heterosexual relationship. The hatred he feels for his victims may be mirrored by an obsessive love for the woman he's chosen to put on a pedestal. Pure. Virginal. He treats her like bone china; she would most probably be quite unaware of his violent impulses. Unfortunately, his repressed behaviour towards her only exacerbates his desire to kill and maim. God help her, of course, if she were to slip off that pedestal. Unfortunately, there is nothing to suggest that Gavin O'Driscoll displayed any of these characteristics. Significantly, however, a further common feature is that many of these men show some signs of sexually deviant behaviour from a very early age. As did Norman Ackroyd.'

Simultaneously, Lambert said, 'Fascinating,' and Whitelaw, 'Bollocks.'

'I'd like to take a closer look at these studies, Medlock.' Lambert turned to Whitelaw with a frosty smile. 'Don't forget to give Chief Inspector

Shenfield my message. My office. Immediately he gets in.'

'You didn't really think Lambert would agree?'

Later that evening, Whitelaw sat in the crowded back bar of the Bricklayers Arms, watching Shenfield stare morosely into his pint. 'Still, look on the bright side. At least the publicity seems to have frightened O'Driscoll off. There's been nothing in four weeks.'

'There was nothing for ten weeks before Goscott and Stewart. Anyway, I don't want to frighten him off, I want to catch him.'

'How did you get on with the Vice Chancellor?'

'That self-important prick?' Shenfield growled.

'That self-important prick happens to be a personal friend of the Chief Constable. Not to mention chairman of Lambert's golf club. It's called politics, Dave. Just be careful. And watch your back with Medlock and all.'

'Medlock? What's he been up to?'

Shenfield shook his head and broke into a grin for the first time since they'd arrived, as Whitelaw passed on the new recruit's latest theories. 'Just humour him.'

'He's dangerous.'

'Come off it! He's a cocky little git who'll probably make a damned good copper after he's been allowed to fall flat on his face a couple of times. Norman Ackroyd?' Shenfield threw back his head and let out a bark of laughter. 'Christ Almighty, whatever next?'

'Just watch him, that's all. We've both met his type before. He knows the right backsides to lick.'

And the right hands to bite, Whitelaw thought to himself. Medlock wanted to be a big fish in a small pond, to make his presence felt, and this investigation was just the chance for him to make a splash. Whitelaw had a horrible feeling that he'd trample on anything, anyone, to do it. He looked across the table with concern. Shenfield was a big man, strong. He'd never looked his age, but he did now. He was pushing retirement and this was bound to be his last big case. He wasn't one to take defeat lightly. Neither was he one to take advice.

Whitelaw sipped his beer and asked cautiously, 'Have you told Lambert about your Christopher?'

'Told him what?' Shenfield growled.

'Listen, Dave. We go back a long way, so I'm saying this as a friend. You've got to let him know Christopher's your son.'

'I don't see why.' Shenfield wore the expression of a truculent mule. 'He took Susannah's maiden name when he was no more than a lad. He made it clear then that he despises everything I stand for. As far as he's concerned, we don't know each other. That suits me just fine.'

'You know the rules as well as I do. He could turn out to be a suspect, for God's sake. He was the first to see the Stewart girl dead. Sooner or later someone – probably Medlock – is going to ask if he was the last to see her alive. Look what he's been saying about that poor sod Ackroyd.'

'Christopher?' Shenfield hooted. 'The only way he'd kill a girl's by boring her to death with his bloody poems. Poems! I ask you!' He swallowed another mouthful of beer. 'I've never read such a load of drivel. They don't even rhyme.'

Whitelaw couldn't suppress a smile. 'You've read his book, then? The wife said he'd had one published.'

'Yeah, well . . .' Shenfield blustered. 'I just wanted to see why anyone would pay out good money for it. And I'm none the bloody wiser. Absolute crap, the lot of it. I couldn't make head nor tail . . .'

'OK, OK.' Whitelaw held up his hands in defeat. 'But look, you've got to come clean with Lambert. You're on dodgy ground, and the Medlocks of this world are just waiting on the sidelines for you to screw up.'

Shenfield's hand tightened around his glass. 'And how would Medlock know?'

'I told him, didn't I? Whatever else he is, he's not stupid. He picked up there was something going on between the two of you.'

'What else did you tell him?'

Whitelaw sighed. 'Nothing. What else would I tell him?'

There was a long pause.

Shenfield tilted his glass and absently swilled the dregs of his beer from side to side. At last he said, 'Susannah meant a lot to me, you know. Sixteen we were when we started going out together. My first girlfriend. Beautiful, she was. All the lads fancied her. I could hardly believe my luck!' His smile faded. 'She was an invalid a long time, Ray. Too long for a man like me to go without a woman. Not that any of them meant anything to me. You'd have thought my own son could have realised how things were. But not him . . .' He shook his head and repeated bitterly. 'Not *him*. Stuck up there in his ivory tower with his head stuffed full of poetry, looking down on us lesser mortals and our needs. I wasn't the best husband in the world, I'll admit that. But I only ever . . .' he coloured slightly and shifted uncomfortably in his seat, before going on brusquely, 'Susannah was the only one I rated. She understood, even if he didn't.'

'Loved'. That was the word Whitelaw knew Shenfield had been looking for. Just as surely as he knew that the other man would never in a million years have told Susannah he loved her. Love wasn't a word he'd feel comfortable with. Whitelaw thought of his own wife, Val. He couldn't even begin to imagine life without her at the centre of it.

''Course she did, mate.' Embarrassed at the tremor in his voice, he slapped Shenfield on the shoulder and gathered up the empty glasses, saying in an overhearty voice, 'My round. Same again?'

The fact that Shenfield hadn't walked out meant that he'd probably taken on board what he'd said, Whitelaw thought. He decided not to labour the point. He caught sight of Shenfield in the mirror behind the bar, his shoulders hunched, his head bowed as though in defeat.

Poor sod.

Medlock was everything Shenfield had wanted his own son to be.

'I thought we might get Dave Shenfield round one Sunday.' Whitelaw stared up at the bedroom ceiling.

Val Whitelaw put down her book and regarded him over the top of her spectacles. 'What's brought this on?'

'Oh, I don't know.' Whitelaw slipped his arm around her and drew her down beside him, shifting his shoulder to make a more comfortable pillow for her head. 'He must get lonely, rattling about in that house on his own.'

Val sniffed. 'He never struck me as the lonely type. From what I've heard, he's never there.'

Whitelaw stroked her soft hair. 'Don't think he goes out much these days. Susannah's death knocked him far more than he lets on, you know. And now all this stuff with his son . . .'

'He should have paid her a bit more attention while she was alive then, shouldn't he?' Val propped herself up on one elbow. 'How's it going with his lad, anyway? You thought it might help them get back together, being thrown into each other's company like that, didn't you?'

'He doesn't say much.' Whitelaw shook his head. 'It must cut you up though, having your own son change his name. Dave was as proud as punch of him, getting into university and all. We got fed up of him going on about it at work. He was like a dog with two tails. It must have been a real slap in the face to him, especially coming when Susannah got so sick.'

'Yes, well if he'd spent a bit more time with his wife and a bit less having a social life, his son wouldn't have had to come back up here to look after her, would he? He could have gone off anywhere, with a degree from Cambridge. I don't suppose it was any sort of a picnic for a lad in his twenties, spending every spare moment with someone with terminal cancer, while his father was off out with God knows who. Hardly gave *him* a chance for a social life, did it? What did Dave expect?'

'I know, I know. The thing is, I reckon he just couldn't handle having to sit and watch her die. He'd always been the sort of bloke to take control, and suddenly . . .'

Val snorted. 'Well, I'm sorry, but it's not him I feel any sympathy for.'

'You never know, they may still get back together.' Whitelaw yawned. ''Course, they're chalk and cheese. I mean, can you really imagine Dave having much in common with a poet?' He chuckled to himself. 'You've not met Christopher. In all fairness, he did strike me as a bit of a drip.'

Val looked at him with real irritation. 'I sometimes wonder if you've been in that job too long, Ray. Just because the man's got a bit more sensitivity than his clod of a father . . . Anyway, I have met him, if you remember. The day of Susannah's funeral. I shall never forget his face, either, when we were standing around the grave. He looked as if he'd have given the world for it to have been Dave inside that coffin. I've never seen such animosity between two grown men. It would have broken Susannah's heart. She told me, you know, that last time I went to see her in hospital, that she hoped maybe once she'd gone . . .'

'Not much chance of that. Their paths barely crossed while she was alive, according to Dave. I remember him saying Christopher even used to ring the ward before he went in to see her, to make sure Dave wasn't there. Don't think they'd set eyes on each other since the funeral, until the other day.'

Val sighed. 'Funny, isn't it? You always imagine that people who can have kids are going to be so happy, and yet . . .' She turned off the light. 'We're lucky, you and me, aren't we, Ray?' She snuggled back down, as Whitelaw reached out for her in the darkness. 'You invite him round if you want to, love,' she murmured sleepily. 'Any time you like.'

Wednesday 4 November

So stupid.

They think they have the answer, but they have nothing.

They think they have stopped me, but it is she who has stopped me.

It was the hair I noticed first. Harlot's hair, cascading almost to her waist. Dangerous tendrils to bind a man and smother him in their amber depths.

But then she turned, and the voices fell silent. For here was purity. An ineluctable warmth of recognition. Renaissance Madonna of a thousand paintings, she smiled on me.

Who could have thought my shrivelled heart could have recovered greenness?

Each day, her image imprinted across the book I read; every line written for her delicate features and shining copper hair. Each night, standing in the shadows, watching over her until she goes to bed. She takes the light with her as she draws the curtains, leaving me only darkness, and I hold my breath, terrified that she has disappeared into my imagination.

But she is real.

My eyes have rested on perfection, and I am saved.

Chapter Seven

The weeks were going by so quickly.

It seemed only days to Flora since she had stepped off the train and caught her first glimpse of Blackport, but October had vanished, and already she was almost half way through her first term.

She loved the flat.

It was cramped, freezing, and steeped in the pervasive aroma of curry. Yet already it felt like home. It was hard to imagine that anywhere else existed on this damp November evening, that at this very moment, life was going on as it always had. At her old school, the bell would be ringing for supper. Girls would be streaming along the corridors from prep, the scent of beeswax from the highly polished floors mingling with the inevitable smells of mince and cabbage, disinfectant and chalk. Sister Euphemia would be at her vantage point at the top of the stairs, exhorting them not to run. On St Mary's, Mrs Menheniott would be clattering around the pristine kitchen, preparing Simon's dinner. Simon would be up in his study, or sitting motionless in the living room, staring out onto the

utter blackness of the downs that ran from the farmhouse to the sea. She imagined the springiness of
the wet heather, the mournful boom of the fog-
horn, the damp mist that, on nights like tonight,
pressed against your face like a veil. It seemed a
million miles and a million years away.

She loved Meg.

In the weeks that they'd shared the flat, Flora
had listened in delight to her long and involved
tales of her huge family, feeling she already knew
the apparently endless stream of older brothers
whose antics had peopled many an evening when
Flora should have been studying. Meg's family ran
a village shop in South Wales, and Flora could
only imagine how proud they must be of their only
daughter. It was obvious she loved them all dearly,
especially Gareth, her eldest brother, who farmed
the next valley with his wife, Bronwen. They were
expecting their first child at Christmas and Meg
had already been asked to be godmother, an
honour she swore she would refuse if the child
turned out to be yet another boy. There were far
too many men in the world already, she said
darkly. She purported to regard the male species
in general as somewhere below pondlife on the
evolutionary scale, a fact that she attributed to
having no fewer than eight older brothers.

'Lousy with testosterone, the lot of them,' she had
asserted cheerfully. 'Take my word for it, girl. You
can't trust any of them as far as you can throw
them!' The one time she'd met Kieran, her only

comment had been that with looks like that, you
could be sure he was up to no good.

Kieran.

Flora had fallen into the habit of meeting him for
a drink before rehearsals. Together, they had ex-
plored areas around the docks where she would
never have dared to venture alone, in search of the
cheapest restaurants. Kieran seemed just as con-
fident there as around the university, quite at ease
in the dark streets, utterly unconcerned by the
gangs that hung around outside the clubs and bars.

'Feel nervous, with your right knee to protect
me?' he teased.

They were never challenged. They would sit in
the shabby gloom of some dockside pub, sharing a
pint and talking the hours away about books, plays,
music. Flora felt that she had talked more in the last
month than in the rest of her life. They would meet,
part, and never once made plans to meet again. But
somehow, the next day, there he would be, in the
coffee bar, outside her lecture room, at the next
table in the library. Now and then he would
take her hand, or lean against her, almost absent-
mindedly putting an arm around her shoulder;
occasionally, fleetingly, he would kiss her. No
more.

It was time to put that right, Flora had decided.
Tonight was bonfire night, and she was planning a
few fireworks of her own.

She slipped out of her dressing gown, to reveal
the lacy bra and knickers she had bought earlier

that day, and gazed critically at herself in the speckled mirror. She might, after a last-minute audition arranged by Myles, have landed the role of Juliet with what had been described as her 'perfect, unsullied image', but she was probably the only virgin in the whole of Blackport, and it was embarrassing.

'There's bold for you!' The lilting accent broke her daydream. Meg strode across the bedroom and pulled the curtains shut. 'Did you realise you can be seen half way down Aigburth Street?' Turning from the window, she eyed Flora and shook her head. 'Those drawers are going to play havoc with your interpretation of Juliet, you shameless hussy!' She picked up the red lipstick that Flora had just finished applying. 'Can I have a go with this? I'm off down the rugby club with some of the lads, see.' She winked at Flora in the mirror as she painted her lips with more enthusiasm than skill. 'If I'm going to be sharing with a wanton woman, I might as well look the part!'

An hour later, Flora was standing on the muddy patch of lawn outside Myles's house, stamping her feet against the cold and wishing she were wearing a thermal vest, as Meg had suggested.

Myles, squatting beside an empty milk bottle, box of matches in one hand, was having a conspicuous lack of success with his fireworks display. Lighting the blue paper beneath yet another rocket, he leapt back dramatically. The flame spluttered, fizzled and died. Amidst boos and jeers, he threw down the matches. Tossing his wind-swept hair, he announced that if anyone thought they could do better, they were welcome to try.

'Go on Kieran, you have a go, before we all freeze to death,' Damien hissed, winking at Flora.

Kieran shrugged and ambled over to the rocket. Within minutes, the garden was ablaze with coloured lights. Flora watched, enthralled, as he moved deftly through the darkness from firework to firework.

'You're shivering. Would you like to borrow my coat?'

The voice behind her made her jump. 'Oh, hi, Dr . . . Christopher. No, I'm fine, really. I'll go in as soon as the display's over.'

Christopher laughed. 'He's in his element, isn't he?'

Kieran was clowning around as the stars burst over his head, turning now and then to take a bow as the others clapped and cheered.

Finally, the last incandescent shower of light faltered and died, and they all trooped back into the house. Flora soon forgot her desire for a thermal vest as the party got into full swing. The noise was ear-splitting, the flaking plaster trembling at the sheer volume of sound from the hi-fi in the living room. Nothing could be distinguished above the vibrating roar of the bass beat. The place was packed, mainly with people Flora didn't know. It was that kind of party.

'Run out of glasses,' Damien bellowed cheerfully

as he edged past, clutching a jam jar filled with beer.

'Do you know where Kieran is?' she yelled, as a couple bundled past her, piled-up plates held high above their heads, but Damien had already been swallowed up in the sea of bodies.

She managed to side-step Myles when he tried to trap her in the corner of the kitchen; she locked herself in the loo when she saw him bearing down on her in the hall. Finally losing patience, she refused him bluntly and publicly as, catching her unawares when she had gone outside for a much-needed breath of air, he planted a damp kiss on her mouth and demanded a dance.

'I can only apologise for that.' Christopher was at her side as Myles flounced off.

'Oh, he's harmless enough.' Flora pulled a face, then laughed. 'I think.'

Nevertheless, she was relieved to see Kieran making his way towards them from the kitchen. The smile he turned on her, as he reached in the darkness for her hand, seemed to exclude everyone, although he was chatting easily to Christopher about rehearsals, then about some work that he was preparing for a forthcoming tutorial. Flora looked on, enjoying the pressure of his grip, still amazed at the casual relationship that seemed to exist between staff and students.

'I wasn't expecting him to be here,' she whispered, when Christopher had gone off to refill his glass. She couldn't imagine Sister Euphemia at a party.

'Christopher?' Kieran shrugged, sounding surprised. He turned, as his name was called from the
kitchen, and waved to a couple of girls who had just
arrived. 'That's Lucy and Kate from off my course.'
He gave her hand a squeeze. 'Come on in and meet
them, they're a good laugh.'

She moved around with him from one knot of his
friends to another, drinking cheap wine, saying
little, content to bask in his reflected popularity and
the warm weight of his arm across her shoulder.

Eventually, people began to drift off.

'Well, that gets rid of the crumblies,' Myles
muttered, as Christopher stuck his head around the
door and made his goodbyes. 'Let the celebrations
commence!' He sat down heavily, opened another
bottle of wine, and produced a joint.

'What's that?' Flora asked Kieran, intrigued.

'You don't want to know.' He put his arm around
her waist. 'Come on, it's time we were going. I'll
walk you home.'

'What a bore you are, Kieran.' Myles, draped on
the settee, shot Flora a contemptuous glance. 'You
want to try it, sweetie. Might loosen you up a bit.'

'Piss off.' Kieran pulled their coats from a pile on
the stairs. 'Come on, Flora.'

'Ooh, very masterful!' Myles's face was flushed
with malice and too much wine. 'Likes a bit of
rough, does she?'

Kieran held out Flora's coat, his knuckles white.

'Is that what turns you on?' Rising unsteadily,
Myles lurched towards her, grabbing her arm and
swinging her around, breathing wine-sour breath

into her face. 'We'll have to find out sometime.'

Dropping the coat, Kieran leapt at him, grabbing him by the throat.

'Leave him, Kieran.' Hot with embarrassment, she pulled him away as Myles fell back against the wall and slumped to the floor. 'He's not worth wasting a punch on.'

She had never seen Kieran angry before. Since she had met him, she always seemed to have been laughing. Now, walking home in silence, she glanced up at his unsmiling profile and the small muscle throbbing in his cheek and felt disturbed and strangely exhilarated. She put her hand in his. He took it, but did not slacken his pace or turn to look at her.

They passed a derelict terrace, the houses standing against the darkened sky like a row of broken teeth.

'It's sad, isn't it, that they're knocking so much of it down?' she said, in an effort to make conversation.

'Why's it sad? Would you like to spend your life in a dump like that?' His voice was harsh.

'Well no, I suppose not. But there's such a . . . vibrancy about it. Do you know what I mean?'

He stopped and turned to look at her, his expression unfathomable. Then he shook his head and said sadly, as he broke into a grin, 'Flora Castledine, you talk the biggest load of bollocks sometimes!'

*

'Do you want to come in for a coffee?' she asked as casually as she could when they got back to the flat. Across the street, she could see the curtains twitching. So far, the evening had not gone entirely to plan; the last thing she needed was for Norman to come over for another of his literary discussions.

Kieran hesitated for a moment, then said, 'Sure, why not?'

She let them in then went through to the kitchen and opened the half-bottle of brandy she had bought that afternoon, while he walked around the little living room, looking at posters and picking up books.

'I shall make it, I just know it,' he said, gazing at a Royal Shakespeare Company poster of *Romeo and Juliet*. 'You'll be seeing me in a real Shakespeare before I'm through, being directed by . . . Michael Bogdanov or someone. I bet you think I'm crackers, don't you?' he asked, turning as she came back in. 'I bet you're thinking, "Daft sod. A couple of plays with some one-eyed university set-up and he thinks he's going to take Stratford by storm." But I'm not daft. And I'm not joking, either. It's what I've wanted since I was a lad, and I'll get there, whatever it takes.'

'I don't think you're daft.' His earnestness touched her. 'I know you'll do it, if it's what you want.'

It was true. He could be anyone he chose. He could switch personalities the way she might change her clothes. When he had first set eyes on Norman, he had seemed to swell until his clothes

85

tightened on him. His hands dangling at his sides, he'd glared at her with narrowed darting eyes and had actually become Norman for a moment; she had even been able to smell the curry. She had seen him staring with rapt concentration at anyone who took his interest, absorbing their mannerisms. Sometimes, when she was fastening her coat, or brushing her hair, she felt him watching her with the same devouring attention.

She shook her head to clear it, and said lightly, 'I wish I was really good at something.'

'You're good at lots of things.'

'No, I mean really good. Better than everyone else.'

He took his glass and raised it to her. 'You're really good at being you.'

'There's no need to be patronising.' She laughed to conceal a prickle of annoyance.

'I'm not.' His face was serious. 'You never put on an act, play games. You're just yourself.'

'I don't know what you mean.'

'I know you don't,' he grinned, sliding down into the settee and picking up the Seamus Heaney anthology she had been reading earlier. 'That's what makes you so special.'

She looked at his bent dark head, waiting for him to continue, but he seemed absorbed in his reading.

'I've bought you something,' she said suddenly, pulling a paper bag from behind a cushion.

He looked up in surprise. 'What, for me?'

'Sorry about the bag. I was going to wrap it. I hope you like it. They said you could exchange it, so don't keep it if it isn't right. I've got the receipt . . .' she babbled, blushing furiously.

He held out his hand, laughing. 'Can I have a quick look, before you take it back?'

It was a scarf of the softest cashmere wool. The colour had reminded her instantly of his eyes; not grey, not green, not blue – a deep, cloudy sea-colour that seemed to change as you looked at it.

'Well, just look at this!' He ran his hand gently over the soft surface.

'It wasn't expensive,' she lied, suddenly embarrassed by the extravagance of the gesture.

As soon as he unfolded it, she saw the flaw; a coarse thickening of the weave, running the length of the scarf like a raised, uneven scar. She could have wept with disappointment. She hadn't thought to examine it in the shop; she had been so attracted by the colour.

'I'll take it back,' she said, snatching it from him, close to tears.

'Hey, it's great,' he said gently. 'I don't want you to take it back.' He folded it deftly to hide the flaw and threw it around his neck with a flourish. 'There you are. Perfect. The perfect English gentleman.'

They sat together on the settee, talking and talking until the brandy was finished. She leant against him and closed her eyes, vaguely aware that the room was swaying gently.

'I should be going,' he said finally, not moving.

'You don't have to. You . . . you could stay.' She felt the tiniest stab of panic as she said the words she had rehearsed so often in her head.

'Are you sure?' he asked quietly. 'Are you certain it's what you want?'

Flora woke first. The lights were still on. Cautiously moving her arm, she squinted at her watch. Nearly five-thirty. She lay quite still for a minute, cramped into her single bed, her head resting uncomfortably against Kieran's bony shoulder, before slowly levering herself up onto one elbow.

Emptied of the grin and the cast of characters always at his command, his face was oddly defence-less. She studied its unfamiliar, shadowed angles and reached in fascination to finger the alien stubble on his chin. His eyes snapped open and he smiled slowly, stretching a lazy arm towards her.

Flora tensed, suddenly conscious of her naked-ness. She was stiff with cold and her mouth tasted sour. Her memory of how they had ended up in her bed together was hazy. Moving away from him, she felt the unaccustomed stickiness of her body and glanced across at the tangled heap of their clothes, appalled. He was sure to have recognised her total inexperience. Mortified, she recalled the infinite tenderness with which he had entered her, stop-ping, holding back, asking again and again if she was all right. God, had it been so obvious? She imagined him sniggering with Myles and the others.

'You . . . you'd better go.' She scrambled up,

dragging a sheet around her as the smile slid from Kieran's face. She was right. He was going to be angry, or worse than that, sarcastic.

'Jesus, Flora, what's the matter?'

'Don't.' She felt his hand on her shoulder and shrugged him off.

'Flora?'

His voice was urgent as his hands gripped her arms and he forced her around towards him. She twisted her head away, but he caught hold of her chin, dragging her around to face him.

'Let me go, you bastard.' She was frightened now, and furious to realise she was crying.

'Flora, have I hurt you?'

She struggled angrily. 'Don't you bloody make fun . . .'

'Oh Christ, I never meant to hurt you.'

She saw the stricken expression in his eyes and reached out her hand to him in confusion.

'Kieran? I . . . I don't understand.'

He didn't say anything. His face was ashen, his whole body shaking.

'You didn't hurt me,' she said slowly. She felt herself blushing. 'It was . . . I thought . . . it's just that I've never . . . and I didn't want you to think . . .' She turned her head away. 'Oh God, I feel so stupid.'

Still he did not speak. His hand, still clutching her arm, was trembling.

She turned back to face him and, looking into his eyes, whispered, 'I'm glad my first time was with you.'

His body relaxed. He looked down at his own nakedness with a helpless gesture, a foolish grin suffusing his features.

'Tell you what,' he laughed shakily. 'We'd not half raise a few eyebrows if we played the bed-chamber scene like this at tonight's rehearsal.'

She sang as she made coffee, knowing that she had never felt so happy. When she went back to the bedroom, he was pulling on his clothes, his back to her.

'What are you doing?' she asked, the song dying on her lips.

'I'd best be off.'

'But . . .'

'I'll see you later, love. Lunchtime. In the Union, yeah?'

She reached out and touched the bare strip of skin between his jeans and tee-shirt as he bent to lace up his trainers. 'It's not even light yet. Come back to bed.'

He turned, taking her face between his hands and kissing her as she twined her arms around his neck, coaxing him back onto the rumpled sheets. For a moment, he laid his face against the soft-ness of her breasts. Then he pulled himself away, shaking his head and mumbling, 'I must go.'

She sat on the edge of the bed as the door closed quietly behind him, cradling his untouched mug of coffee between her hands for warmth, her mind racing to make some sense of things. How could he be so intense one moment, and then disappear with a casual, 'I'll see you later' the next? Had it simply been another of his acts, some private joke with her cast as the outraged virgin? She caught sight of herself in the mirror. Did she look different? Would people be able to tell?

In the mirror, she saw the door open slowly. She swung around, spilling the coffee. Kieran stood in the doorway, twisting the new scarf between his hands, his face troubled.

'Listen,' he said. 'This . . . you and me . . .'

She waited, her heart in her mouth.

'It's more, isn't it?' He ran his fingers over the scarf, as if he were stroking a cat. 'More than sex?'

She put out her hand to him, not trusting herself to speak.

He nodded slowly, looking deep into her eyes with an expression that left no room for words. And then he was gone.

An hour later, on the other side of town, Dave Shenfield was dragged reluctantly back towards consciousness by the shrilling of his phone.

Through half a lifetime of habit, he turned sleepily to Susannah's side of the bed; it wasn't the phone, but the emptiness of the cold sheets that jerked him fully to wakefulness. After more than a year, he still hadn't got used to that emptiness. There had been other women. Lots of them. But he'd never taken any of them into Susannah's bed.

Wearily, he reached for the phone.

'Sorry if I woke you, Guv.' Whitelaw's voice was competing with the wail of a siren. 'I think you'd better get over to the university, fast as you can. Young girl, multiple injuries. Three guesses what colour hair. Right smack in the middle of the campus this time. Looks like O'Driscoll's getting cocky.'

Chapter Eight

Whitelaw was already at the scene when Shenfield arrived.

He pointed towards the shattered window of the bookshop. 'Extensive damage to face, lacerations to the hands and forearms. She fell forwards through the glass. Set off the alarm.'

'Can she give us a description?' Shenfield cut in, when Whitelaw had gone on to recount how the first patrol team on the scene had thought they were dealing with an accident, until they had pulled her out and found the cord around her neck.

Whitelaw pulled a face. 'Attacked from behind in the pitch dark? I wouldn't hold your breath. I've sent Harding in the ambulance with her, just in case. But she was in a pretty bad way.'

'Shit.'

She was the only one of his victims to have survived. Please, Shenfield prayed to whomever might be up there, please let her have seen him. He picked up a blood-spattered copy of Christopher's book, wiping it with the sleeve of his raincoat, before turning to one of the uniformed officers.

'This area should have been sealed off an hour ago,' he snapped. 'Get some cordons up before the vultures get here. Then you can explain to me what you bunch of tossers were doing while all this was going on. No, not now. Save it for later.'

'Eh up,' Whitelaw commented, looking back towards the road as Medlock's yellow MX5 roared around the corner and screeched to a halt. 'Here comes the cavalry.' His face creased into a frown as he looked past Medlock, across the square. 'Someone else to see you as well, by the looks of things.'

A tall figure in tracksuit and trainers was hurrying towards them.

'Get rid of him, for God's sake,' Shenfield muttered, turning away.

Too late.

'Why, Dr Heatherington! You're up bright and early this morning,' Medlock called out as he jumped from the car.

'What the hell are you doing here?' Shenfield growled.

'I couldn't sleep. I sometimes jog . . .' Christopher's eyes strayed towards the broken window. 'What's happened?'

'Someone took a nose-dive through the glass. More than that, I'm afraid I'm not at liberty to say.'

Christopher looked at the book in Shenfield's hand and said acidly, 'I'll take that, if I may. I very much doubt that you would find it of any interest.'

'Evidence.' Shenfield's grip on the book tightened. 'And not your property, either.'

*

Back in his office, Shenfield placed the book on the desk in front of him and stared at it hard. What was it about Christopher, the person he should be closest to in the world, that brought out the worst in him? His own son. He'd had so many plans for him, standing there in the hospital the first time he'd held him in his arms, watching in wonder as the impossibly small scrap of himself scanned his face with its wide, milky eyes, and clamped his finger with its tiny, implacable fist. He'd thought his heart would burst with pride.

'Get a grip,' he muttered to himself, as he jumped to his feet and strode over to the pinboard. He hadn't got time for that sort of nonsense. Harding had radioed in from the hospital half an hour ago. The girl was conscious; he was just waiting for the OK to interview her. I'll have you, O'Driscoll, he thought. The photograph stared mockingly back at him, as familiar to him now as his own face. His desire to nail him, to make him pay for what he'd done, had been more than professional even then. He'd never come down as hard on anyone as he had on Gavin O'Driscoll.

It had been only a few months after Susannah had been given the diagnosis; her cancer had returned, this time inoperably. For the first time in his life, Shenfield had realised that all his strength, the hardness he'd cultivated and valued so highly, counted for nothing. In the face of the insatiable disease, all he could do was stand by, powerless and inarticulate, as the life was inexorably gnawed out of her, even her lovely hair destroyed by vicious, useless chemotherapy. He'd been too red-raw at the injustice and cruelty of death to show any compassion towards a murderer. The contrast between Melanie Loveridge's vibrant hair and the lifeless face beneath it was just too close to home.

And there had been something untouchable, other-worldly, about Gavin O'Driscoll that had reminded him of Christopher. The same mixture of high intelligence and utter lack of common sense. The same infuriating contrast of vulnerability and arrogance, as if the ability to spout Shakespeare by the yard somehow put him above and beyond the common herd. Yes, he'd been hard on O'Driscoll, had beaten him down and broken him with a sense of triumph that was more than simply professional. He'd never regretted more than he had then that the death sentence had been abolished. He'd longed to take an eye for an eye, a tooth for a tooth.

The ringing of his phone brought him back to earth with a start. He shot to his desk and snatched it up, feeling a swooping lurch in his stomach as he recognised Harding's excited voice.

'We've got a breakthrough, Guv. She caught his reflection in the window. Swears she saw several identical images. She's in shock, of course. But she's quite certain of the description.'

Shenfield listened intently, his frown of concentration gradually slackening. Rubbing his hand over his eyes, he said quietly, 'OK. Thin face, receding hairline. Smiling. I've got that.'

Carefully, he replaced the receiver and picked up the book, from which Christopher's image smiled diffidently. Thin-faced. Hairline receding.

'Guv . . .' Whitelaw stuck his head around the door, then ducked as the book crashed against the wall a couple of inches from his head. 'Bad timing?' he queried.

'It was Christopher she saw. Christopher's bloody photograph. That's our breakthrough. God help us.' Shenfield put his head in his hands.

'Fuck,' Whitelaw muttered eloquently. 'Talking of God, Lambert's on his way down. He wants an update. Immediately, if not sooner.'

Lambert was not a happy man. The university authorities had been promised high-profile security around the campus, he reminded Shenfield, jabbing his finger irritably against a map of central Blackport, to which a further red marker had already been added. Neither was his humour improved by Medlock's revelation that the victim was a known prostitute.

'So, we have street-girls parading across the campus under our very noses? One can imagine what the press will make of that, if they get hold of it,' he snapped.

'Oh, they will, you can bank on it. If O'Driscoll hadn't got his act together, I wouldn't have put it past Sid Barker from the *Echo* to knock a couple of tarts off himself, just to keep the pot boiling,' Shenfield said, reaching for his cigarettes.

Lambert took in a sharp breath. 'A little less flip-pancy, Shenfield, if you please. And as far as I'm aware, Gavin O'Driscoll is only one of a number of possible suspects.'

'Oh, come on! You're not *still* trying to make out—'

'The truth is . . .' Lambert held up a hand to silence him, '. . . the *fact* is, we are going into this afternoon's press conference with no more bloody idea who the killer is than we had this time last year. And in the meantime, I have to report to the univer-sity authorities that we're incapable of effectively policing a campus of barely more than one square mile, which it now transpires is a regular right of way for every prostitute in the area. Is that an accurate summary of the position, gentlemen?'

Medlock gave a discreet cough. 'I don't think we should forget Ackroyd, Sir. I've been running some more checks on him. According to my data, we have received no fewer than fourteen complaints since the Loveridge murder from female students claim-ing Ackroyd has harassed them.'

Lambert turned on Shenfield. 'Were you aware of this? And if not, why not?'

'Yes.' Shenfield closed his eyes and said, with elaborate patience, 'Well aware, Sir.' He turned to Medlock, and adopting the sort of tone he might have taken with Christopher when he was about five years old, said, 'I'll tell you about our friend Norman Ackroyd, shall I? After he found Melanie Loveridge's body, he went completely to pieces. Security guard, see? Never forgave himself. He was in High View for . . . it must have been a couple of years. Since they let him out, he's turned himself into a one-man neighbourhood watch. Moved to the student quarter. Taken it upon himself to ensure the safety of every female student at Blackport University. Hardly a month goes by without he rings me up with another sighting of Gavin O'Driscoll. I could paper the walls with the letters he's sent.'

'And if he did but know it, he's produced one or two handy bits of information along the way,' Whitelaw chipped in. 'The lads from Drugs have had their eye on his boss Singh, for a while. I'm not sure they'd be too happy if we started making our presence felt.'

'So,' Shenfield took over, 'there you have it. Special Agent Ackroyd. Nuisance? Certainly. Nutter? Very probably. Serial killer? Absolutely not a bloody chance in hell.'

'I see.' Lambert sounded regretful, but Medlock, far from being deflated, jumped in with, 'Ah, yes. But case studies suggest it's not at all unusual for serial killers to draw attention to themselves by—'

'Stuff your bloody case studies.' Shenfield's patience finally snapped in the face of Medlock's complacent certainty. Had *he* ever been that sure of himself? 'Let's look at the *facts* of the case, shall we? All the murders have happened in term time. Fact. All within a mile radius of the campus. Fact. The majority of the victims have been students, and the others, because of their ages, and the proximity of their patches to the university, could have very easily been mistaken for students. Fact. Now, I may not have the benefit of a college education, but thirty years in the force has taught me that if it looks like a dog and barks like a dog, chances are it is a bloody dog.'

'Ackroyd had a direct link with the first murder. More than a dozen instances of stalking . . .'

'Forget Ackroyd. Someone from that university is the killer, and that someone is Gavin O'Driscoll.'

Medlock examined his fingernails for a moment, before saying, 'With respect, I think you are allowing your personal feelings to cloud your professional judgement.'

Shenfield heard Whitelaw's sharp intake of breath. They both knew what was coming next.

Lambert glanced over quizzically, before saying, 'I think you had better explain that comment, Constable.'

'DCI Shenfield's animosity towards Blackport University . . .'

'My son's a lecturer there. He found Tanya Stewart's body.' Shenfield regretted with all his heart the pig-headedness that had stopped him taking Ray Whitelaw's advice weeks ago. 'We don't . . .' he cleared his throat. 'We don't get on.'

There was a moment's silence. When Lambert spoke, his voice was ominously quiet. 'I think we should have a word, Chief Inspector. My office. Now.'

*

Shenfield stood in front of the desk, shifting his weight from one foot to the other, and studying the pattern on the carpet. He knew he was on perilously thin ice. For years, he and Lambert had enjoyed what could at best be described as a love-hate relationship. Lambert was pompous, and a stickler for red tape. But he allowed Shenfield a fairly long piece of rope, because Shenfield got results, and Lambert knew it. Shenfield usually enjoyed pushing him right to the limit. He realised he was standing with his toes over the very brink of that limit now.

Finally, Lambert looked up. 'Tell me something, Shenfield. Are you deliberately trying to antagonise me, or does this level of stupidity come naturally to you? If this gets out . . . that the son of the investigating officer . . .'

'It won't.'

'You're sure of that, are you?'

'Well I'm not going to say anything. And I'm sure as hell he won't. Admit he's a copper's son? To that bunch of lefties he hangs round with? I don't think so.' Unbidden, Shenfield sat down. 'Listen, I made an error of judgement, OK? I admit it, but at the time . . .'

Lambert shook his head. 'You're off the case.'

'You can't do that!' Shenfield knew only too well that he could. 'We're right on the edge of a breakthrough. Just give me another couple of months . . . Christmas . . .' He heard and despised the growing note of pleading in his voice. 'And as for it all coming out . . .' Casting frantically around, he spotted a possible chink in Lambert's armour. Carefully, developing his argument as he spoke, he went on, 'If I'm suddenly dropped from the case, Sid Barker and his cronies will want to know why. Bound to. They're always looking for a new angle to pump up their readership, right?'

'Precisely my—'

Double or quits. Even to Shenfield's own ears it sounded dangerously like blackmail as he said slowly, 'And when they find out I've remained on the case for over a month after my son first became involved . . .'

He allowed his words to sink in. Lambert was staring at the ceiling. He'd picked up a pencil and was tapping his teeth, a sure sign he was listening.

Shenfield pressed home what he hoped was his advantage. 'Listen, no one outside this investigation knows I'm Christopher's father. I've barely seen him in years. He doesn't even use my surname. All I'm saying is it might be less damaging in terms of public relations . . .' He let his voice trail off.

Lambert looked at him hard. For a moment, neither of them spoke. Then he said, 'Your comments have been noted, Chief Inspector. I will consider the matter. In the meantime, this conversation hasn't happened. Do I make myself clear?'

He got to his feet, and so did Shenfield. Long years of experience had taught him that you could only push Lambert so hard.

The conversation had gone as far as it was going.

Chapter Nine

Christopher's eleven o'clock Yeats seminar was not going well.

Benedict Wolstenholme, a thin boy with spectacles, was attempting to demonstrate that the letters that passed between W. B. Yeats and Maude Gonne, the woman who had so influenced his life and his writing, allowed a deeper insight into their relationship than the many poems he had written about her. The paper was well enough researched, but, like Benedict himself, deeply boring. Not that many of the other students in the seminar group wanted to be there, whatever the subject matter; they were all far more interested in the police cars and press cameras outside.

Christopher appeared just as unable to concentrate as the rest of them. Several times there had been long, uncomfortable pauses while Benedict waited expectantly for some response from him, as he was doing now.

'I asked if you agreed, Dr Heatherington,' he repeated at last, 'that Yeats' letters to Maude Gonne demonstrated more clearly than his poetry the enormous influence she exerted over him?'

Christopher stared at him for a moment. 'Er . . . what does everyone else think? Let's throw it open to discussion, shall we?'

'But in terms of emotional intensity, one can't compare the letters with the poems, can one?' A plump girl leaned forward and looked at him earnestly.

'I . . . er . . . I'm sorry, Eleanor?' Christopher looked flustered.

Benedict raised an eyebrow at her and shook his head, then said, 'You miss my point. The letters were real life.'

'Poetry *was* his life,' the girl responded passionately, glancing towards Christopher for encouragement.

'Poetry isn't life,' Benedict pronounced, 'it's *about* life.'

'Or an alternative. A safer place to live.' Kieran spoke for the first time. Until that point, he had been staring out of the window, apparently locked in his own thoughts.

The clock above the door struck twelve, bringing the seminar to a close. Christopher's students gathered their books together and headed for the door, eager to get back to the gossip in the Union bar. Kieran stood up slowly and began to shrug into his jacket.

'Sorry.' Christopher leant his elbows on the desk and massaged his eyes with the balls of his palms. 'Not one of my better classes, I'm afraid.' He picked up the copy of his book lying next to the Yeats and stared at it hard, then said suddenly, 'I found an injured bird once, when I was a child.'

'Yeah?' Kieran wound his scarf around his neck and picked up his things.

'I can still recall the feel of it, its weightless bones, its wet, bedraggled wings . . .' Replacing the book carefully on his desk, Christopher made a cup with his hands. 'The frantic beating of its wings when I picked it up . . .' He looked at Kieran with a tight, mirthless smile. 'My father wanted to wring its neck. Heartless, instant destruction. That's always been his answer to weakness and helplessness. Either that, or ignore it completely.' He picked up the book again, cradling it as if it were that long-gone bird. 'I tended it for weeks, you know. Fed it, kept it warm, watched it steadily recover its strength and beauty. He couldn't understand that, of course. "*You can't keep that thing here, crapping all over the carpets . . .*"' He looked down at his hands, which were gripping the book so tightly the dust cover was all but torn. '"*Not your property.*"' Christopher spat out the words as if they were shards of broken glass. 'Can you believe that? His great policeman's hands around the book that's taken me most of my adult years to write and he had the nerve to tell me . . .'

Kieran cleared his throat and shuffled towards the door. 'I'd best be—'

'Sorry to disturb you, Dr Heatherington.' The departmental secretary knocked, then, seeing he was not alone, hovered in the doorway. 'A Professor Castledine's been on the phone. Could you ring him back?'

'I . . . er . . .' Kieran ducked past her. 'I'll leave you to it then.'

'Yes.' Christopher massaged his eyes again. 'Yes, of course.' He looked up wearily at the secretary. 'Did Professor Castledine say what he wanted?'

She shook her head. 'He wouldn't leave a message. But he said it was urgent. Is everything all right, Dr Heatherington?'

He tried the number twice and received no reply, then headed for the History department, only to find that Flora's lectures for the day were finished. He went to the Students' Union first, breaking into a trot as he looked from room to room. As he entered the coffee bar, he caught a flash of long, auburn hair, and called her name, only to be faced by a boy with a straggling ginger beard, who stared at him in puzzled amusement. Muttering an apology, Christopher slowed his pace and made his way to the library.

The crash made Flora look up from her books with a frown. It had been difficult enough to concentrate on her overdue essay in view of all the activity outside, without people throwing books around.

Christopher, ankle-deep in periodicals, was attempting to right an overturned bookstand.

'What happened?' she whispered, suppressing a smile as she went over to help him pick up the scattered magazines. The poor man looked utterly mortified.

'I . . . I was just looking for . . .' he stammered,

retrieving some loosened pages from under a table. His voice came out as a bellow. Several heads turned in disapproval.

'Let's get out of here.' She pulled a face. 'I've been trying to think of an excuse to give up on that essay for the last half an hour.'

She looked curiously at the crowds gathered behind the cordons as they walked past the boarded-up bookshop. 'Do you know what's going on? Someone in the library said . . .'

'I . . . I'm not sure. Some sort of an accident, I think.'

'There seem an awful lot of police cars for an accident. And there was an outside broadcast unit here earlier. I heard that—'

'How did the rehearsal go yesterday?'

Christopher didn't seem to want to discuss it further; he must be the only person on campus who wasn't busy speculating and recirculating rumours, she thought, as reluctantly she dragged her eyes away. 'Oh . . . OK, I think.'

'You and Kieran go well together.'

'Do you think so?' She grinned. 'I just wish I could learn my lines at the speed he does. It's sickening!'

'He is exceptionally bright.' Christopher, to her amusement, turned scarlet as he added hastily, 'Not that I'm suggesting you're not just as . . .'

She shook her head, laughing. 'Don't apologise. I don't need telling I'm not in the same league as he is. Not many people are.'

'True. And when one considers his background . . .'

'Background?' She looked enquiringly at him.

'His . . . his late start at the university. Anyway, I'm glad I bumped into you. I wanted to ask if you've been in touch with your father recently?'

She flushed, guiltily. She had barely spoken to Simon all term, answering his frequent, rambling epistles with only the occasional, inadequate post-card. 'I've been really busy, and . . .' She'd ring him this evening, she promised herself, and instantly dismissed him from her consciousness. 'What did you mean, "background"?'

'Kieran's one of the most gifted students I've ever taught, you know. Quite outstanding.' Christopher hesitated, as though about to say more, then added, 'Maybe you could give him a ring. Your father, that is. If this . . .' he looked back towards the bookshop, 'this . . . incident is reported on the national news he's bound to be concerned.' He glanced at his watch. 'I must get back to the department. You will remember to call him, won't you?'

He jogged away before she had a chance to reply.

'It's no good. We've got to get a phone put in.' Flora threw down her dripping umbrella as she entered the flat, later the same night. The cold evening air had brought a glow to her skin and her hair curled around her face in damp tendrils.

Meg looked up from the television and said equably, 'God, there's no justice! My hair goes like a yard of pump-water when it's wet. Can I borrow some of your mousse, by the way?'

'Sure.' Flora peeled off her wet coat. 'Going somewhere nice?'

Meg pulled a face. 'You nine-to-five Arts students don't know you're born. Lecture on forensic pathology. That should put me off my supper.' She sucked her stomach in. 'Still, it all helps the diet. Another two pounds this week.'

'Well done!' Flora gave her a sly grin. 'Are you sure you haven't got your eye on someone?'

Meg seemed to have developed an unexpected interest in her appearance over the last few weeks. She had taken to wearing her hair loose, spending hours in front of the mirror dangerously wielding a pair of curling tongs. Contact lenses had replaced the wire-framed spectacles. And to Flora's secret dismay, the Aztec jacket had been ditched in favour of a coat the same shade of green as her own. The woman in the curry shop below had asked them the week before if they were sisters, a question with which Meg had seemed inordinately pleased.

'Me? What would I want with some love-sick great oaf mooning over me? No, I just decided it was time to take myself in hand a bit. Got to look my best for the christening, see. Did you get hold of your dad, by the way?'

'No. I give up. That's three times I've tried. Oh, God! Is that the time?' she wailed, catching sight of herself in the mirror as the theme tune to *Emmerdale* came on. 'Kieran'll be here any minute.'

'If not sooner,' Meg grinned as the doorbell rang. 'I'll let Romeo in. You go and get yourself ready.'

Kieran stood dripping on the living room carpet

as Meg bustled around, filling the kettle and hanging his sodden coat and scarf over the back of a chair.

'Shan't be a minute,' Flora called from the bedroom, over the whine of her hairdryer. 'Make yourself at home.'

He shook himself like a dog, droplets of rain flying from his hair like a halo, and hissing into the tiny gas fire.

'Cheers,' he smiled, taking the coffee Meg offered him and settling himself comfortably on the sofa.

She switched off the television and perched on the edge of a chair. 'How's it going?' she asked at last.

'Fine, thanks.'

'Enjoying the course?'

'Great. You?'

'Brilliant.' Surreptitiously, she eased off her Wallace and Gromit slippers and nudged them under the chair. 'So what did you do before you came here?'

'Sorry?'

'Flora said you were twenty-four. I just wondered . . . ?'

'All sorts. You know how it is.' He took a swig of coffee and glanced at his watch.

'What, round here, or were you somewhere else?'

'What is all this? Twenty questions?' He laughed, but there was a tinge of irritation in his expression.

'Ready,' Flora called, as the hairdryer went silent.

Kieran stood up and grabbed his jacket. Looking

down at Meg, he said, 'See you later, then.' He grinned suddenly. 'You've got a hole in your sock, by the way.'

By the time they got off the bus at the university, the rain had subsided to a half-hearted drizzle and the moon was breaking through the clouds, its watery reflection wavering on the littered pavement.

'Come for a drink after?' Kieran asked.

'Don't forget Damien's party.'

'Let's go somewhere quiet instead.' He prodded an empty coke can ahead of him with his foot. 'There's something I need to talk to you about.'

Flora glanced at him quickly. 'Is everything OK?'

'Yeah.' He took her hand and squeezed it. 'Yeah, of course.'

'So what is it you want to . . . ?'

'Not now, love. We'll talk after the rehearsal.'

He aimed another kick at the can, watching it roll slowly along the kerb and into the gutter, where it was flattened with deliberate care by a boy on a bicycle.

'Good of you to join us,' Myles remarked waspishly, when they reached the drama studio. He clapped his hands and called, 'OK, everyone. Now that the stars of the show have finally arrived, let's get straight on. Act five, scene three. Let's have you drinking poison, shall we Kieran?' He glared at Flora and added, 'Just lie on the stage and look dead. Think you can manage that?'

Kieran winked at her as they took their positions. Trying not to laugh, she arranged herself on the floor and closed her eyes. Kieran took her hand and began to speak.

'Hold it, hold it!' Myles called irritably, as the door of the studio banged open, letting in a blast of damp air. 'Oh, it's you, Christopher. We were just about to get started.' He sighed dramatically.

Christopher muttered his apologies and took a seat at the back as the lights went down and the rest of the cast fell silent.

Through half-closed lids, Flora watched Kieran as he knelt beside her, rocking backwards and forwards as he wove his magic, his face transforming into a mask of grief. The intensity of his pain was terrifying. He gathered her into his arms, whispering, *'Why art thou yet so fair?'*

She felt herself go limp. She was paralysed. She was in the tomb, the bones of her ancestors mouldering around her, the dank, unbreathed air suffocating her . . .

Suddenly, at the back of the studio, the door banged again. The spell was broken. Kieran released his grip.

'Oh, for heaven's sake, what now?' Myles shouted, slamming down his script.

Flora struggled to her feet and peered into the darkness beyond the footlights, her heart still pounding, as she heard Christopher's startled voice exclaim, 'Professor Castledine! What on earth are you doing here?'

It was as if her two worlds had collided. As the lights in the studio came up, Flora saw Simon's gaunt shape framed in the doorway and felt utterly disorientated. A rustle of conversation had started. She hesitated for a moment, turning towards Kieran with a helpless gesture, then jumped down from the stage and went to him, her cheeks burning with embarrassment.

'Forgive me, my dear.' His cultured tones grated on her and she tensed as he clutched her to him for a moment, before standing back, his eyes searching her face. 'I had to see for myself that you were safe.'

He looked frailer, somehow faded, like an old, half-forgotten photograph. He took off his glasses to wipe away the tears that always came too easily to him. Without them, his eyes looked vulnerable and uncertain.

Behind her, she heard Myles's unconcealed snigger. With a sudden rush of protective pity, she put her arm around Simon's thin shoulders.

'It's good to see you,' she lied. 'I'm glad you've come.'

Christopher took control of the situation, introducing Simon to the rest of the cast as 'the famous novelist, Simon Castledine'. Myles ceased his sniggering. At Christopher's suggestion, the remainder of the rehearsal was postponed. Damien began to round people up for his party, and Flora watched with relief as they gathered their things and began to drift away. Kieran was standing by the door, pulling on his jacket. Flora ran across to him. 'We're going back to Simon's hotel for a meal. Come with us,' she said, taking his arm.

Kieran shook his head. 'No. It's family.'

'Don't be daft! I want you to . . .'

'I'll catch you later, love. You go with your dad.'

'Are you sure?' She glanced back at Simon, who was watching her intently. 'Look . . . I'm really sorry about all this.'

He took off his scarf and put it around her neck. 'Take care of this for me over the weekend,' he said with a smile. 'I'll see you Monday.'

'Kieran, wait!' she called as he ambled off. She caught his sleeve, her face worried. 'You said you wanted to talk.'

'Eh?'

'You coming, Kieran?' Damien called across.

'Right with you, mate!' He turned back and touched Flora's cheek. 'It doesn't matter, love. It wasn't anything important.'

By the time she left the studio with Simon and Christopher, the others were gathered in a reverent circle, examining the long silver Mercedes parked outside.

Simon gestured at it disinterestedly. 'I needed a driver. I have to visit my publisher while I'm over. They organised it for me in Penzance.'

A man with a peaked cap jumped forward and held open the car door for them. Flora turned and looked through the back window, watching Kieran watching her as the chauffeur drove them away.

Saturday 12 December

The voices are in my head again, whispering their lies, but I just say her name over and over and drown them out, as I did when I pushed the whore through the glass. Through the looking-glass. Being saved myself, I saved her from the voices, and now they are angry.

They slide into my head while I'm asleep. They tell me she is no different from the rest.

Roses have thorns, and silver fountains mud;
Clouds and eclipses stain both moon and sun,
And loathsome canker lives in sweetest bud.

I will not listen.

Chapter Ten

Neville Medlock ordered half a pint of beer, sipped it, and pulled a face. Through choice, it would have been a gin and tonic or a well-chilled Chardonnay, but the inappropriately-named Jolly Sailor was not the sort of pub to stock Chardonnay, or any wine for that matter, let alone be able to serve it at the right temperature. The walls exhaled stale decades of chips and cigarette smoke. The cracked linoleum was tacky with slopped beer and the carelessly-discarded chewing gum of its clientele, of which, at six-thirty on a cold damp Monday evening, there was little evidence. The only sign of life came from the fruit machine in the corner. It flashed intermittently and occasionally emitted a series of manic booms and shrieks, which appeared to do nothing to enliven the pot-bellied man who slouched in front of it, robotically feeding in pound coins. Apart from he and Medlock, the only other customers were a middle-aged couple, sitting silent and upright on hard wooden chairs beneath a loop of stringy tinsel that hung limply from the ceiling.

He had selected a table as far away from the bar

as possible, but which had a good view of the door. He took another sip of his beer, as if hoping it might, like a decent wine, have improved by being allowed to breathe. Again his expression implied that this was not the case, as he glanced impatiently at his watch, pulled out his mobile and punched in some numbers. The middle-aged couple, already alerted by his Home Counties accent, could not have regarded him with greater suspicion if he had pulled out a loaded pistol.

He tried another number, then rammed the phone back into his pocket and sat drumming his fingers on the table, his eyes fixed on the door. After a couple of minutes, it swung open, slicing a blast of icy air into the fuggy warmth. Medlock was half way to his feet when a hard-looking man in motorbike leathers entered. He paused, gave Medlock a long, aggressive stare, then went across to the bar.

Medlock subsided onto his stool. The biker watched him for a moment, then muttered something to the barman, who shrugged and pushed a glass over to him. Medlock pulled a newspaper from his briefcase and folded it to the crossword, carefully avoiding the biker's eye.

A sudden eruption of sound from the corner caused a momentary diversion. The fruit machine was spewing out pound coins with a steady, clunking thud. The pot-bellied man watched it impassively until it finally shuddered to a halt, then scooped up his winnings and began feeding them back in again.

Another quarter of an hour elapsed. The biker

left, with one last, suspicious glare in Medlock's direction. The barman slouched across, armed with a greyish dishcloth, aimed a desultory swipe at a few of the tables, then returned to his post. Medlock looked at his watch again. As he did so, the door opened and a bulky figure lumbered in.

Medlock jumped immediately to his feet, pinning a friendly smile onto his face as he held out his hand. 'Norman! Glad you could join me. Sit down and I'll get you a drink.'

He went up to the bar and ordered a lemonade and lime. It was the fourth time they had met here, and he knew what Norman Ackroyd liked, without having to ask.

When he returned, Norman was fumbling with a sheaf of papers. 'I've made a l . . . l . . . list,' he said, carefully wiping the table top with his sleeve and spreading the papers out in front of him. On the top sheet was printed: SUGGESTIONS. Beneath the heading, he had written:

1) Better street lights
2) Better locks on all the front doors
3) More security guards

Medlock studied the list in silence for a moment, then he looked up and said with a broad smile, 'That's very useful, Norman.' He dropped the papers into his briefcase and forced down the rest of his beer. 'I'll see what I can do. Now, why don't you go over the night of Melanie Loveridge's death again for me? You never know, we might just have overlooked a vital piece of evidence that could help us find out where O'Driscoll is.' He glanced around them. The fruit machine was vacant now, the middle-aged couple the only other customers. The pub was silent but for the faint squeak of a glass being polished by the landlord, as he watched them incuriously from behind the bar. 'Tell you what. Let's go somewhere a bit more private. How about your place?'

'N . . . n . . . no!' Norman shook his head, his eyes darting away from Medlock's questioning gaze as he added lamely, 'It's not c . . . con . . . convenient.'

Medlock sighed. It was the fourth time he had received the same response. 'OK,' he said patiently. 'My car then.'

'This really is all extremely helpful,' Medlock said half an hour later, as he beamed across at Norman, who was improbably squeezed into the bucket seat next to him. The gratified smile that flickered across Norman's large face was instantly replaced with a worried frown as Medlock added casually, 'We would have been a lot more comfortable back at your place, you know.' He wiped the misted-up windscreen and blew on his hands, by way of emphasis.

'I'll be g . . . g . . . going.' Norman fumbled for the door handle.

'I was wondering . . .' Medlock looked at his passenger thoughtfully, his head on one side. 'Six accommodation units, was it, with female students in? And all within sight of your own flat?'

Norman gave a cautious nod.

'I know you've been keeping your eye on them for us, and an excellent job you've been doing, as I said before, but I've been reassessing their risk potential.'

Norman paused, his fingers around the handle. 'R . . . risk potential,' he repeated, nodding solemnly, clearly taken by the phrase.

'You're only a couple of streets from where the Stewart girl was murdered, you know,' Medlock went on. 'Now I know you're not keen to have visitors. And why should you be?' he added quickly as Norman opened his mouth to protest. 'An Englishman's home, and all that. But the thing is, if you *were* prepared to allow us to make your place our . . . our operational HQ . . .'

Norman's expression brightened.

'. . . I might be able to organise a bit of extra surveillance. All this is an enormous responsibility for you, Norman. I'm all too aware of that. A break would do you good. In fact . . .' Medlock leant across and pushed the door open for him, as Norman began to protest that he didn't need a break, '. . . I might even be able to help you out myself.'

Likely Scenario: Suspect develops an obsession for the Loveridge girl – most probably fuelled by no more than the occasional glance of her. He stalks her. On the night of the May Ball he witnesses her having sexual intercourse with Gavin O'Driscoll. Enraged that the object of his worship has proved herself unworthy, he kills her once O'Driscoll has *left her there alone, mutilating her to destroy the beauty which he now blames for deceiving him.*

Medlock was sitting at his computer back at Blackport Central. It was Whitelaw's night off, and Shenfield was out chasing his tail somewhere, so he had the office to himself.

Suspect subsequently rationalises his feelings of guilt by completely reversing Gavin O'Driscoll's role and his own he tapped in. *He, not O'Driscoll, has failed to protect her; O'Driscoll, not he, is the murderer. He creates spurious reported sightings in order to reassure himself that O'Driscoll is also responsible for the subsequent attacks, all on women of similar appearance to Melanie Loveridge.*

He scrolled back up the screen, read what he had written thus far with a small nod of satisfaction, then continued.

<u>*Question*</u>: *What has triggered the post-Loveridge attacks?*

He stared at the flickering screen, then added another couple of query marks, before starting a new paragraph.

<u>*Strategy*</u>: *Imperative to gain access to suspect's home address to search for possible incriminating evidence. (Warrant?? Preferable to gain his confidence; move too quickly and we've lost him.)*

<u>*Significant Features of Suspect's Behaviour*</u>: *Classic symptoms of disassociation. Suspect talks freely about the murder, even admitting feelings of guilt, albeit limited to his failure, as one of the security guards on duty that night, in preventing the*

attack! He added as a footnote. *As in Harvard dept. of Criminology study (McKinchy?? – check) 1992 – fascinating to observe at first hand,* then went back to the main text. *Even the apparent passion for poetry (his only other topic of conversation) is entirely consistent with the 'whore / Madonna' attitude to women common in so many of such cases.* He added *Precedent?* to his other footnote, then sat back in his chair, stretched and poured himself some more of the half-bottle of Chardonnay he had treated himself to on his way to the station.

'Thank God for Sainsbury's,' he murmured, then turned his attention back to the computer.

<u>Conclusion</u>: *By his eagerness to talk to everyone and anyone who will listen to him, it would appear that Norman Ackroyd has done as good a job of convincing himself of his innocence as he has of convincing DCI Shenfield and all the other donkeys at Blackport Central.*

Medlock chuckled to himself, then highlighted the final section of his report and regretfully hit the 'delete' key.

In the small hours of the morning, wide awake in his lonely bed, Shenfield could feel the investigation slipping inexorably away from him. He kneaded the pillow that felt filled with rocks. Lambert hadn't repeated his threat to take him off the case – but he hadn't confirmed he was to stay on it, either. And for once in his life, Shenfield found himself afraid to ask.

'Sod this,' he muttered, chucking a pillow at the monotonously blinking green dial of his alarm clock. Four-thirty a.m. He jumped out of bed and pulled on some clothes. By five a.m., he was opening up the Portakabin that had served as the campus incident room for the six weeks since the bookshop attack.

He turned, scanning the blank windows of the halls of residence that loomed out of the shadows across the square. O'Driscoll could be in any one of those rooms. The thought haunted him. He was spending far more time than he could spare on the campus, ignoring the growing piles of paperwork back at Blackport Central, partly to avoid Lambert, but also, he was forced to admit to himself, to allay the irrational conviction that O'Driscoll would make his next move the minute his back was turned. He felt as if they were locked in a game of cat and mouse, and he knew that was a dangerous way to feel, because it meant it was getting to him, getting personal in a way that could really impair his judgement. But he couldn't keep away.

The term was drawing to its close, the students getting ready for the Christmas holidays. If O'Driscoll ran true to form, it should give them a few weeks' respite before he struck again. He should be relieved, he told himself, but the thought of Christmas only added to his general unease. It was the season he dreaded most since Susannah's death. Last year, his first without her in thirty-six years, had been a nightmare. The prospect of rattling around in the cheerless house again this Christmas was not one he relished.

He'd begun to wonder if maybe he should ask Christopher to share it with him. He came across him, occasionally, usually tagging along with some scruffy bunch of students. If ever he spotted his father, he looked straight through him.

At first, Shenfield told himself that the idea of inviting him over was ridiculous, but somehow it wouldn't go away, and the more he considered it, the more sense it made. After all, someone had to make the first move; they couldn't go on like this for ever, each of them carrying on as if the other didn't exist. They could have a few beers, maybe. Watch some old films. Shenfield tried and failed to think of a film they would agree on. OK, no films. But it was only for one day, for God's sake. Surely father and son could manage that much good will between them?

Later that morning, he spotted Christopher going towards the Students' Union and called his name, hurrying over to him before he had a chance to escape. He caught up with him under the giant Christmas tree at the foot of the steps.

'Comes round quickly, doesn't it?' Shenfield commented inanely, nodding at the lights. 'Christmas, that is.' Now that they were face to face, the casual invitation he'd rehearsed had deserted him.

Christopher glanced impatiently towards the group of youngsters he'd been with, who were now disappearing into the building.

'Was there anything in particular?' His cool voice took on a more hostile tone as he added, 'Or are you simply hounding me for the hell of it?'

'Eh?' Shenfield was genuinely perplexed. He hadn't even said anything yet.

'You're really enjoying this, aren't you? "*Maintaining a police presence.*"' Christopher's voice was heavy with sarcasm. 'Well, I should warn you, if you persist in following me around in this way, I shall have no option but to . . .'

'Just shut up and listen, will you? All I was going to ask you was . . .' Shenfield heard the belligerence in his own voice. Why did it always come out like that when he spoke to Christopher? He tried again. 'I was just wondering—'

'This is *my* world,' Christopher cut across him, gesturing towards the library with an angry sweep of his arm. 'Mine, do you hear me? It stands for everything you rubbish and belittle. Poetry. Art. Beauty. I don't want you here. I don't want to speak to you. I don't want to have to set eyes on you. Your very presence contaminates this place. Just leave me alone.'

Specks of spittle had gathered at the corners of his mouth. His face was stiff with fury.

The ferocity of the attack caught Shenfield completely off guard. He opened his mouth, but no words came. In silence, he watched as Christopher turned on his heel and marched up the steps, disappearing into the Union building without a backward glance.

Well, that was that. He stood gazing at the heavy

doors, as though half-expecting his son to reappear.
Then, squaring his shoulders, he turned away and
walked briskly back towards his car, suddenly
anxious to be off campus and amongst the noise,
bustle and the rowdy comradeship of Blackport
Central. He'd done his best. All he could do now
was bury himself in his paperwork and wait for
Christmas to go away.

He almost wished for another murder.

Chapter Eleven

Shenfield was not the only one dreading Christmas.

Flora, battling through the throngs of shoppers, felt her heart sink at the sight of the decorations twinkling in the late-afternoon gloom. The past months had been the happiest of her life. Every minute she could, she spent with Kieran. He had filled her every waking moment, and when she slept, he filled her dreams. He was like no one she had ever met; a magician, brightening colours, making the ordinary fantastic, heightening her sensations like a drug. She closed her eyes against the gaudy lights, and Kieran's bright reflection filled the darkness behind her eyelids. The four barren weeks of the vacation stretched before her like a desert.

She sat down on one of the benches outside the Town Hall and took out her shopping list.

Meg . . . she ticked off the name. At least that one had been easy; for weeks Meg had coveted the floppy green velour hat that Flora had treated herself to at the beginning of term. Thank God they were still selling them on the market.

Simon . . . A book? A CD, maybe? Whatever she bought him would be received with the same restrained display of gratitude masking complete indifference. She stared into the middle distance, imagining the impeccable lunch prepared by Mrs Menheniott, the expensive champagne, the ticking of the grandfather clock in the dining room. Her mother, as every Christmas, a silent, unwelcome ghost at the table. She would think about Simon later.

Kieran . . . She had doodled a question mark beside his name, decorating it with stars and moons, then surrounding it with a garland of holly. She hadn't a clue what to get him. It was hardly that he had everything, more that he appeared cheerfully oblivious to his own lack of material possessions.

A grubby seagull swooped down and landed a few feet away, sidling flat-footedly towards her and staring at the list with hungry, orange eyes. It stood for a few moments, shifting from foot to foot, its head on one side, then, when no bread was forthcoming, it flung back its head and squawked its frustration before flapping away. The sound transported Flora instantly to the Scillies, and in that instant she knew what she was going to buy for Kieran. The idea was so perfect; she couldn't imagine why she hadn't thought of it before.

The bus ride home was spent planning when she should give him the chosen present. Could she bear to wait until the end-of-term ball tomorrow? It was the obvious occasion, the social high point of the term. Fireworks, a fun fair, dancing until dawn, followed by breakfast down at the docks. But there would be so many other people around . . .

Opening the front door of the flat, she all but fell over a mountain of parcels. In bewilderment, she stared around the hall, which was piled with carrier bags from Mothercare and Toys 'R' Us, as Meg burst from the kitchen, her plump face red with excitement.

'It's happened!' she cried, throwing her arms around Flora. 'Joanna Megan. Eight pounds ten ounces. I'm an aunty! The bank manager will probably go into ventricular fibrillation when the cheques come home to roost, but what the hell?' Her delight was infectious. 'Megan, see? They've even named her after me!' she beamed. 'Come and see what I've bought her!'

'There's more?' Flora laughed, as she was dragged through to the living room. On the settee lolled an enormous white rabbit, with floppy ears and a pink gingham frock.

'I know, I know, it's a bit big. But I had to get something a bit special, see. Tell you what, girl, you and me are going to celebrate. There's champagne in the fridge. Well, not *real* champagne. And then we're going out on the town, my treat. There's that new club in Prince's Street—'

'Sorry,' Flora cut in, running her hand over the rabbit's velvety fur to avoid Meg's eye. 'I can't tonight. Kieran'll be here in a few minutes. We're going out,' she added quickly. 'It's the drama soc Christmas do.' Meg had been pretty tolerant about the amount of time Kieran spent at the flat, but Flora had sensed a coolness between them lately.

'Oh.' Meg's face fell.

'But we can still have a drink. Or why don't you come with us? We can all celebrate.'

'Couldn't you put him off, just this once?'

'Oh, come on, Meg,' she coaxed, 'I wish you'd at least try to get on with him.'

'I just . . .'

'You just what?' Flora tried not to sound defensive.

Meg hesitated. 'I just don't want you getting hurt.'

'What?' Flora looked at her in genuine astonishment.

'Look, I can see why you find him attractive; you'd have to be blind not to.' Meg flushed, then went on quickly, 'But how much do you actually *know* about him?'

'Christ, Meg, you sound more like a maiden aunt than my flatmate!'

'All right.' She paused. 'But think about it. He's happy enough to be here all the time, but you never go round to his place, do you?'

'I'm sorry if we're getting in your way.'

'Now don't go all huffy, girl. It isn't that I don't like him, because I do. I . . .' Her voice trailed off. She was blushing even more furiously as, for a second, she caught Flora's eye. Then looking away, she added lamely, 'He's a good laugh. I just think there's something a bit fishy about him, that's all I'm saying.'

'According to you, there's not a man been born that you'd trust, especially a good-looking one.' Flora forced a smile. She was determined not to spoil Meg's evening by letting things develop into an argument. And she was beginning to suspect why Meg had spent most of the term attempting to remodel herself into her double. 'Come on. We should be celebrating.' She gave her a quick hug. 'Don't let's fight.'

'I just think . . .' Meg broke off, then shrugged. 'Oh well, fair enough. It's none of my business is it? Men, eh?' She grinned suddenly. 'They're not worth falling out over, that's for sure. And they're not worth sharing a bottle of champagne with, either! So let's get it down us quick before Romeo turns up.'

Kieran looked surprised to find her waiting out on the pavement for him.

'Meg's got work to do,' she lied.

'We're a bit early,' Kieran said, slipping his arm into hers, as they neared the university. 'D'you fancy a pint?'

They stopped at the first pub they came to. Flora went up to get the drinks. As she took her purse from her bag, she saw the white envelope that held his present and felt a shiver of anticipation. Maybe she'd give it to him now, while they were alone.

Kieran had found a table by the window. She watched him from the bar. He was flipping a pile of beer mats, the long fingers that knew every intimate, secret inch of her body delicately snapping shut to catch them. The sight filled her with a longing so powerful that it knocked the breath out of her. His dark hair fell forward over his eyes and he pushed it back with unconscious, casual grace, his concentration fixed on the mats.

She reached into her bag, then hesitated. What if he didn't want to come? It was all very well organising his vacation for him, but what if he already had plans? She realised how little they had talked about his life away from the university.

She put his drink in front of him and watched as he began to build the mats into a pyramid, before asking cautiously, 'Are you looking forward to Christmas?'

Kieran shrugged, frowning as he added another mat. 'Are you?'

'Not much. It's a bit lonely down there.' Now, she urged herself. Tell him now. She could feel the words like pebbles in her mouth.

'Don't go home if that's how you feel.'

Could he have had the same idea as her? She tried to read his expression, but he was concentrating on his elaborate construction.

'I couldn't do that.' Even if he had, she wouldn't be able to go. She hadn't even dared to break the news to Simon that this year they might not be alone. Why did she always feel so guilty about him?

She was startled when Kieran said, 'Your dad must love you a lot, if he came all the way up here just to see you.' It was the first time he had mentioned Simon's visit; it was almost as if he could see inside her head.

'He does. I'm all he has. The times he's told me that! You can't imagine what a burden it is. It's as if he expects me to be his wife, as well as his daughter. Oh God, nothing like that,' she laughed at Kieran's expression. 'Sorry. I didn't mean to go on. It's the champagne. It's made me maudlin.'

How had they got on to Simon? She steered the conversation back on course, crossing her fingers under the table. 'When will you be going home then?' For all she knew, he might feel equally beholden to his family.

'Who said I'd be going home?'

Encouraged, she said, 'So, not a close family then?'

'Nope.'

Another layer of mats was added while she waited for him to explain, until the silence between them lengthened into awkwardness.

'Tell me about them,' she said at last.

'What, I've shown you mine so you show me yours? Nothing to tell.' He yawned ostentatiously and looked at his watch. 'Can you stand the excitement of another pint here or do you want to move on?'

Meg's words niggled in the back of her mind. 'You sound like you come from round here somewhere,' she pressed on.

'Yeah, but then anyone north of Birmingham sounds the same to you.'

With infinite care, he placed the final mat on top of the pyramid.

Fine, Flora thought, stung by his deliberate elusiveness. If that was the way he wanted to play things, she'd take the bloody ticket back to the travel agent and get her money back.

'I'm off.' She jumped to her feet, causing the beer mats to tremble and collapse.

'What did you do that for?'

'I've got a headache,' she snapped. 'I'm going home.'

'Hang on!' Kieran swigged back the rest of his beer and struggled into his jacket as she headed for the door. 'What about the party?'

Outside, it was sleeting and bitterly cold. Scraps of damp paper flapped and curled around her ankles as she strode along, her head throbbing and her stomach churning as the wine began to take effect.

Catching her up, Kieran took her hand. 'You're freezing, love. D'you not feel well? Here, put your hand in my pocket.'

'I'm fine.' She snatched it away from him.

'Christ, what's eating you tonight?' He rammed his own hands into his pockets and dropped back a couple of paces, his head turned away.

'Don't feel you have to come back with me,' she snapped, as a bus trundled past, its tyres hissing on the wet tarmac.

'OK.' He stopped in the middle of the pavement. 'I won't, if that's how you feel.'

'Suits me.' Taken aback, but determined not to let

him call her bluff, she sprinted after the bus and jumped aboard.

It was only a couple of stops to Aigburth Street. As she got off at the corner, she could see him jogging up the hill towards her. Quickening her pace, she headed towards the flat.

'For God's sake,' he yelled, catching up with her and grabbing at her arm. 'What are you trying to do? Get yourself killed?'

'I can take care of myself, thank you.' She shook herself free.

'No you can't.' His voice softened. 'Come on, Flora. this is daft. Let's go to the party.'

'I'm not in the mood for a party,' she sniffed, knowing she was being childish, but his secretiveness had hurt. She had thought she meant more to him than just a quick term-time fling. She glanced up at him and added ungraciously, 'You can come in for a drink, if you want.'

'Where's Meg?' Kieran asked when, in silence, she had made the coffee.

'I don't know. I'm not her babysitter.' She felt in her bag for the packet of cigarettes that had lain abandoned since the first week of term.

Kieran shook his head when she offered them to him. 'I never knew you smoked.'

'Any objections?'

'Bloody hell, Flora. Give me a break.'

Avoiding his eye, she struck a match, holding it between her thumb and forefinger as she watched it burn. 'Did you do this when you were small?' she asked staring as the matchstick charred down towards her fingers. 'See how long you could hold it before you chickened out and let it go?'

'No.' He leant across and blew it out. 'Listen, that was really stupid, running off like that. Anything could have happened to you.'

She struck another match. 'Maybe I like taking risks.'

'Yeah. Sure.'

'It was one of the reasons I chose this place.' Her eyes didn't leave the flame. 'All that stuff in the papers. Blackport sounded dangerous.'

'Oh yes?' he scoffed. 'And when I came after you that first night, you were bloody terrified, that's how much you like taking risks. Get real.'

She held the blackened matchstick up to him in triumph as the flame dwindled and died. 'Maybe that's what attracted me to you. Maybe I thought you were dangerous.'

He arranged his features into a grotesque leer and whispered, 'I am dangerous, my dear Miss Castledine. But not as dangerous as these bloody things.' Laughing, he grasped her wrist, crushed the cigarette that was still between her fingers, and threw it into the grate. Sliding his other arm around her waist, he dug his fingers into her ribs and began to tickle her. 'Come on, Flora, crack us a smile.'

The pressure of his grip, the sight of his strong fingers so effortlessly encircling her wrist, filled her with sudden excitement. Twisting her face towards him, she kissed him violently, reaching for his zip.

'Hey, steady on,' he laughed and pulled back. Taking her face between his hands, he nuzzled her ear and whispered, 'Let's go to bed.'

'No.' She put her arms around his neck and pulled him on top of her on the dusty, fraying rug. 'Here. I want to do it here.'

He kissed her hair as, slowly, he began to undo the buttons on her blouse.

For once, the tenderness she normally found so endearing infuriated her. Grabbing his hand, she pushed it roughly inside her bra. 'For God's sake, Kieran, I won't break. I'm flesh and blood, not porcelain.'

He looked down, his face puzzled. 'I know that. But you're special. I don't want to hurt you. It should be more than some quick shag on the floor.'

Her eyes half-closed, she arched her back, thrusting her bare breast against the roughness of his palm as she murmured, 'Maybe Myles was right. Maybe I want you to hurt me.'

'That's crap. You've had too much to drink.' He pulled his hand away and sat up, his back to her.

'How do you know?' she laughed recklessly, raking his back with her nails. 'Maybe it would turn me on.'

'Pack it in, Flora.'

'What's the matter?' She flicked her tongue across the raised, red weals her nails had left, her teeth grazing the taut ridge of his spine. 'Frightened to try something a bit different?'

'A bit of rough stuff, you mean?'

The harshness in his voice excited her. 'Sounds like it could be fun,' she murmured, her hands reaching around him to unbuckle his belt.

'Fun?' He was breathing hard, his back still turned to her. 'You reckon?'

She pulled at the button on his jeans. 'Only one way to find out.'

Suddenly, he was on top of her, his weight crushing her as he pinned her arms to her sides.

'Hey, mind my tights,' she giggled, squirming away from him. 'Careful! Ouch!'

Gripping both her wrists in one hand as she tried to push him away, he tore at her clothes, his knees bruising the soft flesh of her thighs as he forced her legs apart and pulled down his zip.

'Is this what you want?' His face above her was distorted, a stranger's face, his eyes full of fury as he clamped his other hand down over her mouth and nose so that she could hardly breathe. Forcing his whole weight down onto her as she struggled and fought, he rasped, 'Still think it's fun?'

Tearing her hands free, she clawed at his face, screaming, 'Kieran, you're hurting me!'

Abruptly, he released her and rolled away, crouching on the rug and gasping for breath, his face white, as she scrambled to her feet, pulling her blouse around her.

'F . . . Flora!' Norman stood in the doorway.

'For God's sake!' She turned on him, venting the shock that had nothing to do with his arrival. 'What

140

the hell do you think you're doing, creeping in on us like that?'

He stared at Kieran, still kneeling on the rug, his face turned from them, then, with a single roar of fury, dragged him to his feet and out into the hallway, pushing him up against the rickety banisters.

'What the bloody hell's going on?' Meg was half way up the stairs, a bag of groceries under one arm, her keys still in her hand.

'Any f . . . fool can see what's going on. This b . . . bastard was trying to . . .'

Scarlet pinpricks of blood were already welling from the scratches on Kieran's cheek. Meg glanced from his gaping flies to Flora's torn clothing, then snapped, 'Leave it, Norman. Go home.'

He let Kieran go. The rage seemed to have drained out of him. His huge hands dangled from the sleeves of his jacket as he turned to gaze wordlessly at Flora.

'As for you,' Meg spat at Kieran, as he struggled with his zip, his hands shaking, 'Get out. Now, before I call the . . .'

'For Christ's sake, leave us alone!' Flora's scream, on the edge of hysteria, shocked Meg into silence. The only sound was of Kieran's ragged breathing. 'Both of you.'

Norman stood uncertainly for a moment, then shuffled towards the stairs.

'And don't keep letting yourself in, either,' Flora yelled after him. 'This is our flat, not yours.'

She turned to Meg. 'Go to bed.'

'I'm not . . .'

'This has got nothing to do with you. Just go to bed.'

'You're a fool. I'll be in my room. Call me if you need any help.' Meg glared at Kieran as she went into the flat. 'I'll leave the door open.'

'What the hell's the matter with you?' Close to tears, Flora hid her humiliation with anger. 'It was only supposed to be a game.'

He looked down at his hands, clenching and unclenching his fists, before saying in a low voice, 'Violence is frightening. It's humiliating. It's no game.'

'Oh, for God's sake! Lighten up, can't you?'

'These are yours.' Meg threw his coat and scarf out into the hallway.

'I'd better go,' he said heavily, stepping away from Flora, avoiding her eye as he bent to pick them up.

'That's right. Bugger off back to the party why don't you? You might find someone you can finish the job with.' She regretted the words before they were out of her mouth. The expression that flicked across his face as his head jerked up was the closest to dislike she had seen.

'That was cheap, Flora.'

The silence between them seemed unbreakable. At last, she said, 'I know.' She could feel her face reddening. 'I . . . I'm sorry. I don't know what's the matter with me tonight. I don't know what's the matter with either of us.'

He ran a light, hesitant finger across the torn fabric of her blouse, his mouth working as if he were searching for the right words.

'Are you OK out there, Flora?' Meg called.

He was at the bottom of the stairs before he turned to face her. 'This isn't a game,' he said. 'Don't you understand that yet?'

Chapter Twelve

Flora got up early the next morning, hoping to escape the flat before Meg woke. Sooner or later she'd have to face her, but for now she just wanted to pretend last night hadn't happened.

To her dismay, Meg was sitting in the living room, spooning cornflakes into her mouth as she watched breakfast television.

'I'm just off,' Flora mumbled from the doorway.

Meg put down her bowl and leant forward to turn the television off. 'We need to talk.'

'Look, Meg, it wasn't what it seemed. You just came in at the wrong time, and . . .'

'So it was my fault?'

'Don't be stupid. All I'm saying is . . . Look, I really don't want to talk about it. I was in a funny mood, I'd had too much to drink, and . . .'

'Oh, so now you're saying it was *your* fault. For God's sake, Flora, you've got more sense than that. We get women coming into casualty covered in bruises every Saturday night with that line. Use your head, girl. What happened last night was no one's fault but that bastard boyfriend of yours.'

145

'You don't know what you're talking about. You don't understand Kieran . . .'

'And you do? You don't know the first thing about him. He could be married for all you know. Well, fine, that's your business. But when he starts knocking you about . . .'

'I've told you. He was *not* . . . Oh, just drop it.' Flora's head was throbbing. Tears of frustration at the injustice of Meg's words pricked her eyes. 'I love Kieran and . . .' she tossed her head back, '. . . and he loves me. Nothing that you or anyone else says will change that. And if you can't find a man of your own,' she added, with a malice she knew she would hate herself for the moment she had calmed down, 'well, frankly, that's your problem, Meg, not mine.'

'Hello there!'

The last person she wanted to see while she was hanging around outside the English secretary's office was Christopher Heatherington. She was feeling so wretched, and he was looking at her with such obvious concern, that she was frightened she might just blurt out the whole story to him.

'If you're waiting for Mavis, she won't be in until nine-thirty, I'm afraid.' As if to confirm her fears, he added sympathetically, 'Can I help?'

'I. . .' She adopted what she hoped was a suitably casual tone. 'I was just wondering if Kieran had any lectures this morning.'

'I've got him for a tutorial this afternoon. Can I give him a message?'

She frowned, chewing at her bottom lip, trying to make up her mind, before shaking her head and saying, 'No. No, it's OK. I'll catch up with him later.'

'There isn't anything wrong, is there?'

'Should there be?' The words came out far more sharply than she had intended.

He looked startled, then said stiffly, 'No problems with the play, I meant.'

She seemed to be managing to upset everyone this morning. 'No, no problems at all,' she said, hoping that her smile was not a little too bright.

He walked over to the History department with her, telling her he had no teaching until ten. It was beginning to snow, and he put up an umbrella, walking close to her so that she could share it.

'Are you going to the ball tonight?' he asked.

She frowned again, then said, 'Yes. Well, I think so.' She cleared her throat to disguise the wobble in her voice and said more firmly, 'Yes, I am.'

'Good.' He seemed genuinely pleased. 'You mustn't miss it. It's quite something. Especially if this snow keeps up. It makes everything seem so much more Christmassy, don't you think?'

'Sorry?'

The university bus had pulled in across the street. Her heart quickened as she caught a glimpse of a greyish-green scarf amongst the muffled figures piling out onto the already-whitening pavement.

'Maybe I'll see you . . .'

'Maybe.' She was aware that Christopher was

147

still speaking to her, but she was gone before the words registered, dodging in front of the bus and running into Kieran's outstretched arms, clinging to him as if her life depended on it.

Christopher retraced his steps, head down against the icy needles of snow. The secretary had just arrived, and waved to him as he passed her office. As he unlocked his study, she stuck her head around her door.

'Dr Heatherington! Phone.'

Sighing heavily, he made his way back along the corridor, 'Who is it?'

She shook her head and pulled a sympathetic face, her hand over the receiver. 'One of the students trying it on about some unfinished course work, I expect.'

'Dr Heatherington?'

The voice was unfamiliar. Welsh. Hesitant. Wearily, he took off his glasses and massaged the bridge of his nose.

'Speaking.'

'You don't know me, Dr Heatherington, but I'm a friend of Flora's. Flora Castledine? I need to speak to you about her. Could we meet? This lunchtime? I think it might be urgent.'

At Blackport Central, Dave Shenfield was feeling more optimistic than he had done for weeks.

'Here, what do you reckon?' he said without preamble as he entered the incident room. 'I've just had Norman Ackroyd in and—'

'I knew it!' Medlock was on his feet. 'He's confessed!'

'*Confessed?*' Shenfield tried to keep the amusement out of his voice. It was hard, when you were young and hungry for your first big success, to face the fact that your hunch had come to nothing, especially when you'd expended as much time and effort on your suspect as Medlock clearly had on poor old Ackroyd. He'd no desire to rub the lad's nose in it, even if he had overstretched himself by going behind everyone's back. At least he'd shown some initiative.

Instead, he turned to Whitelaw. 'He's been keeping his eye on some female students who live in one of Singh's houses – I know, nothing new there – but listen to this. One of them was attacked by her boyfriend last night. Quite nasty by the sound of things. And Norman's claiming he fits O'Driscoll's description. Same height. Different colouring, but you'd expect that. And most interesting of all, he reckons this kid looked a bit old to be a student. Mid-twenties was his guess.'

'It's possible, I suppose.' Whitelaw sounded doubtful. 'It's not exactly Norman's first sighting of O'Driscoll.'

True enough, Shenfield told himself. He had to keep things in perspective. But he just had this gut feeling . . . 'Well, it's got to be worth checking out,' he said. 'I'm going round there to interview the girl. You coming?'

Whitelaw eyed the stack of papers in front of him. 'What, now?'

'No.' Shenfield gave a wry smile. 'You know Norman. Has to make a production of it all. He's got to play intermediary; reckons if a copper turns up unannounced on this girl's doorstep she'll just deny everything. Watches too much television, that's his problem. I'm meeting him at his place this evening.'

'Well, if you think you need backup . . .' Whitelaw sounded distinctly reluctant. 'It's just I promised Val . . .'

'No, you're OK.' That's why Whitelaw would never make Inspector, Shenfield thought. His work would only ever come a poor second to his wife. It was hard to know which of them had got it right. 'It doesn't take two of us,' he went on. 'Not at this stage.'

'I'm free this evening,' Medlock said. No guesses as to which kind of copper he was, Shenfield thought. Work first, last and middle.

'Sorry, mate,' he said. 'Norman said he didn't want to see you.' He watched Medlock take in the implications of this, and added dryly, 'He mentioned you'd met.'

Medlock had the grace to colour. He glanced over at his computer, and said, 'I thought it might be useful to . . .'

'He does tend to take against certain people.' Shenfield ignored Whitelaw's derisive snort. 'Don't take it to heart. It takes years to build up trust with an oddball like him. Right, I'm back up to the university. I'll keep you both posted.'

Christopher walked across the square from the Medical school, his shoulders hunched against the biting wind. Students huddled silently inside their coats as they hurried between the last lectures of term, their frosty breath wreathing their faces with faint haloes. The once-bright carpet of leaves now hemmed the pavements in soggy, blackening heaps, and the skeletal trees angled starkly against the overcast sky. Summer seemed a long time ago; even at two o'clock in the afternoon, it was already half-dark.

Kieran was waiting outside Christopher's study, sitting on the floor and reading a book, his back resting against the door. 'Thought you'd forgotten me,' he grinned, leaping to his feet.

'You'd better come in.' Christopher unlocked the door, his voice as chilly as the wind outside.

Kieran glanced at him in surprise, then followed him into the study. 'Lousy weather, isn't it?' he commented, peeling off his coat and scarf. The sleeves of his sweater were too short, exposing the boniness of his wrists, red-raw with cold. 'Hope it clears up a bit before tonight. Are you going?'

Christopher was fiddling with the mugs and coffee that were part of the tutorial ritual.

'Do we get a mince pie, seeing as it's nearly Christmas?' Receiving no reply, Kieran shrugged, then threw himself down into a chair, scattering papers as he rummaged around in a tattered carrier bag and produced his essay. 'Shall I get started then?'

Christopher placed a coffee in front of him, then sat down without a word as Kieran began to read, sprawling back, his chair tipped to an angle that defied gravity, long denimed legs wide apart, perfectly relaxed, apart from the drumming of his fingers to some jerky, internal rhythm. He had big hands. Strong. The nails were bitten to the quick.

He read for about half an hour, looking up now and then over the top of his notes. Christopher leaned back motionless in his chair, cup clutched to his chest, his eyes closed.

Finally, he turned over the last page.

'. . . and thus forms an unarguable philosophical core to the play, that more than counters Johnson's criticism of Shakespeare as writing "without moral purpose".' He flipped his seat back to an upright position, picked up his coffee, now stone cold, and looked at Christopher expectantly.

There was a long silence.

'Bad as that, was it?' he grinned, his head on one side. When no reply was forthcoming, he asked, more anxiously, 'You OK, Christopher? You don't seem yourself this afternoon.'

Christopher sat forward and put down his cup, positioning it carefully on its saucer, before looking up and saying evenly, 'Tell me something, Kieran. Do you really believe you fit in here?'

'Come on, it wasn't *that* bad.' Kieran's laugh died on his lips, his expression changing slowly from concern, through bewilderment, to shock, as Christopher continued to stare at him unsmilingly. 'I . . . What're you on about?'

'You're bright enough,' Christopher went on, standing up, his back to Kieran 'you have a certain amount of talent, but . . .'

'But?' A dull flush started at Kieran's throat and spread over his face. The long sweep of his dark lashes fluttered nervously.

Christopher turned suddenly. 'I understand that you and Flora Castledine are . . . what's the expression you use? An item?'

Wariness was instantly replaced by defiance. 'So?'

'She's young for her years, wouldn't you say?'

'Not specially.'

'Easily led?'

'What is all this?' Kieran was looking up at Christopher intently, his expression uncertain, as if he were still not sure whether some sort of joke was being played on him.

At last, Christopher said, 'Flora Castledine's father is a wealthy, powerful man. If you want some good advice, keep away from her.'

Kieran put his papers on the table, his head bent for a moment. Then, looking up, he said slowly, 'Oh, I get it. It's OK for me to play at being one of the gang, as long as I don't take it too seriously and start messing with one of your posh friends' daughters. Right?'

Christopher's mouth tightened. 'I have a duty to protect the other students at this university.'

Kieran flinched, his eyes registering the pain, then with an unconvincing laugh asked, 'From me?'

'Let's just say I think Flora might have some difficulty in convincing her father that you were a suitable companion.'

'And I thought you were different. I really thought you understood.' He scanned Christopher's face, then said bitterly, 'But you're not different, are you? You're just like all the rest.'

'I'm a lecturer, not an agony aunt. Flora's father has put me   *loco parentis*. As such, I have her welfare to consider. Are you living together?'

Anger flashed into Kieran's eyes. 'And whose business would it be if we were?'

'I'd imagined, when I gave you a place here, that you'd shaken off your past. Clearly I was wrong.'

'What is all this, for Christ's sake? I don't know what you're on about.'

'Oh, I think you do. I've been talking to a friend of yours. Well, hardly a friend. Meg Evans.'

The colour drained from Kieran's face as quickly as it had appeared. A thin line of sweat prickled across his upper lip.

'I don't have to take this crap.' Suddenly he was on his feet. 'You and your rich mate can kick up all you like. Flora and I love each other. Not that it's any of your bloody business. And as for Meg Evans and her muck-spreading . . .'

'Love?' Christopher spat. 'Kieran Willerton? The star of every show? An uncouth, careless lout, randomly gifted with intelligence and looks, attracting whichever girl you want, then dragging her down with you to your own level. *Love?'* He thrust his face close to Kieran's. 'You don't know the meaning of the word!'

Kieran stepped back, stared at him for a moment, and then said disbelievingly, 'You're jealous, aren't you?' His eyes filled with contempt. 'That's what all this is about. You're jealous, you sad bastard!'

Grabbing him by the arm, Christopher dragged him across to the window. Beneath them, the clean neo-classical lines of the library stood floodlit on the far side of the square. The contrast with the distant skyline of the town, its cranes and factory chimneys picked out by a snake of sluggish yellow street lights, could not have been more stark.

'Look at it,' Christopher shouted. 'Look at it all. I got you into this university. You were special.' His voice cracked. 'I nurtured you, watched you blossom and flourish . . .'

'Get off me!' Kieran tried to shake himself free, but Christopher's grip was vice-like.

'You touch Flora,' he whispered hoarsely, 'you so much as look at her ever again, and I swear to God I'll take your file to the Vice Chancellor and have you thrown out.' He let go suddenly, giving Kieran a violent shove that sent him crashing backwards into the coffee table. 'Now get out of my study before I break your bloody neck.'

'Good God, Christopher!' Clarence Muldoon stuck his head out of the adjoining study as Kieran stumbled off down the corridor. 'What on earth was all that about? I was about to ring for Security. I've never heard such a commotion!'

'Nothing.' Still breathing hard, Christopher rubbed the back of his hand across his mouth, as though trying to rid himself of a bitter taste. 'Nothing,' he repeated quietly. 'It's over now.'

Chapter Thirteen

'Come on, Norman,' Shenfield muttered, stamping his feet against the cold and banging on the front door of seventy-two Aigburth Street. He checked his watch: five to eight. They'd arranged to meet at a quarter to. He banged on the door again. It was odd. Norman had been so eager to arrange the meet that Shenfield had half-expected him to be hanging out of the window when he got there. He bent down and peered through the letterbox. The lights were on, and from somewhere at the back of the house he could hear Radio North West.

'Norman!' he bellowed, thumping the door with his fist. Silly sod must have the radio on so loud he couldn't hear him.

He decided to go round the back. All day he'd been mulling over Norman's story, with the growing conviction that he was on to something, and he was reluctant now to accept the anticlimax of finding he wasn't there.

The side entry was overgrown with weeds, knee-high and sagging under the weight of still-falling snow. By the time Shenfield had trampled his way around to the back door, his shoes and trousers were soaking. He stepped backwards to pull free of a bramble that had become entangled in his turn-up, and trod squarely in a carrier bag overflowing with empty foil containers by the side of the step, releasing, as he did so, an overpowering waft of curry. Cursing, he rattled the knob ill-temperedly, and was taken aback when the door swung open to reveal a cluttered kitchen.

'Norman?' he called, stepping inside and dripping slush and curry onto the cracked linoleum. Apart from Bing Crosby dreaming deafeningly of a white Christmas, the house was silent. The cup and plate that stood beside the radio on the draining board were still standing in a pool of soap bubbles. Shenfield turned the radio down to a less painful volume, then put his hand into the washing-up bowl; the water was warm. If he was out, he'd only just gone, and he'd gone in a hurry, judging by the back door. Norman saw danger around every corner; Shenfield couldn't imagine that it was usual for him to go out leaving doors unlocked.

Warily, he made his way into the hall. The cupboard door stood ajar as if a coat had been hurriedly grabbed on the way out. What was Norman playing at? Shenfield opened the front door and scanned the street in a mixture of irritation and disappointment. Not a sign of him. Another dead end by the looks of things.

He decided he'd better lock the kitchen door and let himself out of the front. If that meant Norman was locked out, it would serve him bloody well right for time-wasting. Not to mention ruining a perfectly good pair of shoes.

Making his way back up the hall, he was seized by a sudden curiosity. What made a bloke like Norman Ackroyd tick? What did he do with himself when he wasn't guarding the womenfolk of Blackport from attack? He stuck his head round the door into the lounge. It was stacked floor to ceiling with books, and not the cheap, mucky paperbacks that Shenfield would have predicted if he'd been asked to make a guess. Norman had said he'd read a lot while he was in High View, but he hadn't expected this. Shakespeare, no less, and a load of other equally boring and unlikely stuff. He flicked through a couple. They'd obviously been well used; some of the pages were turned down, or marked with scraps of paper, Norman's big, childish writing annotating the margins. He should have brought Medlock along after all, he'd have had a field day.

Knowing he was totally out of order in doing so, he went up the stairs, glancing into the cramped, untidy bathroom and what was evidently the spare room at the back, again crammed with books and papers, before opening the door to the front bedroom and turning on the light.

'Jesus Christ!' he gasped.

Every inch of wall space was covered in newspaper cuttings about the murders. Blown-up photographs of each of the victims covered the wardrobe. On the window ledge stood a camera, a pair of binoculars and a notebook; some kind of a log of comings and goings, Shenfield realised as he

glanced at it with growing unease. OK, he'd known
Norman had a few screws loose, but this . . . He
opened the wardrobe, the skin on the back of his
neck prickling as he saw the row of twelve photographs pinned there, below the scrawled message
in Norman's writing: *'who next?'* The photographs
were not good quality; most had been taken from
some distance, and the subjects were out of focus,
some only partially visible. None of them was
familiar to Shenfield. But two things were common
to all of them. They were all young women. And
they all had long auburn hair.

A thousand pieces of the jigsaw rearranged
themselves. And fell into place. Medlock had been
right all along. Which meant . . . Shenfield's brain
was racing in frantic circles like a hamster on a
wheel . . . Ackroyd had got him here deliberately
tonight. Why? Had the door been left open to lure
him inside? He swung around, feeling a cold trickle
of sweat between his shoulder blades as he heard a
noise in the room below. Turning off the light, he
edged his way back on to the landing and down
the stairs, wincing at every creak beneath his feet.
Motionless, he stood in the hallway. The noise was
coming from the kitchen; above the strains of an
inane advertising jingle coming from the radio, he
could hear a dull thudding. His eyes trained on the
kitchen door, he felt behind him into the hall
cupboard, fumbling through a forest of coat sleeves,
until, after what seemed like an eternity, his hand
closed around the handle of a walking stick. Not
much of a weapon, but it was all he had. His only

hope was to take Ackroyd by surprise. Bracing himself, the stick raised above his head, he charged the kitchen door, every nerve flinching from the knife blow that could be awaiting him. In the split second it took him to crash into the room, he could see himself, sprawled in a seeping pool of his own blood, and wondered if he would feel any pain.

The kitchen was empty, the back door swinging idly on its hinges and thudding against the jamb.

Shenfield leant back against the cooker, rubbing one hand across his face, the stick still clutched in his other sweating palm, as his heartbeat subsided. The disembodied voice from the radio babbled on regardless with a traffic update. Reaching to flick it into silence, his attention was caught as the phoney mid-Atlantic twang went on, '. . . And don't forget, folks, that congestion is expected until late tonight around the dockland district, with University Avenue closed to through traffic. So to all you Blackport students getting ready for the Christmas Ball, here's Boyzone with their latest hit . . .'

Christmas Ball. Shenfield felt his blood turn to ice. That's why Ackroyd had wanted him off campus tonight. It was going to be Melanie Loveridge all over again.

Racing out to his car, he radioed Control. 'All available units over to the university. As fast as you can. I'll explain while I'm on my way. And get me DC Medlock. Now.'

Chapter Fourteen

The bus dropped Flora at the end of the street.

She stood for a while, reluctant to go back to the empty flat, watching the snow dancing in the light of the street lamps. Tiny flakes swirled around each other, undecided whether to go up or down, trapped in a small world of glowing orange against the blotted sky. She held out her hand and let the flakes settle on her palm, examining each delicate crystal.

She'd wanted to go to the dance, but that wasn't the reason for her mood of black depression. It wasn't the fact that on this, their last evening alone together, they were *not* together. Anyone could get flu. It wasn't even that Kieran hadn't come to tell her himself, leaving instead a curiously impersonal note in her pigeon hole to say he'd had to go home. Maybe, if he was feeling really ill, he'd had no choice. But she knew in her heart, as she watched the snowflakes blur and melt against her skin, that it wasn't flu. Every time she drew near to him, as soon as she came close to dodging past that heart-stopping smile and penetrating his defences, he gave her the slip. He'd promised her, this morning, that tonight they would talk. That was why he'd disappeared. She had no idea where 'home' was; she knew no more about him now than she had the night she'd first set eyes on him. And he was making sure he kept it that way.

When she arrived outside the flat, she was dismayed to notice that the light was on. Meg must have finished early. The last thing she needed tonight was another confrontation. She recalled her cruel words at breakfast time, and felt sick at the thought of having to face her flatmate.

Across the street, a car revved up, screeched away from the pavement and roared past, drenching her already wet feet in muddy slush. She was almost in tears as she trudged up the narrow stairs, fitted the key in the lock and pushed open the door. The flat was in darkness.

'Are you there, Meg?' she called.

Silence.

'Meg?'

Her other worries forgotten, she stood in the hallway listening to her own breathing. There had definitely been a light on before. She thought she could hear someone moving stealthily in the living room. As she edged back towards the stairs, the doorknob turned and the door swung slowly open. The room was lit by a single flickering candle.

'Surprise!'

'Kieran!' She was faint with relief. 'What on earth . . . ?'

He bowed deeply, a tea towel slung over his

arm. 'Would *mademoiselle* come zees way?'

A tiny Christmas tree stood in the corner of the room and the ceiling was decorated with streamers. The table had been cleared of books and was set with a crêpe paper cloth. A bottle of wine glinted in the candlelight. In the centre of the table, a small sprig of jasmine was balanced precariously in a cracked vase.

'I picked it out the back,' he followed her gaze. In the back yard behind the shop, a stunted jasmine bush had struggled, against overwhelming odds, to produce a delicate lacing of tiny yellow flowers, ridiculously frivolous against the backdrop of black-ened brick. He'd teased the care with which she tended it, pulling back the choking weeds, taking it as a personal compliment when the flowers began to bloom. He shrugged apologetically, and added, 'You'll have to wait a few years for a dozen red roses.'

Flora stared at the scene in amazement.

'Don't get too excited,' he grinned, as he steered her to a chair and knelt down beside her to take off her soaking shoes. 'It's only beans on toast.'

'But . . . what's it all for?'

'What's it for? What's it *for* she asks!' Kieran hit his forehead in mock despair. 'And this is the girl who reads poetry for fun! Have you no romance in your soul?' He looked up into her face, his smile gone. 'You know what it's for. But first, I want you to know how I feel about you.' He pulled a small parcel from his pocket. 'I bought you this. Here, I've marked the page.'

She read the words silently, not trusting her voice.

'I wish I could write you a poem myself,' he grinned awkwardly. 'But you'll have to make do with Yeats. His words, at least. My feelings. Read it out loud.'

She read the beautiful words slowly, her voice wavering and breaking as she reached the final line. '*Tread softly because you tread on my dreams.*'

He took the book from her and whispered, 'I love you, Flora. I never thought I'd say that to anyone.'

She reached down and kissed him, the gentlest of kisses, on his eyes, his forehead, the ragged scratch on his cheek. 'I love you too.'

He rested his head against her knee, staring into the little gas fire as though transfixed by its feeble, popping flame. Then he turned to her and said quietly, 'Are we allowed to be this happy?'

She put her hand on his dark head, not wanting to move, afraid to break the spell, wishing that they could stay here, like this, for ever.

'We've got to talk, Flora,' he said at last.

'Later,' she whispered, slipping down onto the rug beside him. 'We can talk later.'

Nothing could have been more different from his savage anger of last night. But there was a sadness, a kind of finality in the way he made love to her that unnerved her far more. Lying beside him, her head on his shoulder, she felt a prickle of fear like icy water. She couldn't begin to imagine her life without him; whatever it was he was going to tell her, she couldn't bear that. Taking a deep breath, she said quickly. 'Before you say anything, I want to give you this.' She pulled the envelope from her bag. 'Happy Christmas.'

He opened it and looked at the ticket in bewilderment, turning it over between his fingers. 'Who's R. Montague?'

'You! Romeo Montague!' She smiled uncertainly, trying to read his expression. 'Joke? I thought the idea of travelling incognito would appeal to you. I was really lucky. It was the last seat left on my flight. Four o'clock tomorrow afternoon. We can get the train down to Penzance . . .'

Still he stared at the ticket.

'Say you'll come.' She took the ticket from him and rolled over to push it into the pocket of his jeans that were lying in a crumpled heap where he had discarded them. 'Please.'

He pulled himself up slowly, not speaking, and began to dress.

She sat up. 'Please, Kieran. I want you to come home with me. I want Simon to . . .'

'I thought this was home.'

'It is! I've never been so happy anywhere as I've been here, but . . .'

'But?'

She could let it go. Change the subject. Refuse to face whatever it was he was going to tell her. She swallowed hard. 'We can't just pull the covers up over our heads and go on living in a vacuum.'

'A vacuum. Is that how you see it?' he asked quietly.

'I love you more than anything. I want to share everything, know everything. But there are so many things about you I *don't* know. You never tell me anything, not even where you live. You say you love me, but . . .'

He took her face between his hands. 'I do, Flora.'

'Then why won't you let me through?'

A long pause.

'I want to. You've no idea how much. I want to lay out all my dreams for you.' He glanced across at the book. 'All my hopes, all my fears . . . no more pretending. But you've got to give me time. It's . . . hard. There are things . . .'

'This isn't just about what happened last night, is it?'

Silence.

'Look, come back to Scilly with me. We won't have Meg to worry about. We'll have all the time in the world. We can go for walks, take the boat out . . .'

'The boat?' He looked away, gnawing ruthlessly at the raw skin around his fingernails. The cuff of his shabby sweater, she noticed, was badly frayed. And suddenly, she understood. '. . . *But I, being poor* . . .' It was all there in the poem.

'Do you really think it matters? Is that what's been bothering you, you idiot?' Light-headed with relief, she started to laugh. 'The boat, the house, the flash car . . . None of it *matters*. It's what you *are* that counts, not where you come from. Christopher Heatherington was only saying the other day . . .'

'Christopher Heatherington? What's he been telling you?'

'Nothing. He was just going on about backgrounds. Saying how well you'd done, as a matter of fact. Which just shows how little any of it matters. So you see, you don't have to be so secretive all the time. Why should I care where you live or what your dad does?'

'What my dad does?' He turned his face slowly towards her. 'You really think that's what this is all about? Some socio-economic comparison of lifestyles?' His face was hard, the muscle throbbing in his cheek.

She stared at him in amazement. 'Don't be so stupid. I just meant . . .'

'Taken a right load off me mind that has, to know that you could face the peasant masses if you had to. Christ, you haven't got a bloody clue, have you?'

'Calm down, for heaven's sake!' She forced a laugh, shocked at the anger in his voice. 'I don't want to argue, especially not tonight. I just wanted you to know you can tell me . . . well, whatever.' She ran her hand through his hair. 'There's so much more about you I want to know.'

He jerked his head away from her. 'What, like whether I've ever been on a skiing holiday or if I buy my underpants from Marks and Spencer? No, on both counts. Satisfied?'

'I don't understand why you're making such a song and dance about it. You're the one who wanted to talk.' She watched him take an angry swig of his drink, his knuckles white around the glass. This wasn't how she wanted things to be. Lowering her voice, she went on, 'Listen, I know Simon seems

a bit overpowering . . . well, he *is* a bit overpowering . . . But I don't expect things to be the same for
you. All I need to know is who *you* are.'

'Who I am? You think that if you find out what sort
of house I live in, and "*what my dad does*",' he
simpered in a savage mimicry of her accent, 'you'll
find out who I am? And because I've heard all about
your "overpowering" father, and your bloody great
farmhouse, and your precious Isles of Scilly, that
you've told me who *you* are? For Christ's sake,
Flora. Grow up.'

The flat, droning vowels of his own accent were
becoming stronger and stronger as he spoke. For
the first time it irritated her beyond reason. It was
as if he were wearing it like a badge, using it to
claim the moral high ground, when all she'd been
trying to do was to make things easier for him.

'Don't be so damned patronising,' she snapped.
'It's not a crime to have money. I'm not going to
spend the rest of my life apologising for not being
working class, and if you can't handle it, that's your
problem, not mine.'

'Just leave it, can't you?' He stood up and poured
himself some more wine, his back to her.

'No. Why should I? It's you who seems to think it's
some big deal. Well, if your bloody background is
so much a part of you, at least you could tell me . . .'

'It is *not*.' He hurled his glass at the fireplace.
They were frozen, for an instant, by the violence of
the action, as the wine spread crimson into the
plaster.

'Oh, for God's sake!' She jumped up, grabbing a

cloth. 'You tell *me* to grow up. Don't be so bloody melodramatic.'

'My background,' he spat, snatching her arm, 'my *background*, as you call it, is *not* part of me. And it's none of your fucking business. Do you understand *that*?'

'Fine!' she shouted, stunned by the raw fury in his voice. 'Let's just keep it to a quick fuck and no questions asked then. It was never your mind I was interested in anyway. A girl's got to do something to lose her virginity.'

He hit her once, hard, across the face.

'You bastard,' she said in a low voice. She clutched at the table, determined not to fall, too numbed by the unaccustomed shock of pain to hit back.

The jasmine spilled from its vase, the water seeping through the crêpe paper and dripping onto the open pages of her book as he came towards her.

'God, I don't know about you, but I'm done in.' Meg flopped into a chair in the doctor's Common Room and kicked off her shoes. 'Completely knackered, in fact.' She took off her spectacles and rubbed her eyes.

'What happened to the contact lenses then?' Ewan Johnstone, the other medic sharing her shift on Accident and Emergency, handed her a mug of tea.

'And what's wrong with glasses?'

'Nothing!' He raised his hands in mock defence, then grinned. 'They suit you, actually.'

'At least I don't feel like I'm being poked in the eye all the time.' She massaged her aching feet, then yawned hugely. 'Well, better get off home I suppose.' She looked at her watch and groaned. 'I'm on ward rounds in five hours. Christ, why did I ever decide to be a doctor?'

'Come on,' Ewan yanked her to her feet. 'Stop moaning. I'll walk you back as far as the gasworks. I've got to pass there, anyway.'

She rested her head briefly against his shoulder, so tired she almost fell asleep standing up. 'Ewan, you're such a romantic,' she muttered.

Dawn was still a couple of hours away as they made their way through the deserted streets. The curtains of the narrow terraced houses were drawn tightly against the night.

'Seriously,' Meg said, as they walked past a row of darkened shopfronts, 'I do wonder sometimes if it's all worth it. I always wanted to be a doctor. Real battle I had, convincing them at school. But it's just so hard, isn't it? Maybe I should have done as I was told, like all the other girls in the village.'

'*Girls stay home and get married and have babies.*' Ewan looked down at her and laughed. 'I'm from Merthyr, remember. My sisters had the same thing. Four of them I got. Enough to put a man off girls for life. Sorry!' He side-stepped Meg as she swung at him with her bag. 'OK, not "girls", "women". You'd get on well with my sisters, you know. And don't tell me it's not worth it. Just think

172

of your mam and dad's faces when you graduate!'

They walked on for a while in companionable silence. The street lamps cast weird shadows across the silent, slushy pavement. Meg shivered. The snow had turned to driving sleet, needle-sharp as it stung her raw cheeks. 'It's nice to have a bit of company,' she said. 'I hate coming back at this time.'

'Will there be anyone in when you get back?'

Meg frowned. 'I don't know. I'm not sure I want there to be.' Briefly, she described what had happened the night before. 'I'd never have believed Flora, of all people, could be such an idiot. The trouble is, she thinks I fancy him myself, I'm sure she does. So anything I say, she thinks I've got an ulterior motive, see.'

'And do you? Fancy him?'

She shrugged. 'For a while, maybe. Just a bit. But there was always something . . .' she struggled to find the right word, '. . . elusive about him. Furtive, almost. And now I've seen first-hand just what an animal he can be . . .' Her face puckered up in concern. 'I just hope I did the right thing, approaching that lecturer. I felt such a fool, ringing him with a tip-off, like something off the telly. If I'm honest, I suppose I hoped that when we met face to face, he'd tell me I was making a mountain out of a mole hill, or to mind my own business. I just hope he doesn't make things worse.'

'You did the right thing,' Ewan said stoutly. 'She should be grateful to have a friend like you.' He paused. 'I would be.'

'You know what I do when I have to walk back on my own?' Meg said, quickening her pace. 'I cheer myself up by visualising the kitchen at home. Mam will be getting up soon, cooking eggs and bacon.' She grinned up at Ewan. 'Can you smell them?'

He sniffed the freezing air. 'Terrific. Fried bread as well.'

'Why not?' she laughed. 'Then she'll feed the fire with fresh coal, standing back as the egg-shells are thrown on, spitting and crackling. Christmas this year will be great, what with the new baby to welcome into the family. Did I tell you . . . ?'

Ewan pulled a wry face. 'You told me.'

'Sorry, I know I go on a bit. I expect you've seen the photos too then?'

'Yep.'

They both laughed. 'I can't wait to get back.' She gave a little shiver. 'Just think, only another week . . .'

'Perhaps we could meet up over the vac? Have a drink somewhere?'

They had reached the top of Aigburth Street already. Somehow, Ewan had forgotten to turn off at the gasworks.

'Yes,' she said, and grinned. 'Yes, perhaps we could.'

When they had swapped addresses, Meg packed him off home. 'I'll be fine,' she protested. 'You've got a good mile to walk back as it is.' She regarded him sternly. 'Stop fussing.'

She watched him until he was out of sight, then,

with a smile, set off briskly down the road, humming a Christmas carol. Somewhere in the darkness, a cat squalled, a ghostly, unearthly cry like a banshee, and she huddled into her coat, pulling her new hat down over her ears, humming even louder. As if to reassure her, a milk float turned into the street, the whine of its engine punctuated by the muted clatter of milk bottles, its headlights cutting through the gloom. She caught the whistled snatch of an answering carol as the milkman began to load up his crates.

'Dr Meg Evans,' she grinned to herself, fishing in her bag for keys and pulling out a stethoscope. 'Of course it's all worth it.'

'Do you want any today, duck?' the milkman shouted from his float.

She took a bottle from him and pulled a face. ''Fraid so. The rest of the university may be off home today for the vacation, but we medics have to work for a living, more's the pity!'

As she made her way up the side entry, a noise caused her to pause. In the darkened doorway, she caught a glimpse of a tall, silhouetted figure. Flora and Kieran must be back from the dance already. Putting the bottle on the ledge and drawing back into the hedge, she saw what looked like an old coat, lying in a sodden heap at the far end of the flowerbed. In the faint halo of light from the milk float, she could pick out a sleeve.

Or an arm.

She gave an involuntary shudder, then told herself firmly to get a grip. Too much time on A and

E must be playing tricks with her imagination. She craned to get a better look. The yard was set well back from the street. Why would anyone want to dump an old coat . . . ? Cautiously, she made her way across to the inert bundle, her feet skidding and sliding in the muddy remnants of the snow, and bent to take a closer look.

Flailing to keep her balance, she crashed to her knees, tearing a branch from the spindly jasmine as she fell, her face frozen in horror, her mouth opening in a silent scream.

Thursday 17 December

I had sworn thee fair, and thought thee bright,
Who art as black as hell, as dark as night.

Chapter Fifteen

The entrance to the street was blocked by double-parked cars and a BBC outside broadcast unit. A crowd of sightseers had already gathered, huddled into knots, whispering excitedly to one another. Photographers split the sullen morning light with their flashguns; reporters scribbled furiously into notepads.

Shenfield, his face grey with fatigue, watched as the camera monitor zoomed in on the young woman reporter who stood beside him, microphone in hand, before it panned away from the close-up shot to reveal the drab street and the row of shops in front of which she was standing. Across the window behind her were inscribed the words: The Royal Bombay Palace. A make-up girl and several technicians scuttled out of shot as the reporter flashed him a dazzling smile and said, 'Ready?'

'Ready,' he replied grimly.

She pressed her free hand over her earphone, listening intently, then signalled to the cameraman. Pinning on an expression of concerned interest, her voice slightly breathless as though she had just arrived, she said, 'This is Siobhan Doyle, bringing you the latest from Blackport, where yet another university student has been found strangled and mutilated just hours after a man was arrested in connection with the so-called "Beast of Blackport" murders. Chief Inspector Shenfield, you have been in charge of this investigation from its start. Can you give us any information about the victim, and do you believe the man you now have in custody could have been responsible for her death?'

Someone pushed him into shot, and automatically he began to answer the woman's questions. No, they could not reveal any details until the victim had been formally identified and next of kin had been informed. And until forensic evidence became available, it was not possible to establish . . .

He reeled off the answers mechanically. The last twelve hours had been the worst of his entire career. Looking for Ackroyd had been like looking for a needle in a haystack. The campus had been swarming; there had been an estimated two thousand people at the Christmas Ball, most of them in fancy dress. It hadn't even been easy to identify which of the large police presence were genuine. The milling crowds, the flashing disco lights, the blaring racket of the fairground; all had added to the nightmarish sense of unreality. Each clattering explosion from the fireworks display had set his taut nerves jangling. Each scream from the big wheel had brought him out in a sweat. A girl was going to die, he was sure of that, and there was nothing he or any of them could do to stop it.

The sense of relief when, at two-thirty a.m., Whitelaw had radioed him to say that Ackroyd had been picked up without incident, close to the scene of the Loveridge murder, had made Shenfield euphoric. He'd actually grabbed a passing Spice Girl lookalike and planted a smacking kiss on her astonished face. Once Ackroyd had been cautioned and bundled into the back of one of the waiting police cars, they had all piled back to Blackport Central for tea and bacon sandwiches. Medlock had insisted on picking up the tab, and everyone was so elated there hadn't been a single snide comment. Somehow, despite all the odds, they had managed to prevent an eighth murder.

It was nearly five hours later that the news came in. Ackroyd had had the last laugh after all; the murder had been committed not at the university, but practically on his own doorstep. Could the girl have been lying there, just opposite, while Shenfield had been searching the house? Could he even have disturbed the crime while it was in progress? The injuries had been savage, but less extensive than usual: a single blow, made with such force that the scalp was almost severed from the skull. Ackroyd hadn't even turned her over onto her back. What if it had been Shenfield shouting out his name that'd stopped him adding his trademarks . . . ?

It didn't bear thinking about.

He forced his concentration back to the interview. Yes, they were expecting to bring formal charges relating to the earlier deaths later today, but at this stage . . .

He was getting too old for this game. Thirty-six years he'd been in the force, and this was the first time in those thirty-six years that he'd seriously questioned whether he was still up to the job. He pushed the thought from his mind. For now, he could not afford to allow himself the luxury of self-recrimination, to acknowledge the nagging 'if-onlys' that would have seen the girl alive and well this morning, instead of crumpled in the quagmire of her own blood. Time enough for that later.

The interview finished at last, Shenfield bundled his way through the mêlée, dodging umbrellas, and ducked under the cordon at the side entrance.

The backyard was crawling. White-overalled scene-of-crime men appeared and disappeared behind the tent-like construction that covered most of the scrubby patch of lawn. Shenfield closed his eyes. The scene was just too familiar.

Whitelaw was leaning against the wall by the entrance to the upstairs flat. He threw his cigarette to the ground as Shenfield approached, jerking his head towards the stairs.

'No luck with the flatmate. She's in a right state.'

Shenfield sighed. 'Where's Medlock?' he asked.

'Getting in everyone's way and up everyone's nose, same as usual.'

'Ray,' Shenfield said quietly. 'Let's get something straight. Medlock was right and we were wrong. If we'd taken him seriously . . .'

'I hate him.' Whitelaw ground his cigarette into

the muddy grass with his heel. 'No, I hate his sort, with his case studies and his computers and his sodding performance indicators. He's not a copper, he's a bloody machine.'

'An *efficient* bloody machine. He was the only one of us who suspected Ackroyd. All this time we've thought of him as nothing more than a harmless nutter, while he was butchering one girl after another, throwing us sightings of O'Driscoll like biscuits to a dog. And what did we do? We sat up on our hind legs and wagged our tails, that's what. God knows how many more he'd have done if it hadn't been for Medlock and his case studies and computers. You might not like his style. I might not like it, come to that. But he was right. He's the future, Ray.' Shenfield rested his hand on Whitelaw's shoulder. 'Get used to it.'

'So, d'you reckon Ackroyd'll be going for insanity?' Whitelaw asked, after a short silence.

Shenfield lowered himself onto the doorstep. Funny, he thought, however terrible the events surrounding you, the trivial still fought its way into your attention; his feet were killing him. 'God knows. I certainly don't.' He loosened the laces on his shoes and flexed his toes.

When Ackroyd had first been picked up, neither they nor the duty solicitor had managed to get any sense out of him. He'd been raving about . . . willow trees, it had sounded like . . . and Shenfield, his heart sinking, had sent a squad back to search the undergrowth around the lake once more. They hadn't found anything, and Ackroyd seemed to have forgotten about botany the next time Shenfield tried to interview him. He just crouched in the corner of his cell, alternately babbling poetry and weeping uncontrollably. There was no way of telling whether he was putting it on, or whether he'd genuinely gone over the edge, but either way, the spectacle of a fully-grown man sucking his thumb and pissing himself had turned Shenfield's stomach. It would have been kinder simply to put a bullet through his head and have done with it.

'His solicitor's going to push for an insanity plea if he's got any sense,' he said, reluctantly easing his shoes back on and standing up. 'Turn it into a "care in the community" issue, and . . .' He broke off, as a sudden commotion made them both turn towards the entry.

'Excuse me, Sir.' The policeman on duty had put out a restraining arm. 'You can't go in there, I'm afraid.'

'Let me through,' a voice called out desperately. 'I'm . . . I'm a friend of the family. I have to . . .'

Shenfield closed his eyes. As if he wasn't deep enough in the shit as it was.

'Oi, come back, you!' the policeman bellowed. Medlock, appearing from behind the sheeting, made a dive for Christopher who, caught off-balance, tripped against the step, grabbing at a window ledge to save himself and sending a bottle of milk crashing to the ground.

'Sorry mate. I didn't realise he was going to make a dash for it,' the PC explained breathlessly.

Medlock helped Christopher to his feet. 'I do

apologise, Dr Heatherington,' he said, brushing the splashes of milk from his trousers, 'I didn't recognise you for a moment. Do you want to speak to your . . . ?'

Shenfield strode across, and taking Christopher by the arm as he babbled on about the shock of hearing about the murder on the news, hissed, 'Pull yourself together.'

Whitelaw joined them, murmuring into Shenfield's ear, 'I'll take care of this.' He glanced at the PC, then said loudly, 'Good to see you, Dr Heatherington. We've got the victim's flatmate upstairs, in a state of shock. Maybe you'll be able to get through to her.'

Shenfield nodded gratefully. 'That's right. We can do with you here. Friend of the family, you say? Did you know the deceased's flatmate?'

Christopher looked at them uncomprehendingly, then nodded. 'Yes . . . well no, not really . . . she was the one who . . .' He put his hands to his head, his voice breaking. 'Oh, God! Why didn't I report him straight away? I knew he'd been in trouble before, and yet I let him . . . if only I'd realised—'

'Hang on, hang on,' Whitelaw cut in, holding up his hand. 'Just calm down, Dr Heatherington, and let's start at the beginning. Now, have you got an address where we can contact the family? The other girl's in such a state we haven't been able to . . .' He broke off suddenly, and pointed at the shattered glass. 'Just a minute. That bottle . . .'

'The, er . . .' the PC glanced at Shenfield's hand, still on Christopher's arm, '. . . the gentleman knocked it off the ledge. I'll get someone to . . .'

'No, wait. Get the scene of crime boys over here. Now.'

Christopher was pushed aside as an overalled officer hurried across from the garden and knelt to examine the shards of broken glass. A flashgun went off amongst the pack of reporters who jostled beyond the flimsy cordon.

'Can't you get that lot further back?' Shenfield growled at one of the uniformed men. 'It's like trying to work in a bloody zoo round here. And while you're at it . . .' He broke off, suddenly aware that, behind him, Christopher was making impatient, swatting movements with his hands. 'What the hell . . . ?'

'They're like flies.' Christopher was gazing towards the men ducking in and out of the makeshift tent. 'Flies, buzzing around the corpse.' Suddenly, he began to laugh uncontrollably. 'Blue-bottles!' The tears were running down his cheeks. He looked at his father and, helpless with laughter, gasped, 'Bluebottles. That's what they call police-men, isn't it?' His face crumpled and the laughter turned to great, racking sobs. Another flashgun exploded into the damp air.

'Help me get him inside, for Christ's sake.' Shenfield pushed him ahead of them up the stairs. The last thing they needed was some hysterical outburst in front of the assembled media. He was tempted to get a police car to take him straight home, but there was no guarantee that one of the bastards outside wouldn't follow him back. The prospect of Sid Barker, or worse, a hack from one of the tabloids let loose on Christopher didn't bear thinking about. And anyway, Whitelaw was right, he might be able to help them with the flat-mate: at least they'd speak the same language, if Christopher could pull himself together. He beck-oned the policewoman standing at the top of the stairs. 'Get him a glass of water or something.' He nodded towards the closed bedroom door. 'How's she doing?'

The woman shook her head as she followed them into the living room. 'The doctor's with her. He's given her something to calm her down.'

Shenfield glanced around the unfamiliar room. The table was strewn with plates and glasses, but not in the comfortable way of a meal taken and left uncleared. The plates were smashed. A vase was overturned, its water leaching dye from the paper cloth onto the open book that lay beside it, the pages curling and sodden. He picked it up. Poetry.

Christopher was standing motionless in the middle of the room, eyes closed, his hand clamped against his mouth as he took in deep, shaky breaths through his nose, clearly fighting to regain some sort of self-control.

Shenfield handed him the book, more to give him something to do than in any hope of a useful response. 'This mean anything to you?'

'"*He wishes for the Cloths of Heaven*",' Christopher whispered, his eyes blurring again with tears. 'W. B. Yeats. It's one of my favourite poems.'

'Thanks, that's a big help.' Shenfield sighed. He picked up the giant rabbit that was lolling on the settee and glanced at it before throwing it on the floor. 'Sit down.' He handed him the glass of water. 'You look terrible.'

The rug by the hearth was covered in broken glass. Shenfield stepped over it and leant forward to examine the reddish stain above the fireplace.

'Red wine.' Medlock followed his gaze. 'We checked.'

Whitelaw beckoned Shenfield towards the door. Turning his back on Medlock, he lowered his voice to a whisper. 'Listen, Ackroyd was picked up at two-thirty, right? There's no way anyone could have delivered that milk without noticing . . .'

'Not now, Ray,' Shenfield muttered in exasperation. 'Not here.'

'She's sleeping now.' The police surgeon came from the bedroom, closing the door quietly behind him. 'I've given her a pretty strong sedative. She'll be out for at least a couple of hours, I'm afraid.' He glanced towards Christopher and added, 'Anything else you need me for?'

Shenfield shook his head. 'I'll get a car to take him home as soon as it's settled down a bit outside.' He turned to the policewoman as the doctor gathered up his things and left. 'See if you can rustle up some tea, will you, love? And some biscuits to go with it.'

Whitelaw watched her go, then murmured, 'I'll nip down and see if forensic—'

'I don't want a cup of tea.' Christopher cut across

him. His voice was loud and flat as he looked down at the poetry book still clutched in his hand and said, 'I know who the murderer is.' Before anyone could respond, he went on in the same trance-like monotone, 'One of my students killed her. He's attacked her before. His name is Kieran Willerton.'

Shenfield paced the room, nodding, prompting, taking sharp, excited drags on his cigarette as Christopher told his story. So Ackroyd hadn't been spinning them a yarn about the assault; Christopher's account matched it in every detail. And suddenly the 'willow' he'd been raving about took on a whole new significance. His mind raced ahead. Say this Willerton bloke *was* responsible for her death. Were they really to believe there would be *two* madmen stalking the streets of this humdrum northern town? And if not . . .

'How old is this Willerton?' he asked.

'Twenty-four, twenty-five, I don't know. Does it matter?'

Shenfield could see from Whitelaw's expression that they were both thinking the same thing. Taking out a notepad, he began to fire questions. Did Christopher know what part of the country Willerton came from? Could the Manchester accent be assumed, did he think? What had he been doing before he came to Blackport?

Christopher frowned. 'Before?'

'He must have had qualifications, Dr Heatherington?' Medlock spoke for the first time. 'Or an exceptional reason for not having them, surely? English Literature has a highly competitive entry standard, as I understand it. Even at a provincial red-brick like Blackport.'

Shenfield picked up the note of derision. If it turned out Ackroyd had been innocent all along, Medlock would be gutted. He probably felt like wringing Christopher's neck right now. Even so, Shenfield felt his hackles rise. Provincial red-brick, was it? He willed Christopher to bite back, half-tempted to point out himself that it couldn't be so mediocre if it attracted staff with firsts from Cambridge, but Christopher didn't even seem to have noticed the disparagement. Shifting in his seat, he said, 'Kieran's application was . . . unusual.'

'Unusual?' Shenfield said sharply, all thoughts of the university instantly dismissed.

Christopher looked uncomfortable. 'He told me he'd been in some sort of trouble. With . . .' he hesitated, glancing at his father, then said, '. . . with the police. He had no conventional qualifications. No school records. I had to bend a few rules. When he first arrived at the university last year . . .'

'Did he seem to know his way round?' Even as Shenfield asked the question, he knew the answer. O'Driscoll would have been too bright to give himself away that easily. So it was no surprise when Christopher shook his head, and said, 'No. In fact, he was totally out of his depth at first. I even began to doubt the wisdom of my decision; he was so withdrawn, he was practically inarticulate. But as soon as I read his first essay . . . It was brilliant, simply brilliant. His grasp of literature . . .'

Shenfield could see Christopher was off in some

world of his own, but made no effort to interrupt him. How anyone could be spouting on about essays at a moment like this was beyond him, but he had learned, over the years, that it was often when witnesses appeared to be at their most rambling that information of real significance came out.

'You mentioned that he'd been in trouble, Dr Heatherington,' Whitelaw said carefully, when Christopher finally stopped speaking. 'Can you tell us what sort of trouble?'

Shenfield held his breath. He hardly dared to consider where the questions were leading them. 'You don't *know*?' he looked at his son incredulously as Christopher shook his head again. 'You didn't think it appropriate to ask?'

'No.'

Just that. No apology, no anxious query about what he should have done, like any normal person . . . 'Christ Almighty,' Shenfield shouted at him. 'Don't you think you should have made it your business to know? Just what the hell bloody planet are you living on?'

'I thought I could help him.' Christopher's face was white with anger. 'You wouldn't be interested in giving anyone a second chance, I suppose?'

'Oh, sorry. I didn't mean to offend your liberal sensibilities. I don't suppose *you'd* be interested in knowing that this so-called Willerton you let loose on Blackport is most probably a bloody serial killer? Grasp of literature? Christ, you lot make me sick.'

'Steady, Dave,' Whitelaw muttered uneasily, as the colour drained from Christopher's face.

A uniformed officer stuck his head round the door. He glanced at Christopher before asking, 'OK if the body's moved, Guv? The scene-of-crime lads have finished with it.'

Shenfield was relieved to have a change of focus. 'Pathologist given us a time of death yet?' he barked.

'He reckons between five and seven, Guv.'

'Yes!' Whitelaw punched the air. Medlock didn't move a muscle. Whatever he must have been feeling, his expression betrayed no emotion.

Shenfield nodded curtly at the officer. 'And get that bloody travelling circus of reporters cleared before you shift her,' he bellowed after him.

Christopher slumped further into the settee, his head between his hands. Shenfield watched him in silence as he fumbled in his pocket for a handkerchief and wiped his eyes.

'I'm sorry,' he whispered at last, struggling to regain his composure.

'Friend of the family I believe you said, Dr Heatherington?' Medlock asked. 'Just how well did you know her?'

Christopher's head came up sharply. 'I know her father. He taught me at Cambridge. Why?'

'I think we've already established my son's relationship to the deceased,' Shenfield said stiffly. He had hoped it was fatherly intuition, rather than Christopher's transparency, that had raised the suspicion in his own mind. 'This Willerton,' he turned back to Christopher. 'Would there be a photograph of him anywhere? A file on him?'

'There should be.' Christopher ran his fingers through his hair. 'What did you mean, "so-called" . . . ?'

'Can you lay your hands on it? Good. Ray, get a car organised. In the meantime, you're not to discuss these allegations with anyone. Do you understand?'

'He's guilty.' Christopher grabbed his arm. 'I know he is!'

'You know nothing of the sort,' Shenfield said firmly. 'And you'll say nothing of the sort, is that clear?' The last thing they needed was to let O'Driscoll know they were on to him.

'I'll go with Dr Heatherington,' Medlock volunteered.

Shenfield hesitated. Christopher was a loose cannon. Could he trust them out of his sight together? On the other hand, he realised the necessity of minimising his own contact with his son. He had a feeling that Lambert was going to be more than a bit suspicious when he found out just who it was who had provided the lifeline of an alternative suspect now Ackroyd was out of the frame. Shenfield would have been suspicious himself, if he'd thought there was the slightest chance that Christopher might have helped him deliberately.

As Christopher and Medlock emerged onto the street, they were met by a barrage of flashguns and shouted questions from the mob of people who had been moved to the far side of the street.

'And you are . . . ?' A hungry-eyed woman pushed a microphone into Christopher's face.

'Can you tell us the name of the victim?' a voice bawled from the crowd.

'*Daily Echo*. What about this bloke you've got in custody?' a second voice shouted.

'Press conference at eleven. Move back, please,' Medlock called, hustling Christopher towards the waiting car.

He stopped dead in the middle of the pavement and turned back to stare at the cameras.

'Come along, Sir.' Medlock held the car door open for him.

Christopher did not move.

'Dr Heatherington?' Medlock put a hand on his arm.

'Willerton. Kieran Willerton. He's the killer,' Christopher shouted at the top of his voice, as he was bundled into the back seat and driven off at speed.

Chapter Sixteen

'He did *what*?' Whitelaw bellowed into his radio. 'Christ Almighty! And you just stood there and watched? It's no good trying to blame . . . Don't come that one, he was in your . . . No, you listen to me. If you want to be in a job this time tomorrow, you just make bloody sure he doesn't do it again. Got that?'

'Careful, Sir. You'll wake the girl,' the policewoman murmured as he threw the radio down onto the table.

'You'd better bloody wake her before Shenfield gets back. Once that pack of wolves out there let O'Driscoll know we're on to him, we're going to need all the information we can lay our hands on. Christ, Shenfield'll go mental!'

She was paralysed. She was in the tomb, the bones of her ancestors mouldering around her, the dank, unbreathed air suffocating her. Somewhere, a million miles above her head, a voice was calling her name, but she didn't want to answer it. To move a single muscle would send her sliding off the edge of the universe. Sleep. All she wanted to do was sleep.

It was still before ten when Christopher walked down the deserted corridor towards his study. He turned to Medlock, his face still ashen, and mumbled, 'How can it look the same as it did yesterday?' He touched the holly around the notice-board, still green and shiny, the red berries smooth and unwithered.

'This must be difficult for you, Sir.' Medlock's tone was neutral.

Christopher unlocked the door to his study and entered. Christmas cards stood on top of the bookcase where the secretary had arranged them. A pile of marking lay on his desk, beside her neatly-wrapped present to him. 'Port.' He gave a distracted smile as he fingered the little foil gift tag. 'It always is.'

Medlock, who had positioned himself by the door, said, 'If you could find the file, Dr Heatherington? As quickly as possible?' He smiled suddenly. 'I suspect we're both in hot enough water with your father as it is.'

He stood as though on guard as Christopher found the key to the filing cabinet, fumbled with the lock, and jerked a drawer open.

From the office, the phone began to ring, its shrill tone ripping through the eerie stillness, causing

Christopher to start so violently that the drawer crashed to the floor, scattering files. He turned towards the door as if to answer it, but Medlock put out a restraining hand and shook his head.

Kieran's photograph stared up at them from the carpet. Medlock bent to pick it up. He examined it, then slipped it back into the file while Christopher looked on, standing helplessly in the middle of the room. Carefully, he began to gather up the rest of the papers.

Christopher gave a nervous cough. 'I . . . I'd rather you didn't touch any of that.'

'It won't take me a minute.' Medlock looked at him over his shoulder. 'Why don't you go and get yourself a glass of water, Dr Heatherington?'

'That material is confidential.'

'I know. It isn't that long since I was a student myself, remember.' Medlock pushed some of the papers back in the drawer. Sitting back on his haunches, he smiled over his shoulder. 'We've all had the odd puff of dope we wouldn't want the authorities to know about. I'm not going to be rifling through the files as soon as you've gone to see what I can pin on anyone. I'll just tidy this lot up and we'll get off, before we give them an excuse for another bollocking. OK?'

Christopher hesitated.

'Listen.' Medlock pulled himself back onto his feet. 'You've had a tremendous shock today. Just give yourself a bit of a break.' With an encouraging smile, he propelled Christopher towards the door.

'You can trust me, Dr Heatherington. We're not all fascist bastards, you know.'

The crowds looked less purposeful by the time they returned to Aigburth Street. Many of the reporters and photographers had moved off, in the hope of more fruitful interviews elsewhere. The numbers had instead been swelled by curious onlookers, youngsters who should have been at school, men with dogs, women with shopping bags, chatting aimlessly, waiting for something to happen. The atmosphere was not unlike that of a carnival, apart from the steady, drizzling rain.

With a warning glance, Medlock hurried Christopher through the police cordon and up to the flat. Taking a deep breath, he winked and murmured, 'Ready to face the music?'

The air inside the flat was thick with smoke. Whitelaw stubbed out his cigarette as they entered, snatched the file and snarled at Medlock, 'I'll deal with you later. And as for you . . . You pull another stunt like that,' he jabbed Christopher in the chest, 'and I'll have you up for perverting the course of justice, Shenfield's son or not. Got it?'

'What the hell's going on?' As if on cue, Shenfield slammed back into the room. 'Sid Barker from the *Echo* rang me at the station. He's got hold of Willerton's name from somewhere.'

'I told them.' Christopher glanced at Medlock. 'I don't want anyone else to be held responsible for—'

'Jesus.' Shenfield sat down heavily. 'Do you

realise what you've done, you stupid . . . ?'

Whitelaw had taken Kieran's photograph from the file. He looked at it and shook his head as he handed it to Shenfield.

'Two eyes, a nose and a mouth,' Medlock observed. 'And that's where the resemblance ends, if that's what you were hoping for.'

It was a polaroid, head and shoulders, no more than a couple of inches square. It gave no indication of height or build. Not much to hang an ID on. The hair was longish, untidy, dark, the face thin. O'Driscoll had been fair, and heavily built. Even the eyes were a different colour, as far as Shenfield could tell. He held the likeness close, then at arm's length. Was it wishful thinking that made him see a similar set to the wide mouth, the same sweep to the thick lashes? He could have lost weight. Contact lenses would account for the eye colour.

'We'll have to pick him up now,' he said, hoping he sounded more decisive than he felt. 'Before they broadcast. What's the address?'

'You reckon we've got enough on him, Guv?' Whitelaw examined the photograph again, then shot Medlock a look. 'We don't want another Ackroyd balls-up.'

'We'll have to risk it. We don't have any choice. And I want us all pulling together from now on. No point-scoring. Is that clear? Medlock, you take a couple of squad cars and get over there right away.' He glanced back at the file. 'Thirteen Wharf Street. No, on second thoughts, go via the station. Pick up an unmarked car. We don't want the press getting wind of this. Let me know as soon as you've pulled him. Understood?' Medlock nodded. Whitelaw opened his mouth, but one look from Shenfield closed it.

'Is the girl able to give us anything yet?'

'Loudon's with her now, Guv.'

'Tell her to hurry it up.' Shenfield flicked through the file. 'Wharf Street,' He grunted. 'Ironic, when you think about it. All those thousands tied up in Ireland where he can't lay a finger on it, and O'Driscoll's living in some flea-ridden doss-house down by the docks. It must really be pissing him off to think . . .'

Christopher was looking puzzled. 'O'Driscoll?'

'What's happening?' A slurred voice came from behind them. There in the doorway, her hair tousled, her tear-streaked face flushed with sleep as she stared at them in bewilderment, stood Flora.

Christopher's knees buckled, the blood draining from his face as he gripped the back of the chair to steady himself.

'It was horrible,' she sobbed, as the memory flooded back. 'There was so much blood. The snow was all red. And her head . . . her head . . .' She broke off, shuddering uncontrollably.

Christopher stood motionless for a moment, his eyes clenched tightly shut. Then, moving towards her stiffly, as if he were very old, he put out his hand to touch her, testing she was real. He caught his father's eye across the top of her head, and mumbled, 'I thought . . . I didn't realise . . .'

He held Flora to him, rocking her, hushing her,

stroking her hair as he whispered, 'Thank God. Oh, thank God,' but with an awkwardness, a restraint, that suggested . . . Shenfield wasn't quite sure what it suggested. He noticed that Medlock had stopped in the doorway and was watching them both intently.

'Are you still here?' he snapped, clicking his fingers at the policewoman, as Medlock made hastily for the stairs. 'You. What's your name again?'

'Loudon, Sir.'

'First name?'

'Jane, Sir.'

'Look after the girl. This is Jane,' he went on, speaking slowly and deliberately to Flora. 'She's going to get you tidied up, and then she'll make you a nice cup of tea.'

Christopher slumped down into a chair. He was as white as a sheet.

'You OK?' Shenfield asked.

'I don't understand.' The voice came out in the frightened whimper Shenfield could remember from years back. Christopher was rocking backwards and forwards, his hands clutching his elbows. 'I don't understand . . .'

Shenfield perched on the arm of the chair and patted Christopher awkwardly on the shoulder. The younger man shook his head, although whether to clear it, or to indicate displeasure at the gesture, Shenfield was unsure.

After a few moments, he said flatly, 'So it was Meg Evans.'

Shenfield nodded. Whitelaw's muttered, 'Shit,'

told him that he was not the only one who had begun to take on board the implications. When Christopher, and Ackroyd for that matter, had described the earlier assault, no one had realised they were talking about a different girl. Shenfield saw the whole elaborate edifice of his case collapsing before his eyes like a house of cards.

After a couple of minutes' dispirited silence, Whitelaw said, 'You mentioned when you first came here this morning that Meg Evans had made some accusations against O'Dris—' he checked himself. 'Willerton. Do you think it's possible he could have . . . ?'

'. . . killed her simply because she'd witnessed the assault?' Shenfield knew they were clutching at straws. It didn't make sense. He scanned the room, drumming his fingers on the arm of the chair, looking for some clue, his gaze again taking in the wreckage of the meal. Whose meal? Anybody's guess, until he could get a coherent account from Flora Castledine. A confrontation that had got out of hand, maybe? In the garden? At six in the morning? Maybe not. Why hang about in the pitch dark . . . ?

Suddenly, Shenfield's fingers stopped drumming.

'He murdered her by mistake.'

'By mistake?' Whitelaw echoed dubiously.

'Think about it.' The more Shenfield thought about it, the more sense it made. They'd noticed straight away that the girls had similar hair. He'd even been fairly sure he recognised them both from Ackroyd's sinister portrait gallery. 'It was pitch dark. He came at her from behind. She was wearing that deep-brimmed hat, remember.'

'Flora had a hat,' Christopher mumbled. 'Green. Sort of floppy . . .'

'There you go. Similar hat as well. No wonder he got them mixed up. He wouldn't have been able to see her face. And I tell you something else, and all. We think he was disturbed, right? Didn't get as far as turning the body over?' Shenfield's face was screwed into a mask of concentration. 'It's my bet he still thinks it's Flora he's killed. And he'll go on thinking it until we release an identification. But when he does find out he's got the wrong girl . . .' He gave an expressive shrug. '. . . Who knows what he'll do?'

He wondered briefly how Flora would feel when she discovered how narrow an escape she'd had. Relief? Guilt that she'd been taken in by this maniac? He glanced across at his son. She wasn't the only one to have been taken in.

'Maybe we should get Medlock to do us one of his psychological profiles,' Whitelaw observed.

Shenfield gave him a hard look. 'Maybe we should. O'Driscoll's obsessive. He must be to have taken the risk of coming back here in the first place. I reckon he'll come after her again.'

'O'Driscoll?' Christopher shook his head. Then, rubbing his hands over his eyes, and with an obvious attempt to pull himself together, he frowned up at his father. 'That's the second time you've called him O'Driscoll.'

Shenfield looked at him, and then back at Whitelaw, trying to weigh up the risk of letting him in on their suspicions. The situation was close to getting out of hand. Christopher was providing some valuable information, but had already proved himself dangerously indiscreet, and had put Shenfield's neck on the line in the process. And then there was the friction between Whitelaw and Medlock; he couldn't see that getting any easier before the case was wrapped up. But wrap it up he must, and as soon as possible. His fears for Flora's safety were genuine enough.

Finally, he said, 'It's a bit complicated. Do you remember the murder that took place here a few years ago? A student by the name of . . .'

'You mean *Gavin* O'Driscoll?' Christopher stared at him in amazement. 'Are you saying you think Kieran Willerton . . .'

'You knew Gavin O'Driscoll?' It was more statement than question. There was something in the way Christopher had said the name, as if he'd said it many times before. 'Why in hell didn't you say so?'

'You didn't ask.'

Shenfield would have liked to slap him. There was that same cool presumption of mental superiority that had made him slap O'Driscoll so many times all those years ago. His hands trembled slightly as he pulled O'Driscoll's photograph from his wallet, placed it next to the one from Willerton's file, and said, 'Well?'

Christopher studied them for what seemed an eternity, gently fingering each face as if he were reading it in Braille. O'Driscoll's photograph wasn't much of a likeness, even his best friend would have been hard pushed to recognise him, Shenfield told himself. He mustn't expect too much. He tried to read Christopher's expression as he gazed from one image to the other, but Christopher put his hand to his head, as if trying to ward him off. Finally, he looked up and slowly nodded his head. 'It's possible.'

'So if you know both of them, how come you never noticed the resemblance before?' As soon as Shenfield had the response he'd hoped for, he began to question it.

'It's been six years . . . he's done a lot to disguise himself, he's good at that . . . a good actor . . .' Christopher gave the ghost of a smile, then added, with a sudden flash of anger, 'If you suspected Gavin O'Driscoll had come back here, why didn't you make it public?'

'You've got your Vice Chancellor to thank for that,' Whitelaw said dryly.

'Water under the bridge,' Shenfield snapped. 'Right, Christopher. Start at the beginning. Tell us everything you know about him.'

Christopher talked, hesitantly at first, of Willerton's shadowy past, his surprisingly extensive knowledge of literature for one with no formal education, his uncanny ability to absorb the mannerisms of those around him. He described Willerton's passion for the stage; a passion shared by Gavin O'Driscoll, he pointed out, seemingly more and more convinced himself, as he spoke, of his student's true identity. It was through the drama society that O'Driscoll had met both Christopher and Melanie Loveridge.

'All supposition.' Shenfield held up his hand as Christopher started to speak. 'I'm talking about what we can prove beyond reasonable doubt in a court of law.'

Which, he was painfully aware, was very little. And in any case, it was one thing establishing Kieran Willerton's true identity, it was quite another to pin charges on him that would stick; it wasn't even a certainty that a jury would convict him of the Loveridge murder after six years. If they were going to nail the bastard this time, they must start in the present. Produce sufficient evidence to convict him on this latest murder, then work backwards from there.

Biting his lip, Christopher went over his meeting with Meg again.

Shenfield leaned back in his chair and shook his head. 'Can't use it. Hearsay. Come on, Christopher, think. You've accused him not only to us, but to the press. You've got to have more to go on than this.'

'I'm not the one on trial.'

'Neither's he, unless we get some evidence against him.'

The tutorial interested Shenfield. 'He had scratches . . .' Christopher put his hand up to his face. 'I suppose Flora must have tried to. . .' his voice trailed off. 'His behaviour was . . . bizarre.'

'Bizarre?'

'Extremely aggressive.'

'So he was pretty fired up after you'd warned him off?' Whitelaw said.

Christopher looked down at his hands. 'Fired up enough to commit murder, you mean?'

'Don't even think it,' Shenfield said firmly. 'None of this is your fault, Christopher, and you won't help anyone by trying to convince yourself it is.' He turned his attention to Whitelaw. 'I don't think we're going to get much further with any of this. We'll just have to hope Flora can come up with something. Her testimony's going to be crucial.'

Whitelaw grunted. 'If she'll give it. You'd be amazed at what some women, even intelligent ones, will do to protect these bastards,' he went on, speaking now to Christopher, who flushed, but made no reply.

'Which is why we're going to have to go carefully with her. On no account is anyone to hint at Willerton's real identity, is that clear?' Shenfield said, more brusquely than he'd intended. 'We've got to get her to incriminate him before she realises he's a suspect. She's infatuated with this character, remember. She's going to be hostile to questioning.' If Christopher's feelings towards the girl were anything near what he suspected, this must be killing him. 'She trusts you,' he added, with an attempt at compassion that sounded clumsy even to his own ears. 'You can help make things a lot easier for her, and for us, by . . .'

Whitelaw coughed loudly. Shenfield turned as

Flora came back into the room, the policewoman helping her to the settee. Obediently, she took the mug of tea she was handed, but her hands shook so much that it spilt, slopping unheeded onto her skirt.

Shenfield watched his son as he knelt down beside her and dabbed at the tea with his handkerchief. She must be a stunner under normal circumstances, he thought, taking in the bright hair subdued into a tight bunch at the back of her neck. Even if, at that moment, it was as though a light inside her had been extinguished.

Christopher's eyes were fixed on the livid bruise across the right side of her face. He took the mug from her and picked up the rabbit, which she clutched to her, rocking it, her face buried in its soft fur, as if she were a child.

'She never even got to see the baby,' she sobbed, adding, in a small voice, 'Where's Kieran?'

Christopher took in his breath sharply.

'What?' she said, looking from Christopher to Shenfield. 'What? Where is he? What's happened to him?'

Her voice was rising towards hysteria. Shenfield caught his son's eye and said evenly, 'They're trying to trace him now.'

Whitelaw's radio crackled. He turned away, muttering into it and nodding his head as he listened.

'This Kieran,' he asked casually, turning back to Flora. 'Got a bit of a temper on him, has he?'

Flora looked dazed. 'What are you talking about?'

'Only one of our officers has been talking to some of your mates. It seems that not so long ago your boyfriend attacked one of them. A Myles Delahunt. He's prepared to testify that Willerton attempted to strangle him after some minor disagreement. Do you know anything about that?'

The flush started at Flora's neck and travelled slowly to the roots of her hair. 'Myles Delahunt?' she repeated, her hand going to her throat. Shaking her head, she said fiercely, 'Myles Delahunt's an idiot. Everyone knows that.'

'And the black eye?'

The hand moved up involuntarily to her cheek.

'Listen, love . . .' Shenfield put a restraining hand on her shoulder as she struggled to her feet. He hesitated, glancing at Christopher before he went on, 'You'll probably think this is a funny question, but I assume you and he were . . . intimate?'

Flora looked at him blankly.

'Did you notice anything, well . . .' he cleared his throat, '. . . kinky in his behaviour?'

'Come on, Flora.' Whitelaw reached across and took her hand, which she immediately snatched away. 'We know he tried to rape you. What's the point in—'

Christopher jumped to his feet. 'Is any of this really . . .'

Shenfield forced himself to ignore him. They were building up the evidence against O'Driscoll, brick by brick. 'These scratches he'd picked up on his face. Any idea where they came from?'

Lowering her eyes, she mumbled into the rabbit, 'I made them. We were just messing around, that's all.'

Christopher flinched.

'Messing around? Are you sure about that, Flora?'

She looked up into Shenfield's face with a hint of defiance. 'That's what I said.'

'So you roughed each other up a bit sometimes. Is that what you're saying?'

'For God's sake!' Christopher grabbed his father by the arm. 'What kind of question is that?'

Shenfield shook him off, his attention still fixed on Flora, but before he could continue, the door opened and a white-overalled scene-of-crime officer appeared.

'We've taken a cast of the footprints next to the body, Sir. Size eleven. Looks like trainers, from the tread. Quite a distinctive pattern.'

'What sort of shoes was your boyfriend wearing last night?'

Flora put down the rabbit and said slowly, 'Just what are you getting at?'

'And there's this, Sir,' the scene-of-crime officer continued, producing a polythene bag. Pulling on a pair of latex gloves, he carefully opened the bag and removed a scarf, which he unfolded and held up in front of them. Droplets of congealed blood clung to its muddy fringe. 'It was found on the body. It had been used to strangle her. I wondered if Miss Castledine could confirm that it belonged to the victim?'

'No, it doesn't. I recognise that scarf,' Christopher said. 'It belongs to. . .' He looked at Flora, who had pulled away from it, shrinking back into the corner of the settee, and then at his father, before saying in a firm voice, '. . . to Kieran Willerton.'

Chapter Seventeen

The nightmare morning dragged on. No word came through from Medlock. Whitelaw was despatched over to Wharf Street to find out what was going on. Countless mugs of tea were produced by Loudon and left undrunk, as Christopher and Shenfield tried to persuade Flora to tell them what she knew. Did she have any idea where he would have gone? Had he mentioned any detail, however small, of his past? His home town? His birthday, even? Clutching the rabbit, her eyes swollen and red, she stared at them, uncomprehending, as if they were speaking in a foreign language.

Over and over, the same questions. Christopher paced the floor. Shenfield chain smoked. Flora looked exhausted, her face bloodless, her hands still trembling. Every piece of evidence Shenfield presented her with, she parried. Kieran's footprints were in the garden because he'd been picking flowers, she said.

'Picking *flowers*?' Shenfield rolled his eyes. 'OK. What about his coat and scarf?' The blood-soaked jacket on which the body had been lying had also been identified as his. 'Any idea how they got there?'

'I've just remembered!' she said suddenly. 'He didn't have them with him, I'm sure he didn't.' Nursing the rabbit, she stared into space and whispered, 'Poor Kieran, he'll be so cold without them.'

'For God's sake, Flora . . .' Christopher looked at the policewoman, who shook her head and mouthed, 'Shock.'

'We . . .' She looked up at him, then hesitated. 'We had a row.'

Shenfield leant forward. 'So he was in a temper when he left?'

'Upset.' Her fingers strayed to her bruised face. 'I was the one in a temper. And he didn't leave, I did. I said if he didn't want to go to the ball, I'd go alone. I thought he'd . . .' she broke off as the tears started again.

'So you were at the ball?'

'For a while, I . . . there were a lot of others from the drama soc there. Kieran knew I'd meet up with them. I suppose I wanted to make him jealous. I . . .' she buried her head in her hands. After a moment, she blew her nose and went on, 'The . . . the police turned up. Everyone thought it was a drugs bust. Myles and some of the others had been smoking stuff . . . dope . . . so we left. A crowd of us went back to Myles's place.'

'What time was that?' Shenfield asked.

'I'm not sure. Eleven? Eleven-thirty?'

'And you found Meg when you returned here

at . . .' he checked his notes, '. . . six thirty-five. So where were you in the meantime?'

A long silence.

'Come on, Flora. If you saw Kieran, you must tell us. It might help us to eliminate him from our enquiries,' he added lamely.

'I . . .' she looked down at the rabbit and whispered miserably. 'I stayed the night.'

'With Kieran, you mean?'

She shook her head.

'With Myles Delahunt?' Christopher turned his face away from her. In a low voice, he said, 'Oh, Flora, how could you?'

'I was angry,' she sobbed. 'I'd smoked some dope and . . . Oh God, this is all my fault. If I'd just stayed here. Got things sorted out . . .'

A uniformed officer appeared in the doorway. Shenfield took the computer printout he handed him, scanned it, and motioned him out. No record of birth certificate, National Insurance number, or any other official documents in the name of Kieran Willerton. Well, there was a surprise.

The events of the last twenty-four hours were becoming clearer all the time. He remembered what Medlock had said, long before they'd known who the killer was, about what would happen if the girl he'd put on a pedestal lost her footing. O'Driscoll wasn't going to let Flora live after what she'd done to him.

Turning back to her, he asked, 'Does O'Drisc—' he bit the name back. Start again. 'Does Willerton know where you live on the Scillies?'

She started, as if the question had brought her abruptly to her senses. Shenfield noted the momentary hesitation before she lifted her head, looked him in the eye, and said, 'No.'

'Flora, are you sure?' he asked urgently. 'This is very important. You must tell us the truth.'

'Can I get some water?' She was on her feet and out of the room before Shenfield had the chance to reply.

He watched her go and shook his head. 'It beats me. A pretty girl, everything going for her, and within a few weeks of leaving home she's not only shacked up with a vicious little bastard like O'Driscoll, but she's sleeping around and into drugs. Too much freedom, that's the trouble. You think you're doing your best for them, letting them go off to . . .'

What was he saying? He'd felt closer to Christopher in the last few hours than in years, yet here he was, same as always, sounding off as if he was deliberately trying to wind him up. He glanced over at his son, expecting some frosty retort, but it was obvious that he hadn't been listening to a word.

'I reckon I owe you one,' he said, lighting up another cigarette and automatically offering Christopher the packet, to which he absently shook his head. 'If it hadn't been for your assistance, we'd still be none the wiser, you know. Maybe when this is all sorted . . .'

The expression on Christopher's face silenced

him. 'Kieran Willerton was my friend,' he said, his voice shaking with emotion. 'Do you think I want to do this to him? Do you think I'd be telling you any of this if there was any other way?'

For several minutes, they sat at opposite ends of the room, each locked in silent thought, faces averted from each other. Christopher had picked up the rabbit, and was running his fingers gently over the fur where Flora's tears had dampened it.

The silence was finally broken by Whitelaw, who burst back into the stuffy little room and said breathlessly, 'He's gone, Guv.'

'Gone?' Shenfield, galvanised into sudden action, leapt to his feet. 'What d'you mean, gone?'

'He must have been expecting us. His room's empty. Clean as a whistle. No fingerprints, nothing.'

'Why the hell didn't Medlock radio in as soon as he got there?'

'Because he's not been there, that's why. He simply radioed the local beat bobby. No explanation of what it was about. The bloke rang on the doorbell a couple of times and left it at that. He's gutted now, of course.'

'So he bloody well should be.'

'I meant the beat bobby, not Medlock. *He's* spent the morning playing with his damned computer. I warned you not to . . .'

'Christ!' Shenfield banged his fist on the table. 'He could be anywhere in the bloody country by now.' He picked up his own radio and bellowed into it, 'Tell Medlock to get his arse over here right now. And tell him if he hasn't got a bloody good excuse for disobeying my orders, he'll be lucky to have a job as a fucking lollipop lady by the time I'm finished with him. Sorry, love,' he added, as Flora came back in.

'What's happened?'

'Your boyfriend's done a runner.'

'I don't believe you.' Her face was ashen, her eyes closed. But if she felt bad now, it was nothing to how she'd feel when she learned who Kieran Willerton really was.

'I think you'd better sit down, Flora love,' he said quietly. 'There's something you ought to know.'

'Is she going to be all right?' he asked some time later, as the university doctor came out of Flora's room.

He'd really thought she was having a heart attack after he'd dropped the bombshell. Her face, even her lips, had turned the colour of alabaster, every limb shaking as though she had an electric current running through her.

'Traumatised,' the doctor said briefly. 'I've given her another sedative. She'll sleep now.'

'She'll be OK later, though?'

The doctor stared at him with palpable hostility. 'Further interrogation is out of the question, I'm afraid. I think she's been made to suffer enough for one day.'

'I meant, will she be fit to travel?' Shenfield had

218

learned to ignore the attitude, but it still rankled. The police were a bunch of right-wing thugs. But blokes like this one were the first to demand results when their cars were nicked or their gardens vandalised. Or their patients butchered. 'We've got her booked on the morning helicopter to St Mary's. I'd like to drive her down to Penzance tonight.'

'I see.' The doctor sounded slightly mollified. He checked his watch and said, 'Should be. Leave her undisturbed for a couple of hours. She's going back to family, I take it? Well, just warn them to let her take things at her own pace. She's taken one hell of an emotional battering. She's going to need a lot of support.' He turned to Christopher, who was slumped in a chair, nursing a cup of cold tea. 'And how are you feeling, Dr Heatherington?'

Completely done in, if appearances were anything to go by, Shenfield thought as he viewed his son. He had that look of blank-eyed, uncomprehending exhaustion you saw on the faces of earthquake victims or Bosnian refugees on the news. It must have been one hell of a day for him, too. First the shock of thinking Flora was dead, then the shock of finding she wasn't. Not to mention the trauma of realising one of his own students was the killer, and who he was. It was easy to forget, when death was your daily business, just how harrowing it was for those it touched personally. And he'd only had to see how Christopher looked at Flora Castledine to realise this *was* personal. Far more personal than 'friend of the family'.

'Why don't you go home, lad?' he said. 'There's nothing more you can do here.'

'Soon.' Christopher's eyes strayed now towards Flora's bedroom, as if to confirm Shenfield's thoughts. 'I'll just make sure she settles, first.'

The doctor left. Whitelaw came in from the kitchen with the inevitable fresh pot of tea. For the hundredth time, they went over the passenger lists of all outward-bound flights to Scilly. Whitelaw yawned as he checked his watch, then said, 'What makes you so sure O'Driscoll'll come after her anyway?'

'I'll stake my job on it. And what's more, she was lying when she said he didn't know where she lived.' Shenfield took a swig of tea and lit a cigarette from the butt of the last, which he added to the overflowing ashtray.

'Well, the only way he'll get there at this time of the year's by air, and we've got that covered, so I don't see how. The helicopter and Skybus companies know to inform us of any late bookings, and all the local police stations have the photographs.'

'You heard what Christopher said. He's bright. He'll find a way. And when he does, I'll be waiting for him.'

'I still don't see why you need to go. The local police can keep an eye on her, can't they? And I don't reckon Lambert'll buy it, either. Not with all the paperwork we need to shift.'

So that was Whitelaw's beef; he'd got some leave coming up, and didn't want to get lumbered with the loose ends.

'Get Medlock to do it. It'll do him good to settle down to a bit of routine work for a change. And as for Lambert, I don't think he'll want O'Driscoll slipping through our fingers a second time, do you?'

'You seriously think you can trust Medlock while you're gone?'

'For Christ's sake, Ray.' He was beginning to get on Shenfield's nerves. 'Look, he's young, he's ambitious, and he's found it difficult to admit he was wrong. But he's had his bollocking, he's found out the hard way what happens if he ignores orders, and as far as I'm concerned, that's an end to it.'

The written warning would stay on his career record. Shenfield had been reluctant to take such an extreme course of action, but Medlock had to learn to toe the line, same as everyone else.

'I still think I should come.' Christopher flushed as they both turned to look at him.

Shenfield closed his eyes. They'd gone over this a hundred times.

'There you go,' Whitelaw muttered.

It had been Medlock who had put the suggestion into Christopher's head. Whitelaw was convinced he was up to no good. Shenfield told him he was being paranoid; if Medlock had wanted to make anything of Christopher's relationship to him, he'd had ample opportunity before now.

'You heard what the doctor said,' Christopher pressed on. 'Flora's going to need a lot of support. Simon's a nice enough chap, but he's . . . well, he's a bit of an old woman.'

Shenfield put his mug to his lips to conceal the

beginnings of a grin. Trying the old shoulder-to-cry-on routine now, was he? The lad had more guile than he would have given him credit for. Christopher was wearing the same earnest expression he'd had as a child, when attempting to negotiate another half-hour before bedtime.

And why not let him come, he decided suddenly? In fact, how could he stop him? It was the most natural thing in the world for an old family friend from the institution where she studied to accompany her home. He knew Christopher well enough to be certain there had been absolutely no impropriety in his behaviour towards the girl. The one time she'd so much as reached for his hand, as Shenfield broke the news about O'Driscoll to her, he'd pulled it back as though he'd been touched by a live coal. Anyway, it would be a pleasant change for Shenfield to be in favour with him for once.

'OK, you win,' he said. 'Get yourself back over to your place and pack. I'll pick you up later.'

'Thank you.'

It was the first time in more years than Shenfield cared to remember that Christopher had said that to him and sounded as if he meant it.

'See if you can get a couple of hours' sleep,' he added gruffly. 'It's going to be a long night.'

It had been a long day, too. Shenfield called home just long enough to shower and throw a few things in a bag, before heading back to Blackport Central. Lambert was at some conference in London, which saved him the bother of clearing the trip to the Scillies. Norman Ackroyd, he learned, was still in the cells, but only because it was considered unsafe to allow him home. No charges would be brought; he had the best possible alibi for Meg Evans' murder. The press conference had been cancelled, and judging from the activity round the campus when he'd driven past, the media had turned its attention to finding out everything they could about the student they still believed to be Kieran Willerton. And long may they continue, as far as Shenfield was concerned. The less O'Driscoll knew about them blowing his cover, the better.

Before he left the station, he spoke to the police surgeon, and arranged Norman's readmission to High View. Medlock, now painfully eager to please, had volunteered to go round and pick up his things.

With hindsight, it was easy enough to see why Norman had been on campus; he'd got himself into a state after witnessing the assault on Flora, then hearing on the radio about the ball had triggered his old guilt and anxiety. He'd raced from the house, all thoughts of his meeting with Shenfield forgotten, imagining that this time, if he got to the lake soon enough, he could save her. Poor sod. How long would he spend in High View this time, Shenfield wondered?

It was almost six by the time he got to Christopher's flat. The front door was unlocked. He pushed it open and made his way up the stairs. The landing was filled with the mingling aromas of evening meals. Christopher's door was ajar, the flat in darkness, illuminated only by the flickering images from the television, which was spouting out the theme tune to *Neighbours*. Christopher was sitting staring blankly at the screen. Shenfield stood unobserved, watching him for a moment before he tapped on the door and went in.

Christopher, startled, jumped to his feet. 'I was waiting for the news . . .'

'That's OK.' Shenfield put a tentative hand on his shoulder. 'No hurry.'

They watched the headlines together in silence; the latest disagreement at Stormont, a bank-raid in Hackney, another drop in the bank rate. Finally, the rerun of Shenfield's interview outside the Bombay Palace. He found himself grimacing self-consciously into the darkness. It was peculiar; he hadn't realised he looked so old, for one thing. He barely recognised the burly, hard-faced copper who stared unsmiling from the screen. Was that how other people saw him?

'*Police later issued a photograph of a man they would like to interview in connection with . . .*' As the picture flashed up onto the screen, Christopher quickly bent and pulled the plug from the mains.

'Can we go via the university?' he asked, as they got into Shenfield's car. 'There are some important papers . . .'

'Better not. The place is crawling with reporters.'

'I really have to . . .'

Important papers? Shenfield bit back the sarcastic response that sprang to his lips, and instead said mildly, 'Whatever it is, it'll just have to wait a few more days, I'm afraid.'

By midnight, they were on their way. Flora, a blanket around her shoulders, walked to the waiting car as if in a trance. She sat next to Christopher in the back, staring blankly out at the mill of journalists and photographers who pressed against the windows of the car, shouting questions and pointing cameras. She had still not uttered a word. Tentatively, Shenfield asked if there was anything she wanted, but she simply drew the blanket more tightly around her, her head turned away from him.

They sped through the suburbs of Blackport in silence, past rows of windows lit by Christmas trees and decorations, towards the motorway. The streets were white with a fresh dusting of snow. In just one week's time, Shenfield thought disbelievingly, it would be Christmas day.

By five a.m., they were nearing the outskirts of Bristol, the heavy black sky illuminated from below by the dull, distant orange glow of a thousand street lights. They passed signs for South Wales, then the graceful arc of the Severn Bridge, picked out as though by fairy lights. Shenfield wondered briefly if it might be the route Meg Evans would have taken home. Clearing yet another tangle of the roadworks that had impeded their progress all the way from the Midlands, he pushed the car back up to seventy.

Flora stirred in her sleep, muttering Kieran's name. Shenfield adjusted his driving mirror and glanced into the back. She had turned so that her weight was against Christopher, her head resting on his shoulder, that fabulous hair spreading across his chest like a cloak. He felt a sudden lump come to his throat. Susannah's hair had tumbled over him like that, once upon a time. Sleep hadn't managed to rub the sadness from Flora's face. The purple bruise across her cheek was darkening like a stain. She needed someone to care for her now. Someone gentle, sensitive, who would cherish her. As he should have cherished Susannah.

As if sensing his gaze upon them, Christopher half-woke. He stared around, dislocated, and tried to sit up, then eased himself away from Flora, shifting cautiously in his seat until she turned her face away from him, her head flopping awkwardly against the car door. Shenfield felt a ridiculous stab of disappointment.

He'd always feared, in his heart of hearts, that Christopher might be a bit of a . . . his mind shied away from the terms he'd have used at work without a thought: 'pansy', 'bender', 'shirt-lifter'. No, nothing sordid like that. But the fact remained that Christopher had always seemed a bit . . . different. Never a girlfriend. While other lads of his age had been busy chasing anything in a skirt, Christopher had been more interested in writing his bloody poems. Even as a kid he'd been different from the rest. He'd hated sport, terrified, when

Shenfield had dragged him along to football matches, of the noise and the crowds. At school, he'd been an irresistible target for bullies, bookish, slightly-built and sensitive. A walking bundle of nerve-endings. Even the sight of a dead bird could reduce him to tears. They'd found one, once, a bedraggled, half-dead fledgling. The only humane thing would have been to finish it off there and then, but Christopher had insisted on trying to rear it by hand, fussing over it for days, refusing to admit defeat. Susannah had found it, weeks later, hidden in a shoebox under his bed, dead as a doornail. He'd always been a mystery, Shenfield thought, flexing his aching shoulder muscles and blinking hard as a lorry overtook them in a wall of spray.

A sudden gust of wind buffeted them, hurling a sharp flurry of snow against the windows, but the car insulated them from the elements, warm, silent apart from the steady thud, thud of the wind-screen wipers. He snatched another glance into the back. They were both asleep again, leaning into each other, their bodies swaying together with each movement of the car.

By six-thirty, they were nearing Exeter, and the first glimmerings of dawn were beginning to streak the horizon.

'Don't know about you, but I could murder a coffee,' Shenfield said, immediately regretting his choice of words.

Christopher stirred and sat up, rubbing his eyes. They pulled off the motorway and into a service station. Flora woke up as the car stopped, pushing the hair back from her face and staring around her. Shenfield could see from her eyes that memory had returned as instantly as wakefulness. She shook her head wordlessly when he suggested she get out to stretch her legs, and burrowed into the blanket, closing her eyes to shut him out.

They were parked by the entrance to the café. Yawning and stretching, Shenfield got out and leaned against the car. It was perceptibly warmer here than in Blackport, the morning air bland on his face. For a moment, he was reminded of family holidays when Christopher was a kid. The anxious excitement of the journey in whichever clapped-out old car they'd had at the time. Susannah handing out the ritual picnic breakfast of hard-boiled eggs and lukewarm tea tasting of thermos flasks. Christopher tucked up on the back seat, his head in a book.

'D'you want something to eat?' he asked him now, and felt another stab of disappointment when Christopher shook his head.

A surprising number of travellers were about for this time in the morning. A girl hustled a couple of grizzling toddlers past him towards the toilets, looking hardly old enough to be out of nappies herself. Inside the entrance, which was dominated by a huge artificial Christmas tree, a group of hollow-eyed youngsters was clustered around one of the bank of games machines, noisily racing computerised cars. Shenfield observed them with a professional eye while he queued. Waiting for the chance to nick a real one for a spot of joy riding, no doubt.

He grabbed himself a packet of sandwiches and a polystyrene cup of what passed for coffee, and paused to glance at the rack of morning papers. A grainy copy of the Willerton polaroid stared out from the front page under the headline: 'Student Sought in Campus Slaying'.

Shenfield felt himself tense. He hadn't got time to be standing here watching the world go by. Tearing the sandwiches open with his teeth, he wolfed them down as he hurried back to the car. Christopher, seeing him approach, got back into his seat like an obedient child.

Shenfield tried to shake off the weight of responsibility pressing down on him like an overheavy coat as he started the engine and turned the car towards Bodmin Moor. Maybe they should all have stayed in Blackport. O'Driscoll was going to try to get to Scilly. He felt it in his bones. He could be allowing not only Flora, but Christopher as well, to walk into a trap. And only he stood between them and a dangerous killer.

The tickets were waiting for them at the heliport. Shenfield had imagined a scaled-down Heathrow. The small, pre-fabricated building hardly bigger than a shed came as a shock.

A ruddy-faced police constable lounged against the check-in desk, sharing a joke with the baggage-handlers, erupting into a sudden bellow of laughter as they approached. He nodded good-naturedly at the tickets, hardly glancing at them before turning back to his conversation.

'Call that a passenger check?' Shenfield bellowed, bringing the man to flustered attention as he flashed his ID card at him. He pointed to the crumpled copy of the photograph on the desk, half-concealed under a pile of boarding passes. 'Why do you think you were faxed that thing?' He held it under the man's nose and snarled, 'It wasn't a bloody Christmas greeting from Blackport Central.'

'Tickets were all pre-booked long since, Sir. We have checked.' The constable sounded aggrieved. 'And no one's turned up on spec. Course, if they had . . .'

'Can't get on without a ticket, can he? That's how the system works.' The baggage-handler came to the constable's support. He looked Shenfield's crumpled work suit up and down, as if he were recently arrived from outer space. ''Tisn't like getting on a train, you know.'

Flora had disappeared into the Ladies without a word, while Christopher unloaded their meagre luggage. Shenfield ordered a cup of black coffee at the counter of the tiny café, aware that the men at the desk were still muttering about him. He perched on one of the vinyl-upholstered benches, trying not to think of how exhausted he was. He had had no more than a couple of hours sleep in the previous forty-eight. His back ached and his eyes felt full of grit, but he knew he could not relax until they were on Scilly. He looked around again at his fellow travellers, his attention momentarily caught by a tall, dark-haired youth in a bobble hat. O'Driscoll could be here. He could be anywhere.

'Come on, you bastard,' Shenfield muttered. 'I'm waiting for you.'

Chapter Eighteen

It had been easy. Easy to hitch the lifts, easy to
attach himself to a mini-bus full of musicians, over
from Ireland for the Christmas folk festival and
delighted to welcome a fellow Ulsterman to join
them. He'd noticed them in the service station at
Bristol, his ear attuning instantly to the harsh, nasal
accent that still knotted his guts.

Easy.

He'd heard his name on the car radio by then.
Realised, his exhausted brain clicking into action,
that if he were to get to her, he must lose his identity fast, before tomorrow's papers carried his
photograph, as they surely would. And so he had
joined the Irishmen, ridden on down to Penzance
with them, a borrowed hat pulled down over his
long dark hair. Easy to shoulder a couple of ruck-
sacks from the back of the bus and shuffle past the
check-in desk with the rest of them. By dusk, he had
landed on St Mary's.

Easy.

He'd remembered every word she'd told him
about the farmhouse. It stood, as big as a hotel, and

without sign of agricultural activity, on a great outcrop of rock facing out over the Atlantic. Through the lighted windows, he had glimpsed her father moving restlessly from room to room, and had known she hadn't come. Yet.

Now, hidden in the pine woods below the landing strip, he waited, watching. Since dawn, he had stood, stock-still amongst the dripping trees, his eyes fixed on the vacant sky. The mist was rolling in, shrouding the shoulder-high bracken across the downs, muffling the waves that pounded the granite headlands, bleaching the colour from the endless fields of daffodils. Soon, the islands would be cut off by the fog. Gulls circled and wheeled above the cliffs, ghostly shreds of grey-white against the grey-black sea. And on the horizon, a black dot, growing and growing. The distant thunder of rotor blades mingled with the gulls' mewing cries.

Oblivious to cold, oblivious to hunger, he waited for her to come.

'The doctor says it's shock. She'll speak again when she's ready.' Christopher sat in the spotless kitchen at the farm, toying with the huge breakfast that the housekeeper had prepared.

Flora had gone silently to her room when they reached the farm, refusing anything to eat or drink, while her father fussed around her.

Briefly, as he ate, Shenfield sketched in the events of the last twenty-four hours. Simon Castledine had accepted his introduction as Christopher's father without comment or interest. He sat crumbling a piece of toast distractedly between his fingers, grey with anxiety, the fear etched into his thin, lined face. It was impossible to tell whether he was listening or not. Christopher had been right; it was clear the man wasn't going to be of any use to anyone.

They moved through to the drawing room. Castledine went up yet again to check on Flora, coming down to report that she was fast asleep. There were no newspapers; the fog had prevented their arrival from the mainland. Shenfield cursed himself silently for not picking them up in Penzance.

After the chaos of the past twenty-four hours, he found the sudden inactivity intolerable. This place was giving him the creeps already. Castledine sat motionless except for his fingers, which tapped incessantly on the arm of his chair, as he stared out of the huge picture window at the blotted seascape beyond. The panes shivered slightly as each booming wave crashed against the rocks below.

Shenfield wandered around the room. Expensive. Impersonal, except for the book-lined shelves, which must give a clue to his character, if you knew what you were looking for. Not that it appeared the books were read; the shelves were too meticulously tidy, too carefully arranged, unlike the sagging, overflowing assortment at Norman Ackroyd's. The mantelpiece was crammed with the sort of lavish corporate Christmas cards that have the names already printed. It didn't look as if Castledine had many friends.

He picked up the remote control for the television.

'D'you mind?'

Castledine stared at the handset as if he'd never seen it before in his life, and shook his head.

Shenfield flicked from channel to channel in search of a news bulletin. Cartoons, a chat show, a fat West Indian woman making brandy butter. The rest of the world going about its business.

He asked to use the phone, as his mobile wasn't getting a signal, and managed to get through to the incident room in Blackport, but Whitelaw was out.

Christopher was pacing the room like a caged animal when he came back in. His twitchiness was infectious. Shenfield went over to the window, his eyes straining through the seeping whiteness for any sign of movement outside, wishing he'd brought a couple of men over with him to keep guard. The island's police force of two wasn't likely to provide much protection if O'Driscoll came.

When O'Driscoll came.

He pulled the passenger list from his pocket again. There was no boat from the mainland in winter, so he would have had no choice but to fly. Shenfield had read the names on the list so often, he knew them by heart. Yesterday, the eighteenth of December, there had been four flights, all fully booked. Given that Meg Evans had been murdered around six in the morning, and allowing him time to get down from Blackport, the only flight he could have made had left Penzance at sixteen hundred. But he hadn't been booked on, and there had been no last-minute requests for tickets. With the fog, theirs would be the only flight across today. There was no way O'Driscoll could be on St Mary's yet. Relax, Shenfield told himself. Be patient.

He said the same to Christopher, pointing out that if he kept up his present level of stress, he'd crack up long before Flora had need of him. Christopher nodded. For a couple of minutes he sat down, picking up a magazine and riffling half-heartedly through its pages, before throwing it down and going over to examine the bookshelves.

After a while, Castledine joined him. 'Have you read any of my books?' he asked, his voice strained. He had clearly decided to attempt to heed Shenfield's advice as well. He took down a fat, luridly-covered paperback. Shenfield was surprised. It was more the sort of book he'd have expected Val Whitelaw to have; it looked out of place in this elegant room.

'A couple.' Christopher sounded embarrassed. 'I find I don't actually get much opportunity to . . .'

'What did you think of them?'

Christopher hesitated. 'I had expected them to be more . . . literary,' he said carefully.

'Literary,' Castledine repeated. He picked up a slimmer volume, which Shenfield recognised as Christopher's. 'I find I have little taste for literature these days. Would you be surprised to know that, apart from this, I haven't opened a book of poetry in fifteen years?'

'I'd be appalled.'

Castledine nodded slowly, before asking, 'Did

you ever meet my wife? You came up in what . . .
eighty-three?'

'Eighty-two.'

He stared down at the book, passing it absently
from one hand to the other. 'Flora's very like her
mother. Bright. Headstrong. And beautiful, of
course.' He breathed in sharply, as though in pain.
'Very beautiful.' He looked up. 'I met my wife . . .'
A small pause. '. . . My ex-wife, I should say, when
she was my student, did you know that?'

'No, I . . .' Christopher looked uncomfortable.

'Oh yes.' Castledine nodded again. With the
ghost of a smile he added, 'It caused quite a
scandal in the Senior Common Room. I expect you
can imagine. A confirmed old bachelor, falling
headlong for someone half – a third – his age.'

Shenfield, who had been listening with only half
an ear, began to concentrate. What was Castledine
getting at? Could he have seen through Christopher
already? If so, he was more astute than he looked.
Picking up a magazine, he watched his son out of
the corner of his eye, to see how he would react.

'I . . . I believe I met her, once. I came to the
house . . .' Christopher cleared his throat, his eyes
fixed on the neat rows of books. 'One of your sherry
parties . . .'

'Oh, a great many students came to the house.'
Castledine gave a short, bitter laugh. 'A great
many. But I was too stupid, too wrapped up in
the study of other people's lives, other people's
passions, to realise what was happening in my
own home. You see, I thought it would be enough,

238

our mutual love of literature. God knows, I had little enough else to offer her. Except my heart, of course.' He laughed his mirthless laugh again. 'I'm sorry, does that sound terribly trite? You must forgive me, my mind tends to work in such clichés, these days.'

'I would have thought . . .' Christopher bit his lip. He was still staring at the bookcase, his face taut. 'Poetry had been your life. Surely, in the face of your despair, it should have afforded you some sort of comfort, some escape. A safer place . . .' He broke off, his voice unsteady.

'I can see you still put your trust in make-believe, Christopher.' Castledine smiled at him sadly. 'I despise it.'

'I can't believe you mean that.'

Shenfield yawned, put the magazine down and shut his eyes. For a while, the conversation had sounded as if it might be leading somewhere. Now they were back to the intellectual clap-trap, he was getting bored. It was like sitting in on a bloody debating society, he thought irritably, wishing they'd both shut up and let him get a bit of kip in. But no, Castledine was sounding off again.

'So you suggest that rather than confront reality, we wrap ourselves in a cocoon of borrowed emotions?'

'And what is reality? Without literature, what is left? The sordid. The squalid. Pain, ugliness, despair . . .'

Shenfield could tell from the direction of Christopher's voice that he had turned towards him.

He resisted the temptation to open his eyes. If he opened his eyes, he'd open his mouth. Which would get him nowhere. They'd been down that road before. He didn't need confrontation. He didn't need conversation. What he needed was half an hour's nap. He settled himself more comfortably in his chair, beginning to feel himself drifting off, as the conversation droned on above his head.

'And literature can negate those things? Keep them at bay, even?' Castledine sounded suddenly weary. Maybe he was getting bored as well. 'You really believe that? Oh, Christopher! It is the greatest of all intellectual confidence tricks. Don't you see? In the face of *real* pain, *real* despair . . . real love . . .' He paused for so long that Shenfield began to wonder sleepily if he'd left the room. Then he went on in a low voice, 'In the face of real emotion, literature is utterly meaningless. Imagined passions to fill the empty spaces. Just *words.*' He let the book drop to the floor with a crash that made Shenfield, who had been about to nod off, leap from his chair in alarm.

'Flora's mother ran off to Canada with one of my graduate students, Chief Inspector.' Castledine turned to him. 'She holds us both in such high esteem that we have received no more than half a dozen letters from her in the last fifteen years, none of which I have permitted my daughter to see. My books are drivel, as Christopher knows, but is too polite to say. But they are lucrative drivel. They have allowed me to provide a good life for Flora, and it is in Flora that I have put my trust.' His voice shook, as he added, 'She's all I have left. Please don't let anything happen to her.'

It was all getting too heavy for Shenfield. Action, however unpleasant, he could deal with. This sort of confessional emotion frightened the hell out of him. Excusing himself, he went outside for a cigarette, hardly able, now, to see his hand in front of his face. Reaching into his pocket for his lighter, he felt instinctively for the passenger list, realising, as he did so, that he'd left it in the drawing room. He was tempted to go back for it. He felt that as long as he had it in his possession, like a talisman, they were safe. Fanciful rubbish, he told himself firmly. Spending so much time with intellectuals must be addling his brain. What he needed was some exercise, after being cramped up for the last nine hours. His stomach, distended with Mrs Menheniott's breakfast, rumbled its assent.

He decided to risk the path down to the sea as his eyes slowly became accustomed to the mist. A gentle walk, a hot bath, and he'd be ready for a good long sleep. A much-needed calm before the anticipated storm.

He'd gone no more than a hundred yards when he heard Castledine's voice, high-pitched with panic, call out his name. Turning sharply, and cursing as he lost his footing on the uneven ground, he made back in the direction of the shout.

The older man was stumbling towards him, the passenger list clutched in his hand.

'The play. *Romeo and Juliet!*' he babbled, as Shenfield neared him. 'Romeo Montague! That was

his character! I saw him, at the rehearsal, the time I
went up to Blackport . . .'

Shenfield looked at him blankly. First poetry,
now Romeo and bloody Juliet. What the hell was
the matter with the pair of them?

'R. Montague!' Castledine jabbed at the list. 'The
four o'clock flight. He's been here since yesterday,
you fool!'

As Castledine's words sank in, Shenfield's heart
began to hammer. Shouldering past him, he blun-
dered back to the house, taking the stairs two at a
time as he dashed up to Flora's room. The door was
open. The bedroom was empty.

'Tell Christopher to call the police,' he shouted,
tearing back down the stairs as Castledine reached
the hallway.

'He's gone,' the older man panted, clutching
the banister as he gasped for breath. 'He took
Menheniott's rifle. He said he was going after
them.'

Chapter Nineteen

As soon as she had heard Shenfield put down the telephone and go back into the drawing room, Flora had got up, crept down the stairs and let herself quietly out of the front door. She had to get away from Christopher and Simon's suffocating kindness, and Shenfield's relentless scrutiny, before she completely lost her sanity.

She welcomed the cold dampness of the mist against her face. She had slept until she could sleep no more, but still the nightmare remained. She felt like a rat in a maze; every path her brain took led to a dead end. If Kieran – she could only think of him as Kieran – if he were innocent, why had he run away? No. Not 'if '. She must not allow an 'if '. Who would believe him, if she began to doubt him? But how could she do anything but doubt, in the face of such overwhelming evidence?

She couldn't get out of her head a conversation they'd had early on; even before they were lovers. They had been reading through the scene in which Juliet discovers that Romeo has killed her cousin. Kieran had asked her if she could forgive anyone who had taken a life. And she had answered yes. If you loved someone enough, you could forgive them anything. Was it the play they had been talking about?

A movement behind her froze her with sudden panic, until she heard the soft whinny of a pony in the fields, appearing like a ghost as she turned. She held out her hand, desperate to feel the solidity of its warm flank, but it skittered nervously away from her, merging back into the mist as if it had never been.

She stumbled on, following the path up to a group of abandoned outbuildings more by instinct than sight. The bulk of the old barn where she had played her secret, solitary games as a child loomed ahead of her. The fog was a swirling, shifting wall of whiteness as she picked her way along the rutted track.

'Tread softly, because you tread on my dreams...'

He seemed so close. The urge to hold him overwhelmed her.

A twig snapped behind her.

Before she had time to turn, she was grabbed from behind, letting out one high, piercing scream, before a hand was clamped over her mouth.

'Don't be frightened,' Kieran whispered, pressing himself against her. 'Please, don't ever be frightened of me.'

As soon as they were in the barn, he released her. Catching sight of her bruises, he put his fingers to her cheek, but she flinched and backed away from him.

'You think I did it,' he said heavily.

'I don't know what to think.' Her teeth were chattering. 'What am I supposed to think, when you disappear without a trace? I didn't want to believe what they were saying, but you weren't there.' The wall of silence she had built around herself was broken, and all the fear and grief and anger she had been damming up poured out. He stood quite still, offering no resistance, as she hurled herself against him, pounding at him with her fists until, exhausted, she leant her head against him, sobbing, 'Why weren't you there?'

'Look at me, Flora. Do you believe I murdered Meg?'

Shivering, she drew her coat around her as she scanned his face.

'No,' she said at last.

He looked so sad. Grey and diminished. Could it really be an act? Yet the police said there was no record of his existence. No one called Kieran Willerton . . .

'But it doesn't make sense. Why run away? Why go to the trouble of wiping your fingerprints off everything before you left, if you'd got nothing to hide?'

Her head was pounding, her brain still fuddled with too many tranquillisers; the words were out of her mouth before she considered how dangerous they might be. Just saying them aloud made her realise afresh how incriminated he was. What if he'd been fooling her all along? Bewitching her into believing in him as he bewitched his audience each time he stepped up on stage? She had visualised his face constantly in the last two days. In the flesh, he looked different. The magic all gone. And if Kieran Willerton didn't exist, then who was this semi-stranger? She glanced towards the door, trying to judge how many strides it would take his longer legs to reach her.

'If you don't believe me, just go and call the police.' He made no move to touch her again. 'I'll not try to stop you.'

'They're here already. Back at the farm. They're probably out looking for me now,' she added quickly.

'Christ,' he muttered, leaning his head against the wall and closing his eyes, the muscle in his cheek throbbing. 'It didn't take the bastards long.'

She could make a run for it now. His reaction had answered her questions. But still something held her back. Almost pleadingly, she said, 'Just tell me you're not a murderer.'

He opened his eyes. The silence between them seemed unbreakable. Then, in a low voice, he said, 'I can't do that.'

'Oh.' The sound came as though the breath had been knocked out of her. She swallowed hard, feeling the sweat prickle her palms.

He turned his face away from her and said softly, 'I've rehearsed in my head how I was going to do this every day since we met. The first time I saw you . . . those first weeks . . . I tried not to get involved. I told myself it could never work. But I couldn't stop myself.'

She willed him to look at her, desperate to read his expression, search him for lies as he went on, 'That's why I followed you here. I knew they'd pick me up. But I had to see you. Tell you the truth, like I should have done from the start. Because the other way was destroying us both.'

Her eyes flicked between his face and the door.

'Please, Flora.' At last he looked into her face. 'I'm not going to harm you, I swear. Just give me a few minutes to try and explain, before they come. Will you do that?'

His eyes were burning her, melting her. She nodded dumbly.

'Yesterday morning I went to the train station. I was going to come down here with you, see you in your own world. Only you weren't there. So I went to the flat. And there were police everywhere. They wouldn't tell me what was going on, then one of the reporters told me about Meg. Then another bloke said the police knew who'd done it – and said my name. I didn't know what to do. I wanted so much to be with you, but if I stayed, I'd be arrested. You do believe me, don't you? Please, Flora.' He reached out his hand to her. 'Just tell me you—'

'Get away from her!'

They both swung around as the barn door crashed open. Christopher stood in the doorway.

'No!' she screamed, as he raised the rifle.

Kieran stood transfixed, his arms held out as if in supplication.

'Don't shoot!' Instinctively, she moved to Kieran's side.

247

'Don't try to protect him, Flora. You have to face the truth. He murdered Meg, and now he wants to murder you. Walk away from him slowly.' Christopher's finger rested on the trigger. 'Towards the door.'

'Why are you doing this to me, Christopher?' Kieran's voice was scarcely a whisper. 'Whatever you feel about Flora . . .'

Her eyes widened, colour flooding her face as she stared at him.

The gun trembled slightly. 'He's lying, Flora. His whole life's a lie. Just come towards me. You're safe now.'

'Trust me.' Kieran tore his eyes from the barrel of the gun and turned his head very slowly towards her. 'Look into my eyes. You know I'm not lying to you.'

'How can you trust him? He's acting. He acts all the time.'

'He's jealous, Flora. He wants you for himself.'

'He's cornered, and he knows it. He'd say anything. You've heard the evidence. How can you trust anything he's told you?'

Christopher's voice was getting louder and louder, battering at her, confusing her. She put her hands to her ears to block out the merciless words. 'Stop it,' she screamed. 'Stop it, stop it, stop . . .'

'It's all right.' Shenfield's voice, deadly calm and quiet, silenced her abruptly. He moved towards Christopher, saying slowly, 'I can take care of this, lad. You can put the gun down now.'

Christopher half-turned, then jerked back around to Kieran. 'He was going to kill her.'

Shenfield took a step forward. 'Remember me?'

She felt Kieran stiffen. He said in a sneering voice she barely recognised as his, 'I can see the blue light on the top of your head, if that's what you mean, so I know you'll not believe a word I tell you, even if it does happen to be true.'

'You don't fool me, you bastard. I know who you are.'

Kieran turned back to her, looking deep into her eyes. 'Whatever they say to you, I want you to know that meeting you was the best thing that's ever happened to me.' He glanced beyond her and added bitterly, 'Whatever, Christopher, I'll always thank you for that.' The gun barrel came up again towards his head, but his gaze was back on her, mesmerising her, drawing her like a moth to a flame. 'You're the first person in my life that's made me feel like I mattered.'

'Yeah, yeah. Save it for Mills and Boon.' Shenfield took another step forward. 'Think of it, Flora. Think of what he's done. If Meg hadn't turned up when she did, it would have been you lying in that garden with your skull smashed in. Think about that.'

'No.' She put her hands to her ears.

'It's not true, Flora!' He grabbed her arm and pulled her around to face him. 'Don't listen to him.'

'He butchered your best friend, Flora. You saw what he did to her. Take a long, hard look at him and tell me you still want to protect him.' Shenfield glanced at the gun, realising she'd been manoeuvred directly into the firing line. 'For God's sake, put that bloody thing down, Christopher, before you hurt someone,' he snapped, before turning back. 'You followed her to the ball, didn't you? Just like she knew you would. Only you followed her back to Myles Delahunt's, and all. And when you realised what the two of them were up to, you were beside yourself with jealousy. Your innocent, perfect little Flora, being poked by another man.' Shenfield saw the spasm of pain that crossed his face at the coarseness of the words. Flora was crying hysterically. He heard Christopher's strangled sob from behind him, but he knew he could not afford to lose focus now. If he could just get under his skin, provoke him into incriminating himself . . .

'Some other man's hands on her body. Feeling her. Tasting her. Violating her . . .'

Shenfield saw him flinch, put his hand instinctively to his face, as if warding off a blow. As he slackened his hold, Shenfield darted suddenly forward, grabbed Flora by the wrist and dragged her away from him. Then he pulled out a pair of handcuffs, wrenched Kieran's arms behind his back and began, 'You do not have to say anything, but . . .'

'It doesn't matter,' he called over the caution, his eyes not leaving her as Shenfield snapped the cuff onto his wrist. 'I love you, Flora. I'll always love you.' He tried to pull towards her, jerking

Shenfield off-balance. 'Nothing matters, as long as . . .'

The rest of his words were lost as Flora screamed, 'No, Christopher!'

High above the headland, the gulls wheeled and cried in fright as a single shot rang out.

Chapter Twenty

Ray Whitelaw pressed on his false beard and looked at his reflection in the bedroom mirror.

It had become a tradition over the years. Whatever case he was on, somehow he always managed to spare the time to get into the outfit that hung all year in the spare bedroom wardrobe and turn up at Val's school for the Christmas party. The job had made him break a lot of promises to Val in the twenty-eight years they'd been married, but he'd never missed a Christmas party.

He was proud of Val, and her work. A lot of people thought teaching was a dosser's job, but there was no way he would have the patience to deal with a classful of kids, let alone handicapped kids, day in and day out the way she did. Although he could see that it had its rewards; the pure, uninhibited joy on their young faces when he walked into the school hall as Father Christmas was like a breath of fresh air.

He eased himself into his boots. Val always teased him that he must be the only Father Christmas in England who polished his wellington boots, but he liked everything to be just right for the kiddies.

He went out onto the landing, trying to focus on the party and empty his mind of work. He had a precious week's leave ahead of him, and he intended to make the most of it. He'd even taken the phone off the hook, just to be on the safe side.

It wasn't the job he'd gone into twenty-five years ago, when the most important rules were to keep his boots clean and his notebook up to date, when loyalty to his fellow officers was so taken for granted he never even thought about it. Things had been less complicated, then; law-breakers on one side, coppers on the other. Now it was all politics; 'measurable efficiency', clear-up rates. The biggest threats came not from the villains, but from colleagues, and that was corrosive. It made him less sure which side he was on.

He'd been so delighted at Medlock ending up with egg on his face that he'd allowed himself to forget that Meg Evans was just as dead, whoever had killed her. Taking her father to identify the body had brought him up sharp. As if the poor sod could have given a toss about their petty in-fighting. All he'd wanted was his daughter back.

It had made him question whether he wanted to be a part of it any more.

Down in the kitchen, Val was making great plates of sandwiches for the party. The room smelled of warmth and cooking. Racks of mince pies and cakes were cooling on the table. An admiring grin spread over her plump face as she looked up at him.

'You look terrific!' she beamed. 'Do you want something to eat before we go?'

Whitelaw pointed ruefully at the red fabric stretched tight over his stomach and shook his head. 'Either you're going to have to let this out next year, or I'm going to have to go on a diet!' It was impossible to be out of spirits for long in Val's company.

'And to think we had to pad you out with cushions when you first took on the job!' she laughed as she put her arms around his waist. 'We're getting old and fat, Mr Whitelaw!'

'Mature and cuddly,' he grinned, helping himself to a mince pie.

He helped her pack the carefully-wrapped presents into his sack, knowing that this year, as every year, she had supplemented the meagre grant she was allowed for presents with her own money, choosing each gift with love and care. Taking her in his arms, he hugged her hard to him, kissing her soft, greying hair.

'Hey, what's all this about?' she laughed, her face muffled against him as he clung to her.

'I love you, Val Whitelaw,' he said fiercely. 'I don't tell you that as often as I should.'

'You don't need to tell me.' She squeezed him, then pushed him gently away. 'Now move yourself, Santa. You've got work to do.'

They were nearly at the school when Whitelaw's mobile rang.

'Here we go,' Val murmured, rolling her eyes.

'I thought I told you I wasn't, under any circumstances, to be . . .' Whitelaw started, cursing himself for not taking the phone out of the car. He broke off, his face creasing into a frown as he listened intently. 'Christ,' he said at last. 'When did this happen? Well why the bloody hell didn't you get in touch sooner? All right, all right. So Lambert's on his way back now? Jesus. I'm glad I didn't have to break it to him. And Medlock? Yes. I just bet he is. What? No, leave that to me. I'm on my way.' Clicking off the phone, he rubbed his hands across his face before turning to Val apologetically. 'Sorry, love.'

She shrugged, and gave him a determined smile. 'Can't be helped. Trouble?'

'Could say that.'

'Anything I can do?'

He shook his head. 'Go to your party. I'll tell you about it later.' He reached across and squeezed her hand. 'Looks like we've got our Beast of Blackport. Funny, I always thought I'd be dead chuffed to be able to say that.'

'Not one word,' he warned as he strode into the station, tugging at the false beard.

'Right.' The desk sergeant almost succeeded in keeping a straight face. 'Want me to get one of the boys from Traffic over to take care of Rudolph? What's going on in there, anyway? Lambert turned up five minutes ago, looking like . . .'

But Whitelaw was already half way down the

corridor. He changed hurriedly in the Gents. As he reached the top of the stairs, Lambert came out of his office, his face taut. 'In here. Now.'

'Any more news from the Scillies?' Whitelaw asked, following him in.

'Well, let's put it this way,' Lambert snapped. 'He's been blasted in the chest at point-blank range, he's in what sounds like some one-eyed cottage hospital that's probably not used to dealing with anything more serious than sunburn, and they can't get him off the island because it's fog-bound. How would you rate his chances?' He closed the door behind them, looked Whitelaw in the eye, and said, 'Before we go any further, I want it absolutely clear that no one in this station had any reason to believe that Shenfield and Christopher Heatherington were related. Is that understood?'

Whitelaw understood perfectly, even before Lambert underlined his point by continuing. 'Any officer who had that information and withheld it will, of course, be dealt with accordingly. Clear?'

For an instant, Whitelaw was tempted to walk straight back out of the door and down the corridor to the Chief Constable's office, but only for an instant.

'Quite clear.' He met Lambert's gaze. 'I assume that, under the circumstances, I shall be taking over the investigation from Chief Inspector Shenfield?'

It was a very small victory, and they both knew it was the only one he was likely to achieve on Shenfield's behalf, but still Whitelaw was gratified

that it was Lambert who looked away first and said,
'For the moment.'

Lambert sat down, seeming to regain his composure once he had his desk between them. The
matter, his manner suggested, was closed. Impatiently gesturing Whitelaw to a chair opposite, he
went on, 'In the forty-eight hours I've been away
from Blackport, Shenfield has besieged the university campus in order to arrest the wrong man, and
has succeeded in letting the right one slip through
his fingers. Assuming this character actually is
O'Driscoll. And I do hope I'm not going to get any
more nasty shocks when I review the evidence.'

Whitelaw hoped so too. Forensic had failed to
come up with a thing. The Wharf Street address was
a waste of time. And years of student occupation
had plastered every surface in the Aigburth Street
flat with so many prints that analysis was hopeless.
The only firm evidence they had was Christopher's
identification. In which he'd now blown a hole, both
literally and metaphorically.

'I want this debacle cleared up fast. Is that clear?'
Lambert was warming to his theme. 'Let's at least
try to salvage what's left of this force's credibility.
Six years it's taken us to track this man down, six
years, and what happens as soon as we make a
breakthrough? We hand his lawyers enough
ammunition to blow the case clean out of the water,
that's what. If it ever gets as far as lawyers, which I
very much doubt. I take it you've seen this
lunchtime's headlines in the *Echo*? Quite an
achievement, to turn the Beast of Blackport into a

victim of police corruption before we'd even got
him cautioned.'

Whitelaw took the paper from him, his heart
sinking as he saw the headline: 'Student Suspect
Shot in Love Triangle'.

'I think the phrase is "own goal".' Lambert's
voice shook with suppressed fury. 'And in case that
isn't bad enough, the Chief Constable has had
Heatherington's boss, some Professor . . .' He
consulted the memo on his desk, '. . . Muldoon
ringing up claiming he witnessed a scuffle between
the two of them outside Heatherington's office only
the day before the Evans murder. One can imagine
how long that story will take to get out. Just what
kind of an idiot is this son of Shenfield's?'

Whitelaw guessed Lambert wasn't expecting an
answer. With a non-committal shake of his head, he
read on.

'*A young girl watched in horror yesterday as her
lover was brutally gunned down by the jealous rival
who, according to fellow students, had regularly
been seen by her side in recent weeks. Blackport
University student Kieran Willerton was critically
injured on the holiday paradise of St Mary's by thirty-
something lecturer Christopher Heatherington,
author of a recently-published book of passionate
love poetry, and self-styled "family friend" of
Kieran's girlfriend, flame haired history student
Flora Castledine. Flora is the daughter of reclusive
novelist Simon Castledine, who lives on the island.*

'*Two days ago, Heatherington named Kieran as
the Beast of Blackport, following the grisly murder*

of Flora's flatmate Megan Evans. Today, Echo reporter Sid Barker has discovered, in a plot more outlandish than in any of Castledine's string of bestsellers, that Heatherington is none other than the estranged son of the officer in charge of the murders, DCI David . . .'

'It's "Kieran", you notice, not "Willerton". Quite clear where the *Echo*'s sympathies lie.'

'As always.'

'Don't be so bloody naive,' Lambert snapped. 'We all know the score with the press, and that includes Shenfield. What the hell did he think he was doing, allowing the fool over there on police business? Taking a family holiday at the force's expense?' Another rhetorical question. 'Well, we'll find out when you get Heatherington back here. Under arrest.'

'And O'Driscoll, Sir?' Whitelaw risked.

'He's likely to be answering to a higher authority than the courts, if what the doctors have to say can be believed. And you do realise, if he dies on us he's not even going to show up as a conviction? Nine, that's *nine* murders, if we include Melanie Loveridge, wiped off the performance indicators.' Lambert's face purpled at the thought. 'Not that the most incompetent brief in the country couldn't get him off after this fiasco. Take my word for it, Whitelaw. Heads are going to roll.'

And you're going to make damned sure yours won't be one of them, Whitelaw thought, as Lambert snatched back the paper and went on, 'I've already spoken to DC Medlock. He's going with you.' His expression made it clear he was not asking Whitelaw's opinion. 'Now get out, and let me try to concentrate on what I'm going to say at the bloody press conference.'

Whitelaw was still seething when, the following morning, they touched down on St Mary's. All the way from Blackport, Medlock had been fidgeting around in barely-contained excitement, like a kid on his way to a birthday party, at the prospect of arresting Shenfield's son. Of his meeting with Lambert, he would divulge nothing, but Whitelaw was all too aware that he would never have agreed to keep his mouth shut about the whole sorry business if there were nothing in it for him.

The flight had done nothing to improve Whitelaw's humour. He stepped out onto the tarmac of St Mary's heliport with a sense of profound relief. The last twenty minutes had been the most hair-raising of his entire existence. He'd never been happy in planes. Not that you could really call the sardine tin with wings that he'd been forced to board at Land's End a plane.

Medlock was standing by the tiny arrivals building, deep in conversation with his mobile phone, looking ludicrously out of place in his sharp suit and dazzling white shirt amongst the bobble hats and crumpled anoraks of their fellow-travellers.

Whitelaw stretched gingerly, and looked around him. Below the cliffs that made up the terrifying approach to the runway, the sea sparkled a tranquil blue. The small bay was fringed by field upon field of daffodils, the scent of which seemed to fill the balmy air. After the raw chill of Blackport, he felt as if he'd stepped into the pages of a travel brochure. He just wished that what was in front of him was a holiday.

'Sergeant Whitelaw, Sir? I'm Constable Tregannan.' The strong Cornish accent that interrupted his thoughts belonged to an elderly officer who saluted clumsily, before bending to pick up Whitelaw's bags. 'Sergeant Conroy sends his apologies, Sir. He's up at the Castledine place at the moment. Welcome to St Mary's. Did you have a good trip?'

Unable to think of words to adequately describe the journey, Whitelaw said, 'It was different.'

Medlock bounced up, still wearing the same infuriating expression of quiet confidence as he pocketed his mobile and scribbled in his notebook.

Jerking his head towards him, Whitelaw said briefly, 'My DC.'

Tregannan nodded at Medlock, leaving him to pick up his own bags, much to Whitelaw's satisfaction.

As they walked back to the car park, Tregannan brought him up to date. 'We've kept the press at bay so far, Sir. Couple of the papers have had a go at chartering planes to get across, same as you, but Bob Boscombe – he's in charge up here at the heliport – he's not giving landing permission. Not that they'd have got across anyway before now. You've brought the good weather with you,' he observed, crunching the gears as he reversed down a rutted path and away from the landing strip. 'Thick fog all day yesterday. They couldn't even get the air ambulance over, it was that bad. You were lucky to get across.'

Whitelaw glanced back balefully at the plane. 'Very lucky,' he muttered. 'How's the suspect? I assume they'll be transferring him to the mainland, now the weather's cleared.'

'Not unless you're talking about in a wooden box,' Tregannan replied. 'His condition's too unstable to shift him now. That's what Dr Jackson says, at any rate. He's the GP.'

Whitelaw was astounded. 'A GP's treating him?'

'Isn't anybody else, is there? Anyway, he's a good old boy. Been doing it for years.' Tregannan sounded hurt.

'Talking of press,' Medlock evidently considered he had been left out of the conversation long enough, 'fill me in on what's in this morning's papers.'

'Oh, no papers yet, lad!' Tregannan laughed. 'Haven't had those for the last forty-eight hours. They'll be over on the helicopter later. Hopefully.'

They bounced along narrow lanes banked by drystone walls and straggling hedges in the ancient mini van, which passed as the island's police car.

'I suppose I shouldn't say so, but this is all quite exciting for us. We don't usually get anything much more serious than the odd drunk and disorderly, even in the holiday season,' Tregannan went on. 'Bit different from your neck of the woods, I 'spect, Sir?'

'You could say that.' He glanced out of the

window at the flower-filled fields beyond. 'Where exactly did the incident take place?'

'Can't reach it by road, I'm afraid, Sir. I could take you there now, if you want, but I thought you'd probably be wanting to speak to Dr Heatherington first.'

'Where are you holding him?' Medlock asked.

'He's staying with the Chief Inspector. At Mr Castledine's.'

'You mean to say you haven't got him in custody?' Medlock spluttered.

'We've got no proof he's committed a crime, yet, have we?' Tregannan said mildly. 'The suspect made a lunge at them when the Chief Inspector was trying to make the arrest, and Menheniott's rifle went off. I doubt if Dr Heatherington could have hit anyone on purpose with it if he tried. I wouldn't take him for an expert marksman, and most of the guns over here only shoot round corners anyway. There's not a rabbit on the island won't testify to that.' He glanced into the driving mirror. Medlock glared back at him. 'And he can't go anywhere, can he? The whole island's only nine miles round.'

'Is that right?' Whitelaw muttered as they hit another boulder in the road. It felt more like ninety. Any bone that had remained intact during the flight was being shaken from its socket. He didn't add, because he realised Medlock would already have reached the conclusion unaided, that at point-blank range, Christopher would have needed neither a good aim nor a good weapon.

'I thought you might like to go to the guest house

for a wash and some breakfast before you get started, Sir. There's not many open this time of year, of course, but Mrs Pender up at the Garrison's fixed you up. Nice and handy for Hughtown.'

'That's the main town, is it?'

'That's correct,' Tregannan nodded.

They drove on, past a tiny greystone church perched on the edge of a sandy bay filled with small fishing boats bobbing on the calm water.

'Could be the middle of summer, couldn't it?' Whitelaw remarked, as Tregannan honked the horn and waved to a group of children running along the beach.

The van toiled and groaned up a steep hill, and turned into a narrow street, lined on one side with granite cottages and bounded on the other by the ever-present sea. In front of them, a handful of buildings clustered around a small green.

Medlock looked impatiently at his watch. 'How much further is this Hughtown? We need to get on with the interviews as soon as possible.'

'This is it,' Tregannan grinned, as they passed a row of shops and a post office and squeezed into an even narrower street that led almost vertically through a narrow archway and up towards a squat stone castle perched on the cliffs above them. 'Star Castle,' he explained proudly. 'Been here since Tudor times, it has. Did you know that the Dutch declared war on Scilly in . . . ?'

Cutting short the travelogue, Medlock said curtly, 'You've taken a statement from Heatherington I assume?'

'And Miss Castledine and the Chief Inspector. And we've sealed off the scene of the incident, ready for when we can get a forensic team over. We have heard of police procedure over here, believe it or not.'

'I'm sure Constable Tregannan and his sergeant have everything under control,' Whitelaw snapped. The last thing he wanted was to alienate the local force before they got started; knowledge of the vicinity looked as if it were going to be even more vital than usual on St Mary's.

Finally, they pulled up outside a small white-washed cottage. Whitelaw was struck again by the incongruity of the riotous daffodils that shared the front garden with a Christmas tree strung with fairy lights. He'd had enough of this odd, disorderly place already. He missed the organised chaos of the incident room. He missed the filthy Blackport weather. Most of all he missed Val's warm kitchen.

'I'll leave you to have a spot of breakfast, Sir,' Tregannan said, when he had carried Whitelaw's bag inside. 'I'll pick you up in about half an hour, if that's convenient. I'm sure Mrs Pender can fill you in on anything you need to know in the meantime.'

It didn't take Whitelaw more than five minutes to find out what he meant. Vera Pender appeared to be related to just about everyone on the island, and as such was able to fill them in on almost every detail of the case.

'My niece works up at the hospital,' she said, as

she bustled around setting the table in the front room, 'and she said they had the priest in earlier, giving your chappy the last rites, or whatever they call it. Not that he deserves them, in my opinion. Not after what he's done.'

Whitelaw grunted non-commitally, and stared out of the window at the panoramic view of the off-islands. If there was one thing he could do to help Dave Shenfield and his son, it was to play things strictly by the rules. And that didn't include discussing the case with Scilly's answer to Sid Barker.

'Funny old business, that Dr What's-his-name being the Chief Inspector's son, though, isn't it?' She paused, head on one side, marmalade pot in hand, and gave him an inquisitive stare. 'My husband's cousin does a bit of cleaning over at the Castledine house, you know, and she reckons—'

'Just a cup of tea will do fine, for now,' Whitelaw cut her off. He could practically feel the down-draught from Medlock's ears.

'Oh, are you sure?' Vera Pender looked disappointed. 'I got a nice bit of bacon in specially. My lad, the one who works in the Co-op, brought it in earlier, and he was telling me he's heard that . . .'

Whitelaw got to his feet. 'Have you got a phone we could use, Mrs Pender?' He turned to Medlock. 'Give Tregannan a ring. Tell him to pick us up straight away.' He added in as even a tone as he could manage, as Medlock jumped to his feet, 'I'm sure you're as keen to get on with this as I am, Constable.'

*

A quarter of an hour later, Whitelaw was sitting in the mini van outside the small, single-storey hospital built on the cliffs above Hughtown, and realising just how much he didn't want to go inside. Whatever had happened in that barn, he knew he was going to have to take Christopher Heatherington back to Blackport in custody. Anything else would look like a whitewash. But he had a horrible feeling Shenfield wasn't going to see things that way. Reluctantly, he opened the door. Medlock was out already, drumming his fingers against the roof of the van, anxious to be in on the kill.

Well, at least he could deny him that.

'You. Stay here,' he ordered, getting out and drawing himself to his full five feet nine and a half.

Medlock stared down at him. 'No way.'

'Listen, you cocky little . . .' He made a grab for the immaculate lapel, controlling himself just in time. By the rules, he reminded himself. Taking a deep breath, he said, 'I'm in charge of this investigation now. And you'll obey my orders, if you don't want to find yourself on a charge when we get back to Blackport.'

'And what would that be for? Subverting the course of justice maybe? Face it, Whitelaw. Shenfield's at best incompetent, at worst totally corrupt, and I intend to find out which. Either way, he's finished.'

Whitelaw pressed his face very close to the other

man's. 'Crow all you like,' he hissed. 'If O'Driscoll doesn't pull through, you'll be every bit as responsible for his death as Heatherington. If you hadn't let him slip through your fingers in the first place, none of this would have happened.'

'I don't think that would stand up in court, do you?'

'I'm not talking about court. I'm talking about moral bloody responsibility.' He looked hard into Medlock's bland face, then shook his head. 'What's the point?' he muttered as he pushed open the door. 'You haven't got the first idea what I'm talking about, have you?'

'Think about it,' Medlock called after him. 'If you don't take a big step back from Shenfield, right now, you're going to end up in the shit with him.'

'I'll bear that in mind, Constable. In the meantime, you'll stay here. I've no doubt you'll find a chance to put the knife in later.'

'You can depend on it, Sergeant,' Medlock murmured at his retreating back.

Shenfield was in the corridor, dragging surreptitiously on the cigarette in his cupped hand. Stubbing it out hastily, he took Whitelaw's hand between both of his.

'Christ, am I glad to see you. I was afraid they might have sent—'

'They have. He's outside. For God's sake, Dave. What did you expect after your son takes it into his head to play Wyatt bloody Earp? Have you any idea of the capital Medlock can make out of this?'

'They should be giving Christopher a medal. O'Driscoll went straight at him. If he hadn't pulled that trigger . . .'

Whitelaw met his gaze, and held it. Shenfield looked away first, muttering, 'Well, I'm proud of him. I didn't think he'd got it in him.'

Whitelaw felt as if he was kicking a cripple, but it had to be done. 'You'd better see what the papers are saying, Dave.'

He looked away, reluctant to watch his face as he flicked through the press cuttings.

'Do me a favour, Ray,' Shenfield said at last. 'Make sure Christopher doesn't get to see this. He's cut up enough as it is.' To Whitelaw's amazement, a small grin appeared at the corners of his mouth as he went on, 'You've got to admit it, though. She's a bit of a looker. If I was twenty years younger . . .'

'You just don't get it, do you?' Whitelaw shouted, snatching the papers back. 'Medlock's out there, practically wetting himself with glee, and you're—'

'Listen.' Shenfield pointed at the door behind him. 'In that room is a cold-blooded, manipulative killer. So Christopher's put a bullet in him. So what? One less piece of scum cluttering up the prisons.'

'So you're judge, jury and executioner, now?' Shenfield's indifference chilled him. It was the sort of thing they all said now and then. But Shenfield sounded as if he meant it. 'Since when has it been our job to . . . ?'

'Stuff the job. I'll resign.'

'You'll be bloody lucky to get the chance. If you're expecting Lambert to back you up . . .'

'Stuff Lambert and all. I've had it with the lot of them. For once in his life, Christopher's done something worthwhile, and I'm proud of him.'

'We'll talk later.' Whitelaw suddenly felt dog-tired. 'Why don't you go back to the Castledine place? I'll need you both to make a statement.'

'With pleasure.'

There was just the slightest waver of fear, of entreaty, behind the defiance in Shenfield's face. He knew, they both knew, what prison would do to someone like Christopher. Whitelaw closed his eyes. How had he managed to get himself into this bloody mess? Whichever way he jumped, someone was going to get shot down in flames. He put his hand on Shenfield's shoulder. 'You get on back to Christopher. I'd better take a look at O'Driscoll.'

Flora Castledine, her back towards the door, sat by the bed, with its paraphernalia of transfusion bags, drips and monitors. O'Driscoll lay motionless, his head turned towards her, eyes half-open, his tangle of dark hair a shocking contrast against the snowy sheet, his chest swathed in bandages.

Whitelaw looked intently into the bloodless face, searching – hoping – for the resemblance about which Shenfield was so adamant, but what he saw was empty, devoid of any hint of emotion or expression that must once have given it its individuality. A thin trail of saliva dribbled from the corner of the slack mouth. Tregannan had said they'd had to resuscitate him three times on the way to the hospital; it didn't take a brain surgeon to work out the implications. As Whitelaw watched, Flora took a tissue and wiped it away with a gesture of such infinite tenderness that he looked away, an intruder on the intimacy of the moment.

The movement made her start, and she looked up, putting her finger to her lips, as though hoping that the disturbance might wake him.

'He's sleeping now,' she said, 'but earlier on, he moved his fingers, so I know he can hear us.'

'That's encouraging,' Whitelaw murmured, catching the eye of the nurse who was checking the drips. She compressed her lips and shook her head slightly.

Whitelaw looked down, his eyes falling on the arm that lay limp against the starched sheet. He recoiled as he saw it was handcuffed to the metal cot-side.

'For Christ's sake get that thing off,' he rasped.

'Chief Inspector Shenfield gave instructions . . .'

'Get it off.' Pushing the nurse aside, he struggled with the catch. 'Whatever he's done, he doesn't deserve that,' he muttered, as he prised it off and gently massaged the angry red indentation it left behind.

'You'll have to wait outside now, I'm afraid. I can't have you disturbing the patient.' The nurse sounded huffy. 'I'm only following your colleague's instructions, you know.'

'Thank you.' Flora looked up at him with a wan smile.

'I'll, er . . . I'll need a few words, later,' he

said gruffly. 'I'll . . . I'll wait outside, until you're ready.'

He backed out, shutting the door quietly behind him, found a chair and sat down, pulling out the packet of cigarettes he'd promised Val he wouldn't smoke.

He wasn't sure how long he'd been slumped staring at the green-washed plaster, when a small commotion from O'Driscoll's room made him sit up.

'What's going on?' he asked, as the nurse hurried from the room in a rustle of starch and antiseptic.

She eyed his cigarette, but made no comment. Instead, she flexed her back wearily, and shook her head. 'She thinks he moved his eyes. I said I'd fetch the doctor.'

'Did he? Move his eyes?' Whitelaw realised he was desperate for her to say yes.

'No.'

'Will he?'

'She thinks he will. By rights, he should have died by the time he got here, but he didn't. The chances of him making it this far were infinitesimal, but he has. Her willpower's keeping him alive. Who knows? Maybe it'll make him pull through.'

'You believe that?'

She shrugged non-commitally. 'I've seen stranger things. Needs her head examining, if you ask me.'

It was a long time since Whitelaw had prayed, but he prayed now. There had been too much death.

*

'Are you intending to interview Heatherington today, or do you want me to do it?' He looked up from the clasped steeple of his fingers to see Medlock advancing up the corridor towards him, and hauled himself to his feet, casting a glance at the closed door to O'Driscoll's room.

'I was just waiting . . .'

'They'll let us know if there's any change.' Medlock was impatient for action. 'He's not going anywhere. Heatherington might.'

Whitelaw took a last, hopeful look back down the corridor as they reached the entrance, and muttered, more to himself than to Medlock, 'She's just a kid. They're both just kids. I don't know. It seems all wrong . . .'

'Well, of course it does.' Medlock opened his eyes wide. 'It *is* all wrong. Haven't you even worked that out, yet?'

Chapter Twenty-one

After a sleepless night, Christopher had risen at dawn, ringing the hospital, his heart hammering, to be told that there was no change. As soon as it was light enough, he had taken the path down to the sea, walking on across the downs, until he came at last to Porth Hellick bay, the water flat calm in the clear morning light.

It was peaceful here. He climbed out along an outcrop of boulders, scattering the breakfasting seagulls, and sat on the springy turf, looking out to sea. He picked up a pebble and dropped it into the placid water, watching his reflection shiver, break and disappear beneath the surface. He was beginning to understand why Simon, in his own despair, had felt bound to the Scillies. There was an elemental timelessness about the stark granite cliffs and weird, towering rock formations that dwarfed mere human passions. Pulpit Rock. The Loaded Camel. They had stood for thousands of years before he had lived, and would stand for thousands more, unaware of his existence, after he died. The thought was a comfort.

He was unsure how many hours he'd been sitting there. From nowhere, a wind had sprung up, bending the meagre trees on the downs behind him, abruptly filling the sky with heavy, scudding clouds that blotted out the sun and pressed low on the horizon like a black curtain. Christopher pulled himself to his feet as a sudden burst of hail rattled against the rocky path. He welcomed its icy sting against his face.

Eventually, he rounded the headland and found himself in the shelter of a small bay. A tiny, single-storey church, incongruously fringed by a clump of palm trees, stood against the pale sand like a mirage, as unexpected and unreal as everything else in this mysterious place.

He made his way along the beach and into the still churchyard, glad of the solitude, and leant against the wrought-iron railings that bounded the ancient headstones struggling at crazy angles through the dank, overgrown vegetation. Beyond the calm of the bay, the Atlantic ocean crashed relentlessly against the rocks that circled the island like broken glass. How must it feel, to be tossed and pounded by those merciless waves, to feel the last gasp of breath being forced from bursting lungs? Would there be relief, a sense of peace, in that final moment before the water closed above your head for ever and you sank into the black, silent world below the turbulent surface?

He tried to remember what had happened, but the events surrounding the shooting were little more than a nightmare blur of images; freeze-frames from a violent, half-watched movie. Flora's screams, the kick of the rifle, the shock registering on Kieran's ghost-white face. The blood seeping through his jersey and spreading across the stone floor of the barn. The sound of his own blood, roaring in his ears. So much blood.

'They're here for you, Christopher.'

He started violently as a hand was laid on his shoulder.

'I saw you from the road.' Simon Castledine's voice came quietly from behind him. 'I was on my way back from the hospital.'

'He's going to die, isn't he?'

'I don't know. I honestly don't know. Come home now. You're wet through.'

'Is my father there?'

Simon nodded silently.

'He's proud of me. Can you believe it?' Christopher turned towards him, his eyes full of tears. 'That stupid, stupid man is proud of me.'

Whitelaw's small act of kindness had somehow made Flora admit her complete exhaustion in a way that the exhortations of her father, the nurses and Dr Jackson had not, and she had finally agreed to snatch half an hour's rest in a vacant consulting room. She had barely reached the end of the corridor before she heard the crash. Rushing back, heart in mouth, she was in time to see Kieran lying on the floor amidst a tangle of tubes from the over-turned drip stand. The nurse, alerted by the noise, pushed her aside. Calling for assistance, she pulled an oxygen mask over his face. 'All right now,' she said loudly. 'Don't struggle. Just breathe.'

He fought for air, his face a bluish grey, as an orderly ran in and helped to haul him back onto the bed.

'Don't be so rough with him,' Flora gasped.

The nurse shot her a look. 'Go and fetch Doctor, quick,' she muttered to the orderly. 'And get her out of here.'

'Come along.' The man took Flora by the elbow and bundled her from the room. 'You just leave everyone to do their job, Miss Castledine. You'll only be in the way.'

'He sensed I'd gone. He needs me here . . .'

'Come on now.' He steered her down the corridor. 'Don't go causing any trouble, or we'll have to get the policeman back.'

She stood helplessly in the corridor. Doctor Jackson nodded in hurried acknowledgement as he pushed past her. Nurses bustled to and fro. Someone offered her a cup of tea. She was vaguely aware of curious glances, of carols being sung in the main ward. An elderly man whom she recognised from the post office asked her if she wanted him to fetch her father, but her gaze and every nerve in her body remained focused on the closed door to Kieran's room.

'Just let him live,' she pleaded with the God she hadn't spoken to since childhood. Whoever he was, whatever he'd done, the last twenty-four hours had taught her that without him, she had no wish for life.

Finally, Doctor Jackson emerged, grim-faced as he peeled off bloodstained latex gloves, and came towards her. Flora put her hand to her mouth, as the floor tilted abruptly upwards.

'Catch her.' She heard the doctor from a very long way off, before he dissolved and floated away into spangled darkness.

'. . . extremely lucky young man.' She tried to concentrate, as the pink oval blob in front of her slowly took the shape of a face. The mouth was moving. One of the front teeth, she noticed, was crowned.

'Did you hear what I said?' Doctor Jackson asked, helping her to her feet, and sitting her down on a chair with a brisk instruction to put her head between her knees.

She looked up, nodding weakly as he came gradually back into focus, hardly daring to believe what her ears were telling her.

'I'm fairly confident he'll make a full recovery in time,' he went on, 'now we've ascertained there's no brain damage. The fall caused his wound to haemorrhage, but we've got that under control, and I've decided it's safe now to move him to the mainland. It's essential that he's kept quiet, of course. He's lost a lot of blood, and we certainly can't risk another haemorrhage. I've warned him what would happen if he were to make a second escape attempt.' He checked her pulse, then said, 'I'd tell you to get some rest, if I thought there was the remotest chance you'd take any notice.' He looked into her face, professional briskness replaced by concern. 'I know you'll say it's none of my business, Flora, but I think having seen you through measles, mumps and chickenpox gives me the right to ask. Are you sure you know what you're doing?' He sighed and shook his head in resignation. 'Very well. He's refusing sedation until he's seen you. The air ambulance will be here in about an hour.' His tone softened again as he added, 'I'll try to make sure the police are kept out of the way for a while.'

As soon as she entered the room, Kieran pulled himself up in the bed, struggling with the oxygen mask. The handcuff, she noticed, was back in place.

'Hush.' She put the oxygen mask back over his face and pushed him gently against the pillow. 'You must rest. Everything's going to be fine.'

He turned his head towards her, pulling down the mask again, and said with a weak shadow of his old smile, 'Bit dramatic, calling in a priest. Were you hoping it'd appeal to my sense of theatre, or what?'

He's back, she thought, offering up a silent prayer of thanks.

'It wasn't that we thought . . .' she began, anxious not to alarm him. Then, catching his eye, 'All right, but you're out of danger now. As long as you behave. What on earth did you think you were doing? Talk about sense of theatre! That was some way to come out of a coma!' How easy it was to fall into the role of nursemaid, humouring him as if he were a child, when there was so much unsaid that still had to be faced.

'I thought you'd left me.' A shadow across his eyes. 'They'll be taking me off the island soon. There's not long . . .' He pulled himself up again, trying to hide a grimace. 'Listen, Flora. I don't know what the police have said to you, but I'm telling you now. I've done a lot of things in my life I'm not proud of,' he gazed at her bruised cheek, 'including that. But I swear to you, I had nothing to do with Meg's death.'

She held his gaze. 'We've both done things we're not proud of.' A small silence. Then she said, 'I don't think you killed Meg. I've never thought that. But you said . . .' She looked away from him, then back. 'I don't understand what's going on, Kieran.' Another silence. His eyes moved slowly across her face, as if he were trying to memorise every detail of her. She said finally, 'I can't stop myself loving you, whatever you've done. I wish I could.' Then more gently, 'So just tell me the truth. I think you owe me that much.'

He nodded, then ran his tongue over his dry lips and said, 'I've been lying to you since the day we met. I wanted to tell you. Kept trying to screw up my courage. I nearly did, once. Then your dad turned up, and I realised just how impossible . . .' His voice trailed off. After a moment, he took a deep, catching breath and said, 'I've been in trouble with the police half my life. That's why they're trying to pin Meg's death on me. I've done all sorts. Including eight years for killing a bastard who deserved to die.' She started to speak, but he shook his head, holding up his free hand to silence her. 'I got the place at Blackport while I was still inside. I thought I could start again. Changed my sur-name. I was daft enough to think that was all it took. All I had to do was keep out of trouble, act the part, and no one would know me from the real thing. It worked, too. Until I met you.' He glanced at her fearfully. 'There. Now you know. Go, if you want to. I wouldn't blame you.'

She bent and kissed his damp hair. She might not understand what he was saying, but she knew with all her heart that she believed him. 'I told you, I'm not going anywhere.'

He gripped her hand, his head turned away from her, the tears spilling from under his closed lashes.

'Lie down now, sweetheart,' she soothed.

'They'll be coming for me.' His face contorted briefly in pain as she helped him back down the bed, then he said urgently, 'It's not enough just to tell you. I've got to try to explain . . .'

'Later. You're to rest.' How could she ever have doubted him? 'We'll get it sorted, you'll see. The police will have to listen, if you just tell them the truth.'

'I don't need to rest. I'm OK.' The handcuff clanked against the bed rail as he moved. 'See? They obviously think I'm well enough to try and leg it.' The wry grin he attempted couldn't disguise the anxiety in his eyes. As she started to try to reassure him again, he pressed his fingers to her lips and said, 'Please, Flora. Let me say what I've got to. For my sake as well as yours.'

She nodded, smoothing the hair back from his forehead as he stared at a point on the ceiling, swallowed hard and said, 'OK. Potted history of Kieran Henshall. Me.' His eyes flicked to her and then away. 'My gran brought me up. Good Catholic boy, Mass on Sundays, so you guessed right about the priest. She died when I was eleven. I didn't even know I had a mother, until Social Services tracked her down. No dad.' Another painful attempt at a smile, gaze still fixed on the ceiling. 'Could have been just about any bloke in Greater Manchester with the price of a couple of vodka and oranges and a tenner left over.'

Flora thought guiltily of just how often she had complained to him about Simon.

'Anyway, I got sent to live with her. Social Services policy, see. Keeping families together.' He closed his eyes. 'I'd just got a place at the Catholic Grammar. Right little smart-arse, me. I liked school, liked the books. I got a bit of stick from some of the others – free school dinners and that – but I didn't bother. I found I'd a talent for taking off the masters, making the other lads laugh. Then I got into acting.' He nodded absently, seemingly talking more to himself now than to Flora. 'Brilliant. I could be any-one I wanted, live inside my head. I got my first lead at school. *Hamlet*, we were doing. It was great; good write-up in the local rag, big photo of me in all my gear. Really fancied myself, I did. Ophelia.' A faint smile. 'Boys' school, see. Voice hadn't broken.'

His expression darkened, his mouth working as though he was struggling to find the right words.

'She was living with this big Irish bloke. There was a bit of rebuilding going on round Moss Side just then. Anyway, he'd been in the pub, and one of his mates had got the paper. I'd not said anything. If you were found reading a book round our way, they thought you were gay. And there I was in the paper for all to see, dressed up like a lass. You can imagine the way they'd have taken the piss. A macho-man like him, with a fairy in the house . . .' A deep, shaky breath. With effort, he turned his head so that he was looking into her face. 'I've not told anyone this, ever. I'm not sure I can go on.'

She could see he was beginning to tire. But whatever was coming next was something very important to him. 'Do you want to go on?' she asked gently. He nodded, and she rested her fingers on his clenched fist. 'You can tell me anything.'

'He was roaring, by the time he got in,' he went on eventually, his voice so quiet that she had to strain to catch the words. 'I knew I was in for it when I heard him come crashing up the stairs. He'd belted me often enough before. Fell down the stairs a lot I did, after I went to me mam's. Walked into a lot of doors. But what I got that night, you don't get falling down stairs.' He shook his head, staring down at her hand on his. 'I remember him unbuckling his belt, and wondering what I'd done this time. I remember him grabbing me and shouting, "I'll show you what happens to queers, you little gobshite". Then he threw me on the bed, and I remember . . . I remember . . .' His face was wet, with sweat or tears, as he whispered, 'I was twelve years old, Flora. Can you understand what I'm saying?'

She nodded wordlessly, her own eyes full of tears.

He sank back against the pillow, while she shushed him as she might a child, murmuring and stroking his hair until his breathing became more regular. She began to think he'd fallen asleep, and closed her own eyes, trying not to imagine what he must have been through.

His voice, emotionless, made her start. 'Nearly four years, I stood it.' His eyes were still shut. 'I didn't know what else to do. There was no one I could tell. I used to look at the other lads at school, telling smutty jokes they didn't understand, and the masters with their daft, petty rules, and I felt like I was living on a different planet. All that ugliness inside me . . .' He began to shiver.

'Do you need someone?' She made to get up, but he shook his head impatiently, wincing as he suppressed a cough.

'I started acting the hard man. Fights. Drinking. Drugs. I remember the headmaster hauling me in, stood there that smug and bloody clever in his black soutane, going on about the sins of the flesh, and how I should respect the body God had given me, and thinking, "Christ, if only you knew". I'm surprised they didn't expel me sooner. I'd no respect for anyone, least of all myself. I started getting into trouble with the police. Shoplifting first, then cars. I can't remember how many times I was up in court. I'd thought . . . I suppose I'd hoped . . . I don't know what I'd thought, but they didn't send me away. One last chance, they kept saying. Each time, he'd say, "*come back for more, have you?*"'

His voice was hoarse, his breathing laboured. The effort it was taking frightened her, but she felt powerless to stop him. A hundred platitudes came to her lips and were rejected.

'One night I just flipped. We were in the kitchen. He'd come back drunk, as usual. There was this knife . . .'

'But that was self-defence! Why didn't you tell them . . . ?'

He flinched away from her as she put her arms out to comfort him. 'Don't you understand? I was *ashamed*.'

The movement set him coughing again, and he pressed his free hand to his chest.

'Enough,' Flora said firmly, trying to lie him back. She poured water into the glass on the bedside table and tried to feed some to him. He had begun to shake again, more violently than ever. She pressed the call bell above the bed and struggled to fit the oxygen mask over his face, fighting back her panic.

He lifted his hand from his chest and held it out to her, helplessly. Flora was horrified to see that blood was seeping through the bandages. She ran out into the corridor and screamed for help, then rushed back to him. By now, the sheet was soaked red.

'I've had all the tests.' His eyelids fluttered open and he grasped her hand as she bent over him. 'H.I . . .' His voice was fading. 'H.I.V . . . I'd never have slept with you if . . .'

'Don't,' she whispered, the tears pouring down her cheeks. She could hear footsteps running towards them along the corridor. 'Hang on, Kieran. Don't you dare leave me now.'

'I . . . just wanted you to know.' His fingers slackened. The words were no more than a sigh.

Chapter Twenty-two

'Dear me, you're soaked to the skin, Dr Heatherington!' Mrs Menheniott clucked, as Christopher followed Simon into the kitchen. 'You'll catch your death . . .' She flushed, her voice fading.

'Why don't you make some coffee and take it through to the drawing room?' Simon cut in quickly. 'And then you can take the rest of the day off.' He turned to Christopher. 'I'll leave you to it. I shall be out on the downs if I'm needed.' He gave his arm a brief, self-conscious squeeze. 'You were only trying to protect Flora. No one can blame you for that.'

Whitelaw looked at Christopher closely as he came into the room, noting the shell-shocked expression on his haggard, unshaven face. If he was as pleased with what he'd done as his father was, he certainly didn't look it. As gently as he could, and trying his best to control Shenfield's frequent promptings and interruptions, Whitelaw began to draw from Christopher the events leading up to the shooting. It wasn't easy. Time and again, lost in his own private torment, he lapsed into silence, his eyes straying from the rifle which still lay, labelled and wrapped in polythene, on the table, to the turbulent sea beyond the streaming windows. He hardly seemed to know where he was, let alone what had happened.

Medlock observed them from his armchair, smiling slightly, every now and again shaking his head. In some other part of the house, a telephone began to ring. When, after several minutes, Whitelaw jerked his head towards the sound and said irritably, 'Make yourself useful,' Medlock unfolded himself from his chair and walked unhurriedly from the room without a word.

'Please try to understand that I'm not trying to catch you out, Dr Heatherington,' Whitelaw continued when he had gone, more for Shenfield's benefit than for Christopher's. 'We all know you thought you were—'

'Thought? Thought?' Shenfield slammed a fist against the table. 'What is all this crap? I've told you, it was open and shut self-defence. End of story.'

Whitelaw sighed. 'I'm sorry, Dave, but it isn't as black and white as that, and you know it. If he dies . . .'

'He's not going to die.' Medlock stood in the doorway, pausing for dramatic effect as they all turned towards him, before adding, 'That was the hospital.'

'Thank God,' Whitelaw murmured.

'Yes indeed,' Medlock smiled. 'A great relief. And no brain damage, it would appear. His mental faculties, and his memory, seem entirely un-impaired. Total recall of what happened before the shooting. Good news, isn't it? By the way,' he turned to Whitelaw, 'did you realise you'd left your paper in his room? Lucky I spotted it.' He dropped it, folded to display the headline, 'Student Suspect Shot in Love Triangle', at Christopher's feet. Christopher picked it up, his hands trembling.

Whitelaw examined his shoes and wished he was anywhere else in the world but trapped in this nightmare.

Medlock's eyes didn't move from Christopher, as the paper slipped from between his fingers and he hunched forward in his chair, his head between his hands.

'Willerton's bound to see it sooner or later, of course, but there's no reason to hand him his defence strategy on a plate, is there?'

Every muscle in Shenfield's body tensed, the knuckles of his clenched fists white as he gazed at Medlock, but he said nothing.

'Oh, there I go again!' Medlock shook his head in apology. 'Calling him Willerton. A real stroke of luck, Christopher – you don't mind me calling you Christopher? – that you were able to identify him. That's what made me realise I'd been wrong about Norman Ackroyd.'

'St Neville the Infallible? Wrong?' Whitelaw attempted jocularity as he snatched up the paper and placed it, face downwards, on the table. 'Well, that must be a first!'

'Poor old Whitelaw,' Medlock sneered. 'The

twentieth century really hurts, doesn't it? All this new-fangled technology.'

'I'm heading this investigation, in case you've forgotten.' He glanced across at Shenfield, realising that he hadn't been officially informed.

A small exhalation, the merest drop of the shoulders, indicated his acknowledgement. Anxious not to catch his eye, Whitelaw turned back to Medlock and snapped, 'Did the hospital say when O'Driscoll could be interviewed?'

'I ran some computer checks on Kieran Willerton, you know.' Medlock ignored both rebuke and question.

'Kieran Willerton doesn't exist.'

Whitelaw could recognise the dangerous control in Shenfield's voice, if Medlock couldn't. And now Shenfield was officially off the case, he had precious little to lose by letting the precocious little bastard have it right between the eyeballs. Whitelaw couldn't help hoping he would, if only for the sake of his own pride.

'True,' Medlock agreed, pushing his luck still further with a patronising nod in Shenfield's direction. 'But Kieran Henshall does. If you hadn't been so busy handing out official warnings back in Blackport, I could have shown you this.' He took a carefully folded computer printout from his briefcase, opened it out and read, 'Kieran Henshall. Date of birth, tenth of May 1974. Family known to Social Services. Childhood spent on a high-rise estate on the outskirts of Salford. Willerton Heights.' He glanced from one of them to the other, savouring the moment, before reading on. 'Moved to Moss Side 1985. Fifteen convictions before Greater Manchester Youth Courts. Sentenced to nine years, Manchester Crown Court, July 1990, for the murder of one Seamus O'Gorman. Added an extra couple of years to his sentence, apparently, by telling the judge in open court that he was "only sorry the bastard hadn't taken longer to die".' Medlock chuckled to himself and shook his head. 'Sounds a real charmer, doesn't he? Must have been his defence brief's worst nightmare! Didn't toe the line too well inside either, according to Henshall's probation officer, when I spoke to her the other day. Certainly didn't earn much in the way of remission. He wasn't released until September 1998. But she did say that as far as she knew, he'd been going straight since he took up his place in the English department of Blackport University. Certainly there's no record of any subsequent offences, in either name, so higher education doesn't appear to have been a complete waste of time, in his case.' He beamed around at his audience. 'Wonderful things, computers. Rather blows a hole in the Gavin O'Driscoll theory, of course, as Henshall was being entertained by Her Majesty at the time of Melanie Loveridge's death.'

'So they weren't linked at all.' Shenfield sat down heavily.

'Oh, I didn't say they weren't linked.' He looked down on Shenfield. 'I have to hand it to you . . . *Guv* . . .' A slight, sardonic bow.

Whitelaw watched them both with growing

unease. Even Medlock wasn't arrogant – or brave – enough to talk to Shenfield that way unless he had something to say.

'. . . You were on the right lines with quite a lot of it. The killer was from the university, all right. Unfortunately, you were so busy following your nose that you couldn't see the wood for the trees, if you'll forgive the somewhat mixed metaphor.' He cast a sly grin at Christopher, before continuing, 'Tanya Stewart, for instance. That one *was* different. She did know the murderer, as you suspected. And Meg Evans' death must have happened almost exactly as you worked out, too. Mistaken identity.' This time he turned to face Christopher directly. 'No wonder you nearly passed out when Flora Castledine walked in. I thought at first you were acting, but you really *did* believe she was dead.'

There was a moment's stunned silence, then Shenfield said incredulously, 'Have you completely lost your fucking marbles? Tell him, Christopher . . .'

Reaching into the briefcase with the air of a magician putting his hand into a hat, Medlock produced a small leather-bound notebook. 'I borrowed this from your study, Christopher. I guessed that, as a writer, you would feel compelled to commit everything to paper. I take it you will confirm it is your diary?'

Christopher nodded, mechanically. He looked up and said, almost hopefully, 'It's over now, isn't it?'

A volley of hail rattled against the window like gunfire.

Shenfield slumped into a chair, his face ashen.

'What are you saying, Christopher?' he whispered. 'What in God's name are you saying?'

Whitelaw watched them helplessly. It was all beginning to make sense. No wonder Christopher had been so keen to get rid of his bloodstained clothes after Tanya Stewart's murder. Whitelaw had torn him off for that at the time, but had put it down to thoughtlessness, or at worst an unwillingness to co-operate with his father. So much to incriminate him . . . and because of who he was, they had failed to recognise any of it. He'd been on the scene far too soon after the girl was shoved through the bookshop window, but no one had noticed; he was simply Shenfield's son, getting in the way. Whitelaw closed his eyes. Christ, it really had been Christopher she'd seen in the glass, not his photograph. The truth had been staring them in the face all along.

It was worse than his worst nightmare.

'You and your hunches.' Medlock made no attempt to conceal his contempt as he turned back to Shenfield. 'Didn't it strike you as strange that he turned up in such a state at Flora's flat that morning without even asking who'd been killed? That was when I began to realise my error. The psychological profile I had applied to Norman Ackroyd – loner, idealised notion of womanhood, even the confusion of reality with literature – applied equally to someone much closer to home. After that, it was all so blindingly obvious. What did all the girls except Tanya have in common? Their hair. Your wife's hair.'

'For pity's sake . . .' Shenfield mumbled, his hand shielding his face as if he were warding off a blow.

'That's what attracted you to Melanie Loveridge, wasn't it, Christopher? Not as a lover. Never anything as sordid as that. As an icon. Your own, personal Madonna. Your mother was dying, and Melanie had been sent to take her place.'

'Why did she leave me?' Christopher moaned, the stony mask crumbling as he rocked backwards and forwards in his chair. 'Why did they all have to leave me?'

Wordlessly, Shenfield leapt to his feet and crossed to the window, head bowed, his back to them.

'Did Melanie have any idea of your feelings? I doubt it. It was all in your head. In your poetry. But then you realised she had a lover. She was defiled. And that made you very angry, didn't it? She'd tricked you. Melanie wasn't like your mother at all. So you murdered her. Hacked that treacherous hair right off her head. And then you set about framing Gavin O'Driscoll.'

Christopher put his hands to his ears as if to stop Medlock's relentless voice. 'I saw them together, after the May Ball. His great, filthy hands on her, mauling her . . .'

'So, no more trusting girls after what Melanie's done to you. You devote yourself to your mother. And then she dies, and every red-haired whore you see is an insult to her memory. Cut the corruption out of them; mutilate them as the cancer mutilated her, an eye for an eye, a womb for a womb. Until

296

Flora comes along. Innocent. Unspoiled. The re-incarnation of your mother, come to make the world safe for you again. But then Flora deceives you too. And with someone who's confided in you. Someone you've looked on as a friend. That must have made you doubly angry.'

'Is all this psycho-babble necessary?' Whitelaw cut in, but Christopher, his voice thick with tears, had already started to speak.

'He laughed at me. He stood there in my own study and laughed at me. Called me a sad bastard. After everything I'd done for him.' His voice was shaking. 'Everything I'd . . .' He put his head into his hands. 'I thought he understood. He wasn't like the others. The things he said, the way he wrote . . . But when it came to it, he was no different from the rest. I loved Flora. Worshipped her. But he had to take her. Sully her. Not love, lust.' His face twisted. 'And that was what she wanted. I saw the way she ran to him, rubbing herself against him like some cheap harlot. I could have given her so much . . . Why couldn't I have been enough? Why have I never been enough?' Christopher was looking at his father's rigid back.

'So you decided to take your revenge on both of them.' Medlock grasped Christopher's hands to force back his attention. 'You got hold of his coat and scarf and planted them at the scene, just as you'd planted Gavin O'Driscoll's pen all those years before. Then you went to her flat and waited for her to come back from the ball.'

'But he couldn't have known she'd be alone,' Whitelaw chipped in desperately. 'They could have turned up together, and then . . .'

'I'd have killed him too.' Christopher looked at him with something approaching impatience. 'Don't you understand? He betrayed me.'

'You knew he'd been in trouble with the law,' Medlock ploughed on. 'You knew he'd changed his name. When you realised your father thought he and O'Driscoll were one and the same, it must have seemed a gift from God.'

'But wasn't it a risk?' Whitelaw wondered why he was still trying to pick holes when there were none to pick. 'What if Gavin O'Driscoll had turned up? What if . . . ?'

'He wasn't going to turn up.' Christopher's voice was low, his face like stone. 'Gavin O'Driscoll is dead.'

And had been since the day of his release on bail. Six years they'd been searching for him, following one false lead after another, and all that time he'd been in the lake near where Christopher had found him, laying flowers for Melanie.

'So,' Medlock said triumphantly, his attention now on Shenfield, 'that establishes why your son was so keen to keep the spotlight on O'Driscoll. What's your excuse?'

Shenfield turned, at last, from the window. Without a word, he walked over to Christopher and put a hand on his shoulder.

'Was it only bad judgement?' Medlock went on. 'Or had you begun to suspect . . . ?'

'Leave it!' Whitelaw's voice was shaking. 'We've heard enough. You've done what you came here to do. For Christ's sake leave it now.'

From the corner of his eye, he could see that Shenfield had edged towards the table, and instantly read his intention. Their eyes met in a moment of unspoken understanding. The choice was his. Whitelaw could alert Medlock to what was coming, or he could look away.

Very deliberately, he positioned himself to block Medlock's view.

As Medlock began to speak again, Shenfield made a grab for the rifle.

'Run, Christopher,' he shouted, ripping off the polythene and aiming the gun at Medlock.

Christopher hesitated, then scrambled to his feet.

'Go on,' Shenfield urged, 'Run!'

'Do you think you can get away with this?' Medlock's blustering tone was belied by his pallor.

Behind him, Shenfield heard the crash of the front door being flung open, followed by the crunch of Christopher's running footsteps across the gravel path, dwindling, after what seemed like an eternity, into silence.

'Do you think I care?' Shenfield backed towards the door, the gun still aimed. 'You knew it was Christopher before we came over here, didn't you?'

'I didn't know. I had reason to suspect.'

'What kind of a creature are you, Medlock? That kid could have *died*. Come after me, and I'll shoot you.' He lined up the gun with Medlock's head, his eyes glinting, and closed his finger round the trigger. 'Or maybe I'll just shoot you anyway.'

Whitelaw, not even daring to breathe, looked from one of them to the other, and at the dark, wet stain spreading across the front of Medlock's trousers.

Shenfield saw it too. Lowering the gun fractionally, he whispered, 'Except you're not worth the bullet.'

'I knew it. He's been shielding him all along,' Medlock muttered, fumbling to button up his jacket in a vain attempt to hide the stain, when Shenfield had backed out of the room and they heard the key being turned in the lock. He ran to the door, testing his weight against it and rattling the handle, before pulling the mobile from his pocket.

As he began to jab the numbers in, Whitelaw snatched it from him. 'Reason to suspect?' He made no effort to keep the contempt from his voice.

'It's watertight. Even without the diary. Ackroyd recorded every coming and going at Flora Castledine's flat since October. Heatherington spent hours hanging around outside the place. There's even a bloody photograph of him. I just wanted to establish how implicated Shenfield was, and now I have. Give me that phone.'

'Crap. All you wanted was to destroy Shenfield and take the glory. You could have stopped this days ago. Instead of which, you allowed a sick man to stay on the loose, and put other lives in danger. Think that's going to get you a promotion, do you?

You can just thank God that lad's pulled through, or I'd personally be bringing a . . .' He stopped, and looked closely into Medlock's face. 'That *was* the hospital on the phone?'

'It was someone wanting to speak to Castledine.'

Whitelaw felt his mouth go dry. 'Why?'

'How the hell should I know? Don't look so shocked. I took a gamble and it worked. Once Heatherington believed Henshall had regained consciousness, he knew the game was up. I got a result, didn't I? That's all that counts. We don't need his evidence. Heatherington's confessed.'

'Look at yourself.' He stared in disgust at Medlock's trousers. 'Call yourself a policeman? You make me want to vomit.'

Medlock made a lunge for the phone. 'You're in this deep enough already, Whitelaw, without adding accessory after the fact.' He knocked the phone from Whitelaw's grasp, sending it skidding across the polished parquet tiles. Whitelaw was after it in a split second, smashing it under his heel as Medlock made a dive for it.

He looked up, from all fours, and panted, 'You bloody fool. I'll finish you for this.' Pulling himself up, he ran to the window, tried the catch, then grabbed a heavy lamp, hurled it through the glass, and began to climb out.

Whitelaw dragged him back. 'They can't go anywhere, for God's sake. Shenfield's got to bring him in himself. This is between the two of them. Father and son. It's a matter of honour. Can't you even understand that?'

'Honour?' Medlock stared at him in disbelief. 'I'm a detective, not a Knight of the fucking Round Table.' He shook himself free and hauled himself onto the sill. Whitelaw spun him around, feeling the satisfying crunch as fist contacted with jaw and Medlock crashed backwards onto the floor.

'No,' he muttered, looking down at the prone figure of his young colleague. 'You wouldn't understand in a million years.'

Sobbing for breath, Christopher battled his way across the cliffs. He ran by instinct, without hope or reason; like a fox, with its lair sealed and the pack on its heels. Below him, the sea boiled and crashed, hurling up great plumes of drenching spray. A million splintered, nightmare images collided in his brain and fell inexorably into place. The tiny voices that had started as an itch thundered inside his skull. They had seemed like the seed of a new poem at first, exciting in their insistence. But they had grown and grown, no matter how hard he had tried to ignore them, until the only way he could silence them was to do as he was bidden. No music, no poetry on earth could keep them at bay now. The fragile lacquer of his ordered life was shattered.

He'd tried so hard. He'd poured his life's blood into trying so hard to make them love him, but each of them in turn had betrayed him. Even the little bird, its bright eyes filled with scorn as he tried to nurse it, tearing his finger with its sharp beak. Even his beloved mother, dying not with his name on her lips, but his father's. They'd all betrayed him. All whores at heart.

On and on, he struggled over the rocks, as the hail beat down on his bare head, a jumble of poetry the taunting counterpoint to his thunderous heartbeat. *O the mind, mind has mountains; cliffs of fall. Frightful, sheer, no-man-fathomed . . .* He pushed through drifts of dying bracken, scratching his hands on the needle-sharp gorse that grew waist-high across his path. At last, across the headland, he could see in the distance the small greystone church, its spreading trees and ancient, lichen-covered gravestones spilling down almost to the water. Maybe there he could find sanctuary. His lungs bursting, his legs like lead, he stumbled on, until at last he reached the shelter of the bay. The wind dropped abruptly, the deafening roar of the waves reduced to a distant rumble. His mind was becoming mercifully numbed by exhaustion, now. He entered the silent churchyard and sank to the ground. Sooner or later, they would come, and this limbo would be over. Maybe then, the voices would be silenced at last. A sudden shaft of sunlight burst like a laser through a break in the lowering clouds as the rain dwindled to a standstill. He felt peaceful, now. Ready to sleep. Curled foetus-like amongst the weathered granite headstones, he waited.

'I thought I might find you here.'

He looked up to see his father towering above

him, black against the sun. He felt very calm. All he wanted to do now was sleep.

'There's nowhere to run,' he said simply.

Shenfield knelt down beside him. On a level with him. Face to face. For the first time since he was a baby. Shenfield took his son in his arms and held him to him, pressing his face against his hair as he whispered, 'There never was, lad. There never was.'

Whitelaw heard the shot, throwing himself the last few hundred yards towards the churchyard, his heart in his mouth. He stood inside the lychgate, his ears straining over his own ragged breathing, then edged gingerly down the overgrown path towards the church.

He found Christopher's body almost at once, his head resting against a mound of grass, eyes closed, his hands folded over the jagged hole that had been his chest. He looked curiously peaceful.

The wet grass was flattened in a narrow, steep trail leading towards the cliffs. Cautiously, his heart contracting with fear, Whitelaw followed it. Overhead, the gulls wheeled and squawked. Above them, the red air-ambulance clattered its way back towards the mainland.

Shenfield was standing on the edge of a high outcrop, which overhung the rocks below like a massive granite pulpit, silhouetted against the sky. He looked quite calm, like any other visitor admiring the vastness of the sea. He turned around as

Whitelaw called out his name, and raised the gun. It seemed more a greeting than a threat.

Whitelaw inched his way up the steep, stony path, scrambling blindly over the treacherous rocks, his eyes never leaving the gun. At last, he was within a few yards of Shenfield; close enough to see the tears.

'Put it down, mate,' he said quietly. 'It's over now.'

Shenfield nodded. He bent and placed the gun carefully on the ground between them. Whitelaw breathed out slowly. 'Come down, now,' he coaxed, trying to calculate his distance from the trigger, frightened of startling him with any sudden movement. 'We can get it sorted out.'

'Like a mad dog.' Shenfield nodded, talking more to himself than to his friend. 'I said, didn't I . . . ?'

'I know, mate, I know. Here, give me your hand.'

Whitelaw was within a couple of feet of him now. Almost close enough to touch him. As he extended his hand, Shenfield looked him in the eye.

'Like a mad dog.'

He pulled himself to his full height, shoulders back, head high, as if standing to attention, then stepped backwards, his large body describing an arc of surprising grace through the clear air, seeming to hang for a moment in flight like a bird, before it smashed onto the boulders below.

Chapter Twenty-three

Christmas came and went. People ate too much, drank too much, and watched too much television: cartoon films; repeats of Morecambe and Wise; maybe the odd carol service. They didn't want tragedy. They didn't want scandal. By the time the New Year had been rung in, the Beast of Blackport was yesterday's news. With no trial to fan the flame of public interest, the case was history.

For Ray Whitelaw, Christmas was a succession of endless, harrowing funerals. The chapel had been packed for Meg Evans. The whole village had gathered to give what comfort it could to her grief-stricken family. Her medic friends from the university were there, more accustomed than most of their age to death, but still numbed at the loss of one of their own. Everyone had been there. Even the tiny, ginger-headed baby who bore her name, and would provide them, in the months to come, with the hope and strength to carry on without her.

Blackport Central had turned out in force to send Shenfield on his way. Even Lambert had made an appearance, worried by what the press would make of it if he stayed away. The chilly, impersonal church was packed with coppers. Colleagues, rather than friends. No family. An appropriate send-off, Whitelaw had thought, as they filed out and headed thankfully back to work.

Only Whitelaw had been present for Christopher's cremation, a secret, early-morning affair a hundred and more miles from Blackport. The chaplain had muttered a few hasty words about God's infinite mercy. The two of them had sung a hymn. *'Father-like he tends and spares us / Well our feeble frames he knows . . .'* Whitelaw had watched the cheap coffin disappear on its final journey, and wondered if the irony was intentional.

Had Shenfield suspected, in his heart of hearts, that his son was the Beast of Blackport?

Medlock thought so.

Lambert thought so, too; Whitelaw could see it in his eyes. Not that Lambert would ever admit it. Not publicly. Damage limitation, it was called. The case was closed.

They'd never know the truth, because they'd never known Shenfield the way Whitelaw had known him. And integrity was a word they didn't understand.

So Blackport returned to normal. The girls still plied their dangerous trade around the docks. A new university term started. St Neville Medlock, Blackport's own Elliott Ness, would receive his promotion, the written warning quietly excised from his file. In today's police force, his sort would always rise to the top, like scum on soup.

Whitelaw had considered, and rejected, the idea of early retirement. Someone had to try to keep the Medlocks of the world in check. He felt he owed Dave Shenfield that much. So he took over Shenfield's desk at Blackport Central and submerged himself in his work. When the dust had settled, he would put in for the Inspector's exam. He and Medlock reached an unspoken agreement: Medlock wouldn't put anything in the report about the broken phone or the bruised jaw; Whitelaw would forget the wet trousers.

Life went on.

There was just one more service for Whitelaw to attend, before he too could finally close the case. A ceremony he was dreading, in a place he had fervently hoped never to see again.

He stepped down from the helicopter and looked around at the tranquil scenery. Was it really only four weeks since he'd stood here before? Focusing his mind on what was ahead of him, he picked up his bag and set off. The air was heavy with the mingled scents of daffodils, salt, seaweed and the white garlic flowers that grew wild in every hedgerow. He passed a field of flower-pickers, bent low over the nodding yellow heads like grazing cattle. A gnarled old man with a beard straightened up with a grimace and rubbed his back, glancing at him with an incurious, 'Mornin'.'

Here, as in Blackport, it was as if nothing had happened.

*

Simon Castledine was waiting for him when he reached the church. Flora, huddled into her coat, a black headscarf covering the brightness of her hair, stood at his side. Whitelaw had seen her just the once since Shenfield's death, at Meg Evans' funeral.

Why was it you only saw some people at funerals?

'Just the three of us,' he said, when they had shaken hands.

'Four.'

Whitelaw turned to see Kieran Henshall levering himself with difficulty from the bench inside the porch, his face pale and drawn. Flora was at his side in seconds, slipping her arm around his waist, taking his weight on her shoulder to support him.

At least there was to be one happy ending. The air-ambulance had got him to an operating theatre on the mainland. He was out of hospital now, and on his way to recovery. With a new-found family of his own by the looks of things, Whitelaw thought, as Castledine took his other arm protectively.

He'd been through the probation files. It didn't take much reading between the lines to see the lad had been handed the dirty end of the stick all his life; if anyone deserved a break, Kieran Henshall did.

'You're sure you won't use the wheelchair?' Castledine fussed. 'There's still some way to walk.'

Kieran shook his head. 'I want to be standing on my own two feet for this.'

310

And so the little procession followed the path out from the churchyard, and up to the cliffs.

Whitelaw faltered as they trod the last few steps to the edge, and looked out at the clear, empty sky and the timeless expanse of sea, his mind's eye filled with his last sight of Shenfield here a month – a lifetime – ago. Then, squaring his shoulders, he took the two casks from his bag.

He'd had to take responsibility for the ashes; there wasn't anyone else. For a couple of weeks, he'd kept them locked in the drawer of Shenfield's desk, wondering what the hell he should do with them. It had been Val's idea to bring them down here, to lay the remains of Shenfield and his son to rest on the spot where they had finally reached some sort of peace.

Fighting the lump that was forming in his throat, he went to the very edge of the cliff, and opened the casks.

'Should we be saying a few words?' Simon asked, as Whitelaw held them out over the water and emptied them.

He shook his head. 'There aren't any.'

He watched, as the breeze took the ashes and mingled them. For a moment, they danced together in the sunlight. Then they floated down onto the still surface of the sea and slowly disappeared.